The Osiris String

A Sam Buckner Adventure

By Leo J. Audette

Notice: This version uses imperial measurements. For the Kindle international market version, go to www.amazon.com/dp/B009I4T9EW .

Revised by Dolores Garon
Contributing Editors: Henrietta Wasik and Wayne Jesseau

www.leoaudette.org

ISBN 978-0-9917047-2-9

Other books by the author:

The sequel to The Osiris String: **The Divine Formula**

The third installment to the trilogy: **SlipTime**
        (Available October 2015)

A medical breakthrough that could save hundreds of thousands of lives...

Members of a sinister organization, hell bent on converting the invention into a weapon: the ultimate weapon, which would give them the power to control world politics...

It all starts with a series of strange deaths reported in the Middle East...

Sam Buckner, a biogenetic researcher at the University of Toronto, receives an unusual visit from three agents looking for answers to solve the mystery around the strange deaths. He is plunged, along with Melinda Gordon, a beautiful agent of Homeland Security and Agent Cohen, of the Israeli Secret Services, into a series of missions to find the cause of the deaths and to stop any more from occurring.

They soon realize that they are just touching the tip of the iceberg. Hints to what is really behind the killings point to a powerful Islamic organization with plans to use a new type of weapon to take control of world politics. At the top of their list is the President of the United States, followed by powerbrokers from around the world, who stand in the way!

Dedicated to

Shirley, my best friend, my one and only love!

With Thanks

This novel was in the works for several years. When the bulk of the novel had been written, it became evident that I would need to have others read it and comment on the concept, as well as on my storytelling skills.

That's where family and friends came into the picture. To that end, I have to thank Mark and Adrienne, my children, Gene, my brother-in-law, my son-in-law Darren, Menny and Tony, family friends, for their critique, encouragement and comments on the story. A special thanks to Henrietta, Gene's sister, who graciously agreed to first edit my novel.

Since the original publication a year ago, I realized it should be revised. With the help of a friend, Wayne, and especially my cousin Dolores, who put in so many hours to help me, I believe I have a better novel to offer you.

It seems the novel is still a family affair.

Prologue

He was finally here!

It felt so strange to be between the silk sheets on Monika's bed. Sergeant Benjamin Oliver had just spent three months on a tour of duty on the Israeli/Palestinian border, just west of Ramallah, in the West Bank. As he lay here, his chest heaving up and down in a slow rhythm, it struck him that he now better understood Einstein's theory of relativity. The three months of loneliness, on a lumpy army cot with only rough linen sheets to keep him warm at night and nothing but dust and sun during the day, all collapsed into but a few moments compared to the eternity of the past hour with Monika. A feeling of elation spread throughout every cell of his body, bringing a huge smile to his face and causing him to shudder in contentment.

Two years had passed since Israel successfully concluded peace talks with the Palestinians and one year since the inauguration of the new Palestinian state. Some of the more radical elements still active in Al Fatah and Hamas tried to stir things up by taking the occasional shots at the Israeli soldiers patrolling the border or at the many check points. Suicide bombings were still part of Israeli life, but they were fewer and farther apart. President Jabali would denounce the attacks as misguided, but they were meant to show that not all Palestinians could be lulled into complacency.

Sergeant Oliver had, in fact, been wounded during one of these incidents. Lying there under the soft white sheets, he half-consciously massaged the scar on his left shoulder, inflicted by a bullet fragment that had ricocheted off a wall while on one such patrol. The rest of the troop had quickly surrounded the area the shots had come, only to find their prey gone, evidently having disappeared through a hidden tunnel system, that had yet to be found and obliterated. Benjamin's wound wasn't serious enough for a medical evac, and much to his dismay, he was ordered to finish his patrol once he was treated.

He hated this part of his military duty feeling it was boring. He was, however, called upon from time to time, to take part in special duties as a member of a crack military unit.

He loved the exhilaration of the surprise *call to action* and being sent to an undisclosed location to complete a black ops mission: that was more to his liking. They usually had to coordinate their actions with the regular army units, but only to the extent that they did *their* job and the regulars would come in to clean things up, and much to his chagrin, take the credit. How did the Americans put it, "It sucked!" He couldn't share what he did, even with Monika, though he was sure it would mean he would get more of the passionate lovemaking he had just experienced.

Monika Ruben and Benjamin Oliver had known each other since childhood. Their parents had immigrated to Israel during the sixty's; Monika's parents coming from New York and Benjamin's from St. Petersburg, both settling in a kibbutz in Nahf, in northern Israel just south of the Lebanese border.

As children do everywhere, they had teased each other. Unlike other kids in the world, they knew they were special just for being there and because they were making a difference. Or at least that is what they were told on a daily basis. Over the years they grew to understand the meaning of their purpose for Israel and they embraced it.

As they grew from adolescence to adulthood, they found each was special in other ways. Monika was developing into a beautiful woman, alive with vitality and spirit. Benjamin was becoming a handsome, picture-perfect poster boy: the type the U.S. army would have loved to have for their recruiting campaigns. He had actually posed for an Israeli poster, just prior to signing up himself, not that Israel needed to *recruit* its military personnel because of the

2

mandatory military duty policy. A handsome soldier in uniform was eye candy for the young women, and a model to emulate for the young men thinking about the duty expected of all young Israelis.

Benjamin had joined the army in the fall of 2009 and had quickly been pressed into combat. The Palestinian issue had proved frightfully difficult, threatening to become an all-out war between Israel and the Palestinians. Suicide bombers struck often and stealthily in Israel, constantly undermining the peace process spearheaded by the U.S. and its allies. It wasn't until the summer of 2004 that the situation truly began to change and hope for a peace settlement seemed attainable. Formerly the Chairman of the Palestinian Coalition, President Jabali, was finally able to convince the radical groups within and outside his organization that the militant approach to achieving a Palestinian homeland would not work. Peace talks based on compromise might not be the hoped-for-method of achieving their goals, but they would surely be a better alternative to the never ending tit-for-tat reprisals of the past several decades.

As he lay there reminiscing, Benjamin smiled at the thought of the changes in his relationship with Monika, from the first hesitant kiss to the passion they presently shared. Now, if she would only hurry from the shower and get into bed once more!

"What's taking you so long?" he yelled. The only response was the sound of water in the shower.

"Hey! I've been told I could be looking at a promotion! Captain Baruck says the higher-ups have been keeping an eye on me and that they feel I have potential."

Again, there was only the sound of water.

The bedroom itself was simple enough. It was typical of those found almost everywhere in the Eastern Mediterranean: basic white plaster walls, terra-cotta floors and Spartan in its decor. Its main source of lighting during daytime was a narrow French style double door with green privacy shutters that opened onto a small second storey balcony. Sheer curtains hung across the opening, undulating slowly back and forth as if dancing, providing some level of privacy but allowing the warm sun and gentle breeze to come through.

The temperature seemed to have risen somewhat and beads of sweat started to form on his brow and chest. He thought of joining Monika in the shower, both for the fun of it and to cool off, but decided to wait.

"It's a little warmer than usual! Maybe we should buy an air-conditioner for the bedroom!"

The water stopped. "What was that?" Monika called, her head poking out from behind the shower curtain.

"I said I think you need to consider an…"

That's when he bolted upright in bed! Every part of his body seemed instantly to be on fire, the pain excruciatingly ripping through his chest, radiating outwardly. A million needles were pricking every part of his body, as if being tattooed by a hundred tattoo artists, all at once. Some invisible sledge-hammer was pounding at his head and he felt the warm ooze of blood trickling from his ears and nose. And try as hard as he might, he could not breathe. Though he did not yet realize it, he had just inhaled his last breath of fresh air! His joints had seized up tight, leaving him in a sitting position, in instant rigor mortis. Even as his sight began to fade, he sensed he was unable to close his eyes. And though he could no longer move or breathe, he could still taste. And the only taste he could recognize was that of burnt meat!

As his body slowly tipped over onto its right side, his brain stopped thinking and processing. It could only now reveal the last images he would see before dying: the curtains swaying in the open doorway to the balcony and in the distance, bats!

A colony of bats had escaped from an empty bombed out building across the street, swirling upward in a perfect cyclonic shape, just as Benjamin quickly fell into his own downward vortex toward eternal darkness.

What had felt like hours of torture had in fact only taken a few seconds. Einstein was right again!

Tantalizingly naked and drying her hair in a towel, Monika was just coming out of the washroom, rounding the corner to the hallway which led to the bedroom.

"So what was it you were trying to say? We need a …."

She stopped dead in her tracks at the bedroom doorway, not quite sure of what she was seeing. She had expected to see a handsome naked man in her bed, a devilish smile on his face!

But what she saw was horrific! It looked like a dismantled, charred manikin…

"Wait a minute," she thought... "is this some sort of sick joke?"

But that smell?

Reality slowly dawned on her…

From behind the curtains leading to the balcony door came such a frightful scream that most of the passers-by on the busy street below froze on the spot, with only a few having the common sense to run into the house and stream up the narrow stairway to search out the source of the wailing above. Others looked up and pointed at the strange midday sight swirling away.

No one however, noticed the black panelled van slowly making its way around the corner.

Part 1

Chapter 1

(CNN News)

"This is a CNN newsbreak:

It was reported this afternoon that President Alexander's late morning trip to the Walter Reed National Military Medical Center was the result of a toothache. A source close to the President indicated that he had been bothered by a pain in one of his molars for over a day and that the ensuing procedure was a minor one. White House doctors decided that he should have it dealt with before he required pain medication.

The same source said the President was alert and smiling when he left the hospital and that he was back in his office, hard at work, with but a slight slur to his speech due to freezing. In fact, he is reported to have said he would have to lay off *somewhat* from his favorite candy, both for the sake of his teeth and that of his waistline.

And now the weather...."

*****

(Six months earlier)

Ra'id al-Eissa was alone for the first time in months. He, too, could not believe he could finally take some time off his project. Lying in his lounge chair, taking in the sun at Paradisius Beach on Mykonos, he felt twinges of guilt, but only fleeting ones.

Ra'id felt comfortable in his black swim trunks. Though he wasn't the jock his younger brother was, he certainly had nothing to be ashamed of where his body was concerned. Standing at five foot eight, with black curly hair trimmed short and dark brown eyes, women considered him handsome: a young Omar Sharif but without a moustache or a gap in his front teeth. A dark and mysterious aura seemed to emanate about him. Women unwittingly gravitated to him, not quite understanding the attraction. He was the male version of the *femme fatale*!

Though Islam did not prohibit going to the beach, it obviously frowned upon topless or nude beaches. Contrary to the rule of abstinence from alcohol, Ra'id also allowed himself to indulge in a bottle of locally brewed beer. The beer was cold and the view... Well, it was very nice indeed! Two young women, clad only in the bottom portion of their bikinis, sat surrounded by several young male admirers who were talking loudly, laughing, trying to impress one another and especially the two girls, as if in some sort of mating ritual which Ra'id found too primitive for his liking.

The well-tanned young woman lying in the sun chair next to him, rolled over from her left side onto her back. She too was topless, exposing two well-rounded breasts. She certainly was not new to the beach, as no tan lines were evident, other than the one which peeked out of her bikini bottom.

Ra'id had met the sultry young Greek girl while sipping his espresso at a café bordering the picturesque harbor of Mykonos Town. He had been attracted to her by her deep, dark eyes and silky black hair, reminding him very much of Samihah, his only real love. In spite of his feelings of remorse, his need for companionship overshadowed his feelings of guilt, even though Samihah had been dead for only a year now.

He had brazenly smiled at the young woman as she passed by and was surprised when she responded. Two hours sped by as they sat under the canvas awning and shared trivia, feeling as though the rest of the world and its problems had disappeared. When she invited him to join her on the beach, he agreed on condition she would be willing to join him for supper at the restaurant of her choice. He secretly hoped she would be with him for breakfast as well.

These liberties, he thought, he could permit himself. Allah would not judge him too harshly. Was he not, in fact, doing Allah's will and would he not be considered the greatest of Allah's servants, next to Mohammed of course.

Here, on this beach, the struggles of the world seemed so far away, and yet, he could not help but feel somewhat apprehensive... Off to the left, across the bay, he could see a single house on a rocky peninsula, standing alone against the elements. A simple stone wall surrounded it, creating a large empty courtyard devoid of any vegetation other than a single misshapen olive tree. In spite of this, the house seemed alive and alert. With three sides facing the sea and the two adjoining bays, the floor-to-ceiling windows gave it had an unimpeded view. The house seemed to be on guard and prepared for any onslaught from the elements. Ra'id empathized with the house. He, too, felt alert to the dangers he would face and to the impact his work would have on history. He, too, was ready for any storm. He, too, would stand defiant and triumphant!

But enough of that for now! All he wanted to do for the moment was to take a few weeks of rest before going back to fulfill his destiny. Mykonos was renowned for its beaches, its restaurants and nightlife, and he planned to immerse himself in the ambiance of the island.

Yes, Allah would forgive him...

Was he not the *sword of Allah*?

Chapter 2

"And finally, from #10 Downing Street, Prime Minister Barber is reported to be doing well after an emergency appendectomy. The Prime Minister collapsed as he left his office on his way to defend his new immigration bill in the House of Commons. He is said to have fared the operation well. Barring any complications, his aides have indicated that doctors expect him to be able to assume some of his duties within a week.

Prime Minister Barber's new immigration bill is heralded as long overdue by many who want to restrict even further the flow of immigrants into what they call an 'already racially-divided Great Britain'. Critics of the bill have stated that it goes too far and that valuable expertise will be diverted to other countries, hungry to compete with Great Britain…"

＊＊＊＊＊

"Hey Sam! You won't believe this one."

Jalal Ulfayad was Sam Buckner's partner in crime so to speak. That is, he was his project partner, and lately, one of Sam's few links to the outside world. As he entered the biogenetic lab at the University of Toronto, he almost tripped over a stool which had been left in the walkway between the counters by the door. He was just returning from McDonald's with two orders of fries and burgers, a shake and a coffee, double-double. He and Sam had been living on this staple diet for the past three months.

Sam had been able to secure a prestigious research grant from the Rockefeller Biological and Health Sciences

Foundation. The premise of his thesis had caught the imagination of the selection panel, in part because it proposed a uniquely new approach to genetic investigation and because three of the five panel members had varying degrees of interest in things *occult-like*.

Born and raised in Moncton New Brunswick, close by the banks of the Petticotiac River, he had witnessed daily one of the strange natural wonders of the world: that of the great tidal bore of the Bay of Fundy. As a boy, he had spent many hours watching the waves of water rolling in against the current, raising the surface of the muddy river by as much as a dozen feet, twice every day, followed by the gradual drop to its usual low-tide level. He had learned early that this was caused by the gravitational pull of the moon on the Bay of Fundy, raising its level and creating a reverse flow in the low lying river.

As he grew older, also learned two more important lessons: the first is that one had to delve more deeply into immediate and obvious events to look for the un-obvious in order to find the reasons why they happened: what was more important than the *Why*, was the *How*. The second is that things happening close to ground level could be caused by things far above.

Some twenty years later, his childhood musings led him to believe he could demonstrate a relationship between the gravitational fields of celestial bodies and the way the genes in the DNA molecule combine at the moment of conception. He felt that much of our evolutionary history could be explained by studying how gravity could influence the sequencing of amino acids in our genes. It wasn't that he was trying to debunk Darwin's theory of evolution! On the contrary, he was a firm believer in evolution, but felt that in and of itself, it still left many gaps in our understanding of the big picture. Though Darwin could explain why an individual species could change or adapt to its surroundings, he could not explain some of the major changes which had occurred in humans, as well as in a large array of animals. Every now and then, it seemed as though *something* had kick-started completely new branches of species. Sam felt the answer was not Intelligent Design, but less *divine* celestial events.

In a sense, he believed there was some truth to the mumbo jumbo of Astrology, but he could not accept the supernatural elements now associated with this pseudo-science. Truth be told, if he were correct, he would be giving Astrology some credibility for claiming to be able to predict personality and physical traits based on the alignment of the moon and the stars at the moment of birth. What astrologists overlooked was that, if the stars had any effect, it could only happen at the moment of conception, or nine months before birth. This is what had impressed the panellists at his funding hearing.

He felt he might be able to find some explanation for the differences in human traits and ultimately, for human evolutionary patterns. The impact of lunar and solar gravity could possibly determine which gene combined with which, setting into motion common traits Astrology capitalizes on. On a grander scale, the gravitational impact of passing *rogue* stars, the motion of the Milky Way around the center of our galaxy, and even the proximity of other galaxies could not only influence individual embryos, but any number of newly-fertilized eggs around the world and in all species.

To do this, he had enlisted the help of Jalal Ulfayad, probably the most brilliant of the graduates the astronomy department had produced in the last decade. With his help, they would chart the position of celestial bodies which came through our neighbourhood of the Galaxy over the past ten million years. By comparing the DNA of present day humans and that of our ancestors who lived during each fly-by, they believed patterns would reveal themselves.

12

"Far out! There's news about a mysterious death: a case of spontaneous combustion in Israel."

"Where did you get that bit of information, the National Inquirer?" was Sam's response, not even looking up from his microscope.

"No, no! This was reported in Aljazeera. They claim it is proof Allah is sending a sign to his people."

"Sounds more like one of those things you find in the Bible: *And he breathed upon them and fire came forth to destroy the non-believers,* and stuff like that!"

"Right!" Jalal said scornfully. "Anyway, get this. The poor bastard, a captain in the Israeli army, was at home for lunch with his wife and kids. While they were having their main course, the wife said that her husband and children were not feeling well; while she was tending to the kids, her husband went rigid and simply *crisped up*; my words not hers. Whoosh! All that was left was a pile of ashes where he had been sitting. Nothing else was touched and the kids stopped feeling ill!"

Now Sam looked up. "You surprise me sometimes. You'd think that if any part of that were true, it would be reported in more reputable news services than Aljazeera."

"Do you think all *real* news only comes from CNN?" responded Jalal, shaking his head in disbelief. Looking up at Sam, he continued with some sarcasm, "And everyone knows Fox News is the model of unbiased journalism! So why would you necessarily think they can relay the *truth*, while other sources such as Aljazeera, can't?"

"OK, point well taken!" conceded Sam. "But if it is true, I feel sorry for the wife and kids. Can you imagine the panic?"

"No kidding! Still, pretty freaky if you ask me, especially since there are rumours of another similar incident."

13

Jalal could see that Sam was preoccupied and becoming a bit impatient with the topic.

"Look, let's get serious here. I need you to get in touch with John over at the computer department and see where he is with the simulation model of the solar system he is working on. I hope the data you provided him didn't also come from Aljazeera!" Sam couldn't help but chuckle.

Jalal frowned. "Look, as long as the model is built according to my calculations, it should be one hundred percent accurate and predictable to a hundred thousand years in the past. With a few further refinements to my computations, I'll get the model to reach back the ten million years you are looking for and possibly much, much farther back!" And with a smile that was more a smirk, and a flutter of his brow, he sat back, put his feet up onto the counter and attacked his Big-Mac.

*****

(Moscow)

The phone rang!

Mufid Ashrawari rolled over lazily toward the sound, his eyes not yet opened, not quite conscious of what was happening or where he was.

Ring!

Peeking between his eyelids, he realized it was still dark. "Who could be calling me now? And what time is it?"

The clock showed it was four in the morning.

The phone rang once more. Mufid reached for the receiver.

"Yes…"

"Yes, I am. Who is this?' His eyes opened wider and he quickly sat up looking down to make sure he was dressed appropriately! "Dumb reaction!" he thought to himself, half smiling.

"No, no. It is all right. You know you can call at any time."

"No, I am not scheduled for work today…"

"Certainly… What do you need me to do this time?"

"That could be somewhat difficult, but I think I can manage it. Which hospital? Yes I know that one. Which floor and which room?"

"Yes, yes, I understand. Getting the uniform shouldn't be too difficult. Getting the item out might be more problematic but I know how it can be done."

"Yes, I know where to send it… By the end of the day."

"You know I am always prepared to serve you. You have been most kind and generous to me. I know you do Allah's biding. Goodbye, my friend and may Allah bless you and protect you. I know He will guide me."

He replaced the receiver on its cradle and immediately got up. He had information to get and specifics to put together to complete his plan. This would be the second task he had been asked to complete and he would not fail this time either.

One hour later, Mufid was out on the street, heading toward Moscow's beautiful subway system where he would be whisked away to within three blocks of the hospital.

Taking the subway at the Universitet terminal, not far from his flat, Mufid proceeded to the exchange hub at Biblioteka Lenine and then onto the northbound train, up to the Vladykino terminal.

He constantly marvelled at the elegance of the Moscow underground. For a city whose architecture was for the most part nondescript and functional, the palatial décor below astounded him with its beauty and extravagance. He knew that, were it not for the ever-present security guards, half the population of Moscow would probably move into the subway to escape the dreariness of the view above it.

Arriving at the hospital some twenty minutes before the regular shift change, Mufid blended in barely noticed by anyone, in spite of his mid-eastern complexion. As it was, more and more immigrants looking for work had come to Russia since the collapse of the Soviet Union. And though there were muggings of immigrants of color and a few beatings by groups such as the "Russia for Russians First" faction, Mufid felt relatively safe in Moscow.

He had come six years ago to study medicine and to learn Russian. Funding had been provided by the Foundation for the Promotion of Islamic Culture, which professed to support Muslims willing to settle in other countries and live the Muslim faith as an example to others. They had paid for his university training and helped him settle into his apartment. In return, they had simply requested that he assist them on occasion. Mufid knew there was probably a darker and more sinister purpose behind the façade, but he would not question it, nor would he turn down the monthly stipend he would pick up at the local mid-eastern deli and grocery store.

Though he did not train in this particular hospital, he felt comfortable with his surroundings. The need for conformity by the Communist philosophy of old required that all hospitals look and operate in a similar fashion.

He had selected one of the service entrances closest to the elevator leading to the first level basement area. There, he knew he could find an orderly uniform in one of the lockers.

He was in luck! In the third locker he found one his size and because there was still some political paranoia in the system, lockers were required to be left without lock to allow for easier scrutiny. It was of no great consequence if a uniform was *borrowed* for a shift. No one would report this incident either.

He took the elevator back up, this time up to the male medical floor on the fourth level. As the doors slid open, Mufid quickly assessed the area. Everything seemed routine!

Across from the elevators was the nurses' station where two of them sat behind the counter, peering over patient charts, already assessing the type of day they would have before passing it all over to the next shift.

Hearing the bell on the elevator, the nurse-in-charge looked up briefly and just as quickly resumed her reading. Mufid walked over and spoke to her. "I'm here for the disposal pick-up."

She looked up again, seeming a bit annoyed at the interruption. "A bit early aren't you? And where is Serge?"

He realized quickly that Serge must be the regular orderly who did the morning disposal pickups. "He was called up to the sixth floor for some major cleanup. So I was sent to complete this part of his duties. My orders were to take one container down for disposal."

Mildly satisfied with the answer, the nurse simply pointed down the hallway to the left. The container would be found in the secondary nurses' station.

As he made his way, he nonchalantly checked the room numbers. He really didn't need to do so in order to find the target's room, for sitting on a chair just outside the door, looking bored and tired after a full night on duty, was a giant of a man. The juxtaposition of this *missing link in a suit* sent chills up Mufid's spine; and he could tell by the cold stare he was getting, this man was not the type you underestimated or crossed.

As he walked by, Mufid smiled and tried to look as if he belonged there. He made quick work of finding the Nurses Station B and located the plastic container with all the discarded syringes, tongue depressors, and used dressings.

They were individually wrapped and labeled, indicating the room number and patient's name. Mufid could just as easily have picked up the single package he needed and walked away. But he thought it might look suspicious to the *giant*. Luckily, just behind the door leading to a utility closet at the rear of the station, he found a two-wheel cart. Loading the bin onto the cart, he made his exit.

His pace was well-measured as he passed the Neanderthal. Other than another curt smile, he tried to match the ho-hum expression that seemed to be painted on the giant's face. Mufid kept his eyes well away from the patient in the room. He really didn't need to see him. The leader of the opposition was doing well and would be back on the campaign trail in a few weeks. In spite of his absence during this portion of the election campaign, organizers thought it was early in the hustling and would have little negative effect on his popularity.

Andrei Sarquorf was leading in the polls and would surely be the next President of Russia in six months. His aides had wanted to keep his hospital stay very low key. By randomly selecting the hospital where he would be sent and delaying his arrival until the last moment, security could be maintained with a minimum number of agents. To ensure peace and quiet, all the patients on the floor had been moved to a different floor on the pretext that a serious staph infection had broken out and needed to be eradicated.

Another smile for the crabby nurse-in-charge, and into the elevator he stepped. As the doors closed and the down chime rang, Mufid sighed with relief. He heard the up chime from the elevator next to his as its doors opened onto the fourth floor.

Now in the process of dispensing the day's drugs for her only patient, the nurse-in-charge looked up once again. "Serge?! I thought you were assigned to the 6th floor!…"

It took Serge several minutes to discover the dressings had been taken. Security was brought in and a search for the *other* orderly was launched. When the search proved to be a dead end and because only the missing item was the dressing, it was decided to sweep this one under the carpet.

Chapter 3

Ra'id Al-Eissa

As a child, Ra'id demonstrated tremendous intellectual abilities. His father, owner of an import/export business out of Yemen, was extremely proud of his son's brilliance and hoped he would some day take over the reins of the company.

Imad Al-Eissa was a well-respected member of his community. Over a twenty year period, he had built a huge business conglomerate, importing and exporting dry goods traveled around the world. He regularly traveled to Europe, the Caribbean and the U.S. to find new products to add to the list of goods he could offer to his many clients.

The fact that he had not yet attempted to penetrate the oriental market was because he was not interested in doing so until his sons were of age and ready to assume their rightful roles within the family business. Every spare moment was spent with them, helping with their studies, reading from the Quran or discussing issues related to world events or his own affairs. But the two boys especially enjoyed the times when they would simply play games with him.

Whereas Ra'id's strength rested with his intellect, his younger brother, Ali, was destined to become Yemen's answer to David Beckham. Agile on his feet and propelled by an explosive speed, Ali had an innate sense of knowing where the soccer ball would be at all times. His timing intimidated goalkeepers, who most often failed to anticipate his moves. Imad felt certain Ali would be a star.

It was Ra'id, however, who was being groomed to take over the family operatio. In fact, it was Imad's dream that Ra'id would set up and run the future oriental division.

But Ra'id had somewhat different ideas. His skills in mathematics were more attuned to calculating cosines than price mark-ups.

He had been mesmerized when he happened to read a book on Nikola Tesla, the inventor of the alternating current. This book became the catalyst in Ra'id's dreams of climbing the ladder of greatness in the name of Allah. Tesla's research into this new form of energy opened Ra'id's eyes to the possibilities of science and humanity's ability to delve into the mysteries of life. Tesla's biography was also an education on the issues of competition and jealousy on the part of rivals, especially if one's own ideas were from those of a superior mind.

Tesla had worked on the production of electricity for use by the emerging American industrial might at the end of the nineteenth century. Unlike Thomas Edison, his employer and later his rival, Tesla believed that if electricity were to become the foundation on which the modern world would be built, it would have to have an inexpensive and suitable delivery system.

Edison championed direct current as the solution. Tesla reasoned, and correctly so, that DC current would either require unusually thick copper cables for long distance transmission, or a power plant on every corner. The beauty of AC current was that it could be delivered on much thinner cables over incredible distances by simply converting the current to high voltage and low amperage for transmission purposes and then stepping it down to lower voltage and higher amperage nearer to the end user. The irony of the story, and the lesson learned, was that even though Tesla died poor and Edison incredibly rich, Tesla's ideas became the foundation of the world we now know.

Though images of Tesla, sitting in a room surrounded by bolts of lightning during one of his demonstrations, peaked Ra'id's imagination, he was more intrigued by

Tesla's experiments in harmonic vibrations and frequencies. Tesla had discovered that with the right frequency, he could undermine the integrity of whole buildings. In fact, Tesla had witnessed the power of these vibrations with his invention, the harmonic oscillating device. When attached to a steel girder, his oscillator shook the building so dramatically, he had to use a sledgehammer to destroy it before the building collapsed.

In 1895, Tesla concentrated his efforts on building a power broadcasting system that would transmit electricity over great distances without wires. In 1899, he built a prototype power broadcasting device at Colorado Springs and used it to energize light bulbs stuck in the earth more than twenty miles from the power transmitter.

Tesla's story had given Ra'id a new direction to his life, and he felt a renewed and more focused interest in his studies. This drive and self-discipline would be his trademark while in university and during the whole of his research.

It wasn't until halfway through his final year of high school shortly did Ra'id dare to discuss his real hopes with his father. Imad was at first deeply saddened that Ra'id was looking at furthering his studies in physics rather than in business. But after three weeks of sometimes frigid talks with his son, Imad finally acceded to Ra'id's pleas to study physics at the University of Frankfurt. And by the time Ra'id was to leave home for his first term, Imad had completely accepted Ra'id's decision and embraced him with all the fervour he could muster. Perhaps Ali could step up and assume the role Imad had created for Ra'id. After all, there could surely be some advantages to having an ex-champion soccer player running an importing/exporting division!

Ra'id's research had shown him that the Physics department at the University of Frankfurt was best known for its work in non-linear dynamics, as well as highly-correlated electron systems. It did, however, also post an impressive curriculum on laser technology and, more particularly, on masers. Obsessed as he was with Tesla, Ra'id preferred courses related to this less *sexy* area of study, similar to the laser but producing and amplifying electromagnetic radiation, mainly in the microwave region of the spectrum rather than in the light spectrum. This was, in fact, the reason Ra'id had selected this university as his first and only choice. It was also the reason he had chosen German as one of the three languages he studied during his secondary school education. With thoughts of Tesla in mind, he felt sure that maser technology would help him make great contributions to humanity. He just didn't know quite how yet!

The first three years of his studies were uneventful. Ra'id preferred cloistering himself in his room, deepening his understanding of physics rather than following the party circuit.

During his third year, he had befriended another young Yemeni who had enrolled in the molecular bioenergetics program at the university. Between his heavy course schedule, his long hours of study and the time spent with Mohammed Al-Kammin in prayer and discussion, Ra'id had little time for anything else. When he could, however, he would return home to be with family and even join his father on some of his business trips. He graduated 'Summa cum laude', a fact his father never failed to brag about to his clients and friends.

It was at the beginning of the first year of his Master's program that Ra'id ran into Samihah Utbah: literally! Both were late for their class in German. The outward opening door happened to be on the northeast corner of the classroom facing east, with hallways intersecting at that very juncture. Ra'id had come running from the corridor on the north side, while Samihah hurried from the east corridor. Coming around the corner from the blind side, Ra'id ran into the door Samihah had just opened, creating a ricochet effect. First, he struck the wood-paneled door *head on*, followed inevitably by the rest of his body. The door flew back from the impact, only to bounce open again after striking Samihah with the full force of Ra'id's momentum. Dazed, both saw multi-colored worlds, moving in slow motion, their books flying through the air just a few feet above their own flight paths to the floor. The initial impact had created a loud *bah-boom*, echoed by the thud of two bodies falling on their rears, and again by the clatter of the airborne books as they also crashed to the floor.

As if drugged, the pair sat there looking at each other, too stunned to say anything or move. The door opened once more, and the professor and several students came running out to see what the commotion was all about. Soon they were on their feet, Ra'id with a bloody nose and Samihah a bruise on her forehead. The professor suggested they go to the university medical services and perhaps take the balance of the day to recuperate. He sent a couple of students to accompany them. However, though they were shaken and rather sore all over, the Ra'id and Samihah decided to decline the first suggestion and opted for the latter. Having released the two students accompanying them, they ended up in the university cafeteria, getting to know a little about each other over coffee.

Born in Kuwait, Samihah had traveled extensively with her parents as a result of her father's position as ambassador in no less than fourteen Kuwaiti embassies around the world. Her mother had died when she was just eleven and her father had decided he was going to be both mother and father to his precious daughter. He knew his many posts could create a sense of insecurity and lack of stability, but he was determined to be there for her every day. If the confidence and emotional balance she demonstrated were any indication of his efforts, he had surely succeeded in raising a very special young woman. She had been awed by the different cultures she had been exposed to and this had sparked in her an interest in languages, which was the program in which she has registered. She was hoping to become an interpreter for an organization such as the United Nations or a large multinational corporation. By now, she was already fluent in French, English and could hold her own in Italian and Spanish!

Samihah was petite: about five foot four in height and weighing only one hundred fifteen pounds. What she didn't have in stature, she more than compensated with her beauty: flawless, olive-colored skin, large dark eyes that would put Bambi to shame. Her oval face was framed by a beautiful mane of long, black hair that fell to the middle of her back.

As much as Ra'id could be comfortable regarding topics such as light and sound amplification, he had to concentrate on every word he uttered in order not to sound like a complete moron when he was around her.

Samihah sensed his struggle, pleased with herself that she could have that effect on him. She, too, found words difficult to come by, but was thankful her upbringing in the world of embassies had well prepared her for those awkward moments. Over the next weeks and months, the problem of being tongue-tied was no longer an issue for either of them. Every moment together was filled with talk on every subject under the stars.

One topic which became a focal point of their discussions, was that of a concept Ra'id and Mohammed were developing and which they believed would make them famous. They thought they could have a possible cure for Aids, or at least, for people who were HIV positive.

Yes, life was great and full of wonder! Allah had directed him to physics and Mohammed. Above all, Allah had brought him Samihah! He felt exhilarated and capable of taking on the world, as though time itself had stopped to allow them to savor the moments. Reality, however, struck with devastating clarity about five months later.

Ra'id was told by a teary-eyed Ali that their parents, Imad and Amineh Al-Eissa, had been found robbed and murdered while returning from their second pilgrimage to Mecca. Police reports indicated that their rental car had been discovered just off Highway 40, on the road to the airport in Mecca, and that no suspects had been found to date. Truth be known, the police really did not believe anyone would be arrested, since similar incidents were relatively common. As holy as were Mecca and the Great Mosque surrounding the Kaaba, pilgrims going or returning from their *Hajj* could be easy prey for the less religious and unscrupulous types.

Life seemed to collapse for Ra'id as he felt the weight of family responsibilities fall upon his shoulders. Ali, too, was devastated and gravitated to his older brother for the strength he needed to get through the funerals. Ra'id, in turn, found his strength in Samihah.

Strangely enough, another individual was there to help the two brothers through their tragedy. Umayr Al-Eissa, Ra'id's uncle, stepped in as a surrogate father. Long considered the black sheep of the family, Umayr had established himself as an import/export genius in his own right, providing his ultra-rich clients with their dream cars.

During the two weeks following the burial of his parents, Ra'id had spent a lot of time talking to Umayr about his future. He had decided to forego his studies and take an active role in his father's business, as ill-prepared as he might be for the task. They spoke again of his concept and the fact that he would have to postpone any plans he and Samihah might have had.

To his surprise, his chain-smoking uncle had offered to set his own business aside for a while, to look after Ra'id's and Ali's interests. He had insisted Ra'id needed to continue with his studies and that he would cover the cost of his tuition for as long as Ra'id needed. He admitted that he found Ra'id's concept difficult to understand, but not being a man of science, he had to defer to Ra'id's talents and vision. Besides, Umayr needed to do this for his brother, in that he had to pay retribution for years of strained relations between himself and Imad. The Koran required him to look after his new family; he planned to leave his life as a bachelor behind and become a pseudo-father and a good provider for the two boys.

After another week with Ali, Ra'id left for Frankfurt to rejoin Samihah who had left five days after the funerals. He was secure in the fact that Ali would be looked after by his uncle and he hoped his own life could resume, somewhat in the direction he had planned. Yet, he would give it all up if he could have his mother and father back in his life.

He returned to his studies with a renewed commitment. He and Mohammed had begun to focus on courses which would help them fine-tune their doctoral research, beginning the following year. They also needed to find funding for their ambitious project; there would be little time for anything but their research.

Ra'id did make time to spend with Samihah. Every moment with her became more and more precious to him; she became his security blanket. Taking time to walk along the busy streets of Frankfurt, stopping in the cafés along the way, talking about their likes and dislikes, their hopes and goals in life and their feelings for each other. As important as his project was to him, Samihah had replaced it as his number one concern and priority. Somewhere in the back of his mind, was a plan to make his relationship with Samihah more permanent. Sadly, he would now need to talk to his uncle about the wedding plans rather than to his beloved father.

Chapter 4

It wasn't that others couldn't provide the Arab royals and oil magnates with the vehicles of their dreams! Rather, what made Umayr Al-Eissa stand out above the competition was that he provided his clients with entertainment as well.

It had all started in 1972 when he had taken his first order to deliver cars to three wealthy Yemeni contractors. The first was a classic 1936 model 810 Cord convertible coupe. More specifically, the Cord the client wanted was one produced for the New York/Chicago/Los Angeles shows in late 1935. The appearance of the Cord in November of that year shook the automotive world at its foundation. The designer, Gordon Millar Buehrig, had demonstrated a unique sense of form and dramatic modernism. Frantic spectators had actually stood on top of their cars in order to get a first glimpse of the auto. This particular car was the only one of one hundred produced for the shows that had been operational. Mothballed at the Connerville plant in Indiana shortly after the shows, the car had sat idle until 1937 when it was modified with one of the new supercharged engines. This was just before E.L. Cord sold the corporation in August of that year to a group of New York financiers. One of the partners rifled the car to his winter home in Florida, where it remained with the rest of his collection of classic cars until his death in 1971. His grandson and only heir, had tried to sell the vehicle to other collectors, but his greed had prevented him from asking a fair market price. Umayr got wind of the situation through an employee of the Auburn Cord Dussenberg Museum in Indiana, and immediately contacted the grandson. Price was no object and for a car that originally sold for $1,995.00 in 1936 (without modifications),

Umayr thought the asking price of $250,000.00 was a travesty. After intense negotiations, he had the price reduced to $175,000.00. However, he did not care since he would sell it to his client for an additional $150,000.00.

The second car on his list was a 1967 original 428 Shelby AC Cobra. The car was black with a black leather interior. Not that there was much of an interior to speak of: it came stripped of every standard option, other than the two bucket seats, the steering wheel, the gear changer and rollbar. Cobra enthusiasts, however, only cared about its speed and handling. And there was no doubt this muscle car stood in a class by itself! It was the fastest production car ever made at the time: it was capable of doing zero to sixty mph. in 4.2 seconds, and a top speed of 180 miles per hour with the *pedal to the metal*. The 490 bhp baby was going for $500,000.00 and would bring in an additional twenty-five percent commission to Umayr.

The last car on his list was the 1960 Ferrari 250 Cabriolet. This twelve cylinder car was in mint condition and boasted a Pinin Farina body with a removable hardtop, dual exhausts and knock-off wheels. Although it was a little more sedate than the Cobra, its asking price of $650,000.00 was still impressive. Again, another sizeable commission would be tacked on.

Umayr's flare for the dramatics was the key to his success. For his initial sale, he decided to dazzle his clients with a demonstration of their cars' abilities, but more so to demonstrate his own. Umayr flew all three clients to Paris where he had them chauffeured to the Arc of Triomphe at the west end of the Champs Élysées. There they were escorted to the observation deck at the top, where the spectacular view of Paris could be appreciated. He had a caterer bring an ample supply of 1949 Dom Pérignon Champagne and beluga caviar all served by model-like waitresses wearing white gloves, white tuxedo shirts, bow ties, cummerbunds and tight-fitting black slacks.

He had worked several months at preparing what followed. Three of the top Formula One racers were hired to drive the cars at breakneck speeds down three separate avenues converging on the Place de l'Étoile circling the Arc of Triomphe. They drove around it twice, meet up and rocketed down the Champs Élysées in a south-east direction, whizzing past all the high-end boutiques and apartments, with a multitude of Parisians and tourists, all stretching their necks in order to get a better look at the commotion in the street. They made a half loop to the right around the Place de la Concorde, onto the Voie Georges Pompidou by the famous Jardin des Tuileries on one side and the Seine on the other, veering slightly to the right on the Quai des Tuileries in order to miss the approaching tunnel. The classic cars careened down the Quai François Mitterrand until they reached the intersection at the Pont du Carrousel and made a sliding left turn through the third archway below the southern wing of the Louvre, which led to the large central courtyard of the Place du Carrousel. The finale be was to be a spectacular spinning stop just before the Cour Napoléon, placing the cars in a zero degree, a ninety degree and a one hundred and eighty degree position facing each other, all perfectly poised for pictures with the Louvre's Glass Pyramid as a backdrop. The media had been alerted to the stunt just forty-five minutes beforehand, giving them little time to do anything but race to get their cameras into position.

Umayr had courted one of the police dispatchers and had convinced him to participate in this ten-minute stunt. A sizeable portion of his commission was used to pay off the forty-two selected policemen who were needed. Each was dispatched to the proper intersections and, in sequence, they stopped traffic from interfering on the targeted route. Drivers and onlookers were not surprised by the disruption, being used to similar situations involving the many heads of state convoyed through Paris at any given time. Because the plan was executed flawlessly, each intersection was blocked for only five minutes, after which the police simply relocated to their usual stations, as if this were just one of the many special escort duties they had performed for so many dignitaries. As for the dispatcher, when his superior got wind of the stunt, he was summarily suspended without pay for one month. This had been expected by Umayr, who had agreed to pay the dispatcher any salary he might lose plus a stipend of ten thousand dollars U.S. He had also made arrangements to deposit another ten thousand dollars as payment in the dispatcher's superior's private bank account, to help sweep the incident under the rug.

Of all the stunts he had pulled off over the next thirty years, this remained his favorite. His clients were elated with the experience and were ready to praise Umayr to all their associates. He always dreamed of attempting a similar stunt, but this time in Dubai and for ten new clients. He would use the Burj Al Arab Hotel, the only seven-star hotel in the world, as the end destination and backdrop!

*****

(Ottawa Spectator)

"Simon Ormont, Chair of the Bank of Canada, who four months ago was diagnosed with prostate cancer, was pronounced clear of the disease by his doctors. He has undergone surgery followed by chemotherapy to eradicate any cancerous cells which would have remained. During a press conference yesterday, he reported he was as optimistic about his prognosis as he was about the future of the Canadian economy.

Speculation is that he will raise interest rates by point two five next Tuesday, in order to slow down the heated economy and maintain the under two percent rate of inflation we've experienced the past three quarters...."

Chapter 5

Their Masters completed with honors, Ra'id and Mohammed turned their attention to the project they knew would not only earn each one of them a doctorate, but also revolutionize medicine. Hell! It would get them the Nobel Prize for medical contributions to humanity! Ra'id could see himself and Mohammed, walking up to the podium and being presented with the coveted prize while hearing: "Ladies and gentlemen, I am proud to present to you, the winners of the Nobel Prize in medicine, Ra'id Al-Eissa and Mohammed Al-Kammin!" He pictured Samihah and his brother Ali in the front row of the spectator gallery and the standing ovation from the crowd. The thought exhilarated him!

But his mind drifted back to reality and the fact that competition for research dollars was fierce. Though a portion of their initial research would be covered by the university, Ra'id knew they needed a substantial infusion of funds in order to continue. His uncle had taken a keen interest in Ra'id's project and had suggested he might have a contact who could prove to be of benefit.

Three weeks later, Ra'id got a telephone call from Sheikh Asim Wadi Al-Kabir, chair of the *Foundation for the Promotion of Islamic Culture.* He was hoping to meet with Ra'id and Mohammed to discuss their project and determine whether it would fit the foundation's criteria for funding. The meeting was set for two weeks hence, with Wadi Al-Kabir coming to Frankfurt on his way through to London.

Waiting in front of the hotel on the appointed day, Ra'id was expecting a tall, elderly and sophisticated type. As he stepped out of the limousine, Wadi Al-Kabir gave Ra'id a hearty smile and an embrace, after introducing himself.

Surprisingly, the Sheikh was shorter than Ra'id's own five-foot-eight stature and seemed a little *rough around the edges* in his appearance and demeanor. Even his two thousand dollar Italian suit did not do much to give him a look of classiness.

Stepping back slightly, he said "It is good to meet you at last, young *ibn Imad*. For a split second, Ra'id's heart sank as he realized that it had been a long time since he had been addressed as his father's son.

"You knew my father, then?"

"I knew of him through your uncle. First allow me to say how I am grieved by the death of your parents. You have shown true strength, worthy of them. Furthermore, I am also quite impressed by the concept you have brought forth."

Turning toward Mohammed, Wadi Al-Kabir embraced him as well in the same manner, with a traditional kiss to both cheeks. "And you are the partner in crime so to speak. Of you I have heard many words of praise. The two of you make a solid team."

Ra'id stepped back and gestured toward the covered entrance and to the doors leading into the lobby. Hoping to impress the Sheikh, he had reserved a suite at the Meridien Park Hotel. He had also planned the meeting around a traditional Yemeni lunch, which he had taken great pain in describing to the chef. The latter had taken up the challenge with gusto, seeing an opportunity of attracting more business from the Arab community to his dining room.

Using some of his father's contacts, Ra'id had been able to furnish the chef with the raw ingredients shipped in from Yemen. They would have *salta*, a highly-spiced lamb dish with lentils, chickpeas, beans and coriander, on a bed of rice. An assortment of *khubz tawwa,* or homemade breads, would be used to scoop up the *salta*, in lieu of knives and forks. *Lahuh*, pancakes made from sorghum, added a touch of festivity to the lunch. The *mal* was to be accompanied by *shay*, a very sweet tea, flavored with mint. As a final touch, *gat,* a leaf grown locally in Yemen, would be offered to chew while conducting business: tradition held that it aided the thought process. Ra'id had been present for many of his father's business lunches and hoped he could replicate the atmosphere.

If Wadi Al-Kabir was impressed he did not show it, taking it all in stride. He opened the business at hand while sipping on his glass of *shay*.

"Your uncle was sparse in his description of your project. But he more than made up for it in his enthusiasm. Please, describe the concept for me and do not spare the details."

Ra'id and Mohammed had rehearsed their parts a hundred times. This now, was for real!

"The concept is relatively simple. It is in the details that its complexity will reveal itself. We believe we can identify the HIV's DNA sequence and develop a multiple harmonic frequency attuned to that, and *only* that specific sequence, in order to stimulate the genes into an extremely high state of vibration. The heat created would be instantaneous, localized and sufficient to destroy the virus' genetic code, leaving the host undamaged and free of infection. What is as important, is that every HIV virus in the patient's body would be neutralized."

Ra'id could see a heightened level of interest in Wadi Al-Kabir's eyes. "Mohammed is the expert on genetics and he will be able to explain the biology behind our concept in a more understandable fashion than I can."

Realizing he was now *up at bat*, Mohammed slipped into his team leader mode and began. "Since HIV and Aids were first identified back in 1983, researchers have made a superhuman effort to fully understand how the virus works and devise a way to destroy it. They were successful on the first count, but failed on the second. It became clear to them that this virus was quite special, in that it attacked by becoming part of the host cell, giving its orders from within. Destroying the virus, meant you destroyed the host cell. Now, if you take into consideration the fact the virus can make as many as ten million copies of itself in one day, you can see why it is so invasive and how destroying all of these copies would be lethal to the patient.

"As well, since current medicine is based on the development and use of pharmaceuticals, established procedures have proven to be ineffective. Because pharmaceuticals are effective when the goal is to destroy a complete entity, HIV can only be treated at very specific stages, and only contain rather than cured."

"May I describe how HIV works? It will make it much easier for you to understand why others have failed and why we believe we will succeed."

Wadi Al-Kabir simply nodded.

"The first stage of infection is called *binding*. This comes after the introduction of the virus through sexual or blood-to-blood contact. The virus locates the CD4+T cell, or T4 cell for short, which are the immune system's key infection fighters. It attaches itself to the outer wall of the T4 cell, then proceeds to empty its content into the host, i.e. the infection stage. Because the process begins relatively soon after the introduction of the virus, the window for treatment is incredibly short, especially when one considers just how an individual is usually infected. Even if we might consider this just retribution by Allah for the infidels' decadent lifestyles, this is the only moment a cure could occur. Once begun, however, the process is irreversible."

"The next stage is called reverse *transcription*. Normally a cell will replicate itself through the process of transcription, which means the DNA converts to RNA when it splits to recombine during reproduction. With a retrovirus, the process is the reverse. Using its own RNA as a model, and with the help of reverse transcriptase enzymes, the HIV RNA is changed into DNA. It then proceeds to integrate itself into the DNA of the T4 cell. As long as the host cell survives, it will remain infected, meaning a lifelong battle against the disease.

The third stage begins when the T4 cell begins the process of transcription to replicate itself. The DNA moves closer to the outer wall of the cell. In this assembly stage, the new genetic material begins to *bud* on the surface of the T4 cell, preparing to separate itself, taking some of the T4 cell's membrane with it. Up until this point, the HIV DNA fragment is still intact and has not developed into AIDS. From the time the HIV RNA changes to HIV DNA, and up to this point, the virus is vulnerable to our process."

"What is responsible for the final stage is the cleaving of the DNA strand into smaller pieces by protease, another enzyme present in the cell. The body is then vulnerable to any disease of convenience, which leads to death. Most of the research and efforts to cure the HIV/AIDS virus have concentrated on this final stage. Protease inhibitors have been developed to block cleaving. As effective as they might be, they are expensive and very powerful compounds, requiring a lifetime commitment on the part of the patient. The HIV virus is always present, ready to move on to the final stage of maturation."

Mohammed paused, waiting for some response or comment.

Wadi Al-Kabir queried "So there is *no* cure for AIDS?"

"Yes and no. Not if pharmaceuticals are the focus of the research. Also no, if we are talking about AIDS. Unfortunately for those afflicted with it in the final stage, not even our *cure* will work. Our process targets the HIV, therefore preventing AIDS."

Wadi Al-Kabir seemed sobered by the information. If he did or didn't understand the presentation, he wasn't letting on. Again remaining silent, he simply made a motion with his hand, hinting that Mohammed needed to move on.

"As you may be aware, the DNA of all living entities is formed of strands of genes, connected in a specific sequence. This sequence can be mapped and compared to others in order to determine similarities or differences. The Human Genome project, completed a few years ago, has mapped out the complete sequence of genes responsible for every aspect of human development. It contains information about every characteristic of the human body, reaching back to the dawn of life itself. What the researchers have done is to map the DNA in a series of codes which can be represented by sequences of letters. Until now, most them have been concentrating on finding specific DNA codes or sequences, depending on the type of research they have been involved in. They need to know *what* each means or does. We don't!"

"We have to be able to compare the sum total of the genetic sequences of a particular individual, taking into account the codes that control hair color, size, eye color and the rest, and compare the genetic code of the HIV DNA in the T4 cells to ensure our process will not damage *innocent* sequences. We also need to map out exactly where in the T4 cell the HIV DNA sequences have grafted themselves."

"The Human Genome project and the data produced have advanced our work by a quantum leap. It has literally sped up our work by a decade or two. We, or that is I, need only determine the genetic code of the HIV DNA to be able to move ahead."

Sitting up in his chair and seemingly frowning, Wadi Al-Kabir interjected. "I was told that up until now, you have been working with microbes and fruit flies! How does this fit into the picture?"

Mohammed was ready for the question. "Yes, we have been working with, more specifically, viruses and fruit flies! As complex as their DNA is, fruit flies have shorter codes than humans and other mammals. So we decided to use the simplest example of the phenomenon we want to understand: therefore, the fruit fly. We needed to develop an expertise in identifying their genetic makeup and an ability to compare them to one another. Let me give you some perspective: we know chimpanzees have about ninety nine percent of our three billion DNA letters or genetic makeup. The remaining one percent is what makes us, us. With the computational power we have at our disposal, we needed to deal with four letter sequences no larger than ten million letters in total. As well, the limited funding we had available to us, would only allow us to remain at this level: hence, your presence here."

Again just another nod, but Wadi Al-Kabir added, "So, where does all this information leave you and how would you benefit from a grant from our foundation?"

A quick look between Mohammed and Ra'id told each other that they could be close. "We have been able to decode some of the HIV virus, but not all of it. To do so, we will need to introduce the DNA of an infected individual and that of the retrovirus itself. Then, we *primalign* them with the genetic map of a healthy individual in order to find the differences. We are talking about specialized lab time, computer time and certainly, specimen samples."

Wadi Al-Kabir turned toward Ra'id. "I assume then, that most of the costs will be associated with your contribution to the project."

"You assume correctly, I'm afraid. Though I have had some success with the process, using equipment available at the university, the next step will require very special equipment: some of my own design, some off the shelf. I will

39

need large blocks of time with the computer. This will not come cheaply."

Wadi Al-Kabir again sat back into his chair. "What exactly does this specialized equipment do?"

Ra'id breathed a quiet sigh of relief. For a moment he thought they had lost control of the flow of the presentation. Now they could get back on track. "Simply put, it will take the data provided by Mohammed, that is, the letter sequences which will allow me to create an oscillation of harmonic frequencies, each attuned to a grouping of the target DNA fragment. This pulse of microwaves will cook the fragments within an instant, like a microwave oven, leaving the rest of the DNA intact. But it will only work during the time the HIV DNA is intact and not integrated into the host cell."

"You say you have been successful in doing this already. Why would you need further investment from us?" inquired Al-Kabir. Another shot from left field! Ra'id needed to stay calm and regroup.

"Yes, I have been successful, but only with a few sequences we introduced into fruit flies infected with a simple retrovirus. I had to modify a hydrogen maser, short for Microwave Amplification by Stimulated Emission of Radiation. The university physics department used it as a precision clock for some of its experiments. I was able to have it amplify and emit up to four highly-focused resonant frequencies between twenty-four and thirty-two GHz. The DNA fragments vaporized leaving the fruit fly uninfected."

"What we need to do now is to build a maser which will allow us to broaden the frequency spectrum to encompass the range needed to vaporize the HIV virus in humans. To put it into perspective, it would mean taking the maser I have modified, already unique in the world, and multiplying its capabilities by one hundred thousand times. It can be done, but it is a question of design and money. The design is ready but the funding needs to come next. The costs are listed in Appendix C of our concept paper."

Wadi Al-Kabir picked up the folder in front of him and quickly leafed to the correct page. Not that the list meant much to him as he quickly scanned the page:

#1.   Coaxial Waveguide Combiner for Ultra Broadband Power Amplifier

#4.   Tuneable Raman up-converter

#6.   Sixty GHz Unplanar MMIC 4x Subharmonic Mixer

#10.   Full Waveguide Band MMIC Tripler for seventy-five to one hundred GHz

#13.   Novel Planar Array Smart Antenna System with Hybrid Analog-Digital Beamforming

He looked up at Ra'id, raising his right eyebrow, in part as a sign of bewilderment, in part as a sign of astonishment.

"Then all you need is this equipment and you can cure HIV?"

"There is one more component. Based on Mohammed's data and our experiments with retroviruses, including the HIV virus, I have created a software program capable of identifying the DNA groupings which need to be eradicated. Because each human being is slightly different from another, the program needs to make a new computation for every individual. With some of the letter groupings being close in the different segments of the DNA, you can understand that it will be vital for the patient that *only* the HIV fragments be affected. To do this, I estimate it will take the university mainframe computer at least seventy-eight hours of computation per case. Even if done at night, the cost of leasing all these hours will again be high."

For the first time since the beginning of the presentation, Wadi Al-Kabir gave the two young scientists a huge smile. "You make me believe this is possible. May I bring this copy of your concept paper to my Board of Directors?"

Ra'id stood and leaned across the table, taking Wadi Al-Kabir's hand and shaking it firmly. "You honor us with the request. We have been so taken with the research, knowing of its potential, yet not knowing if anyone would take us seriously."

"My plane leaves for London in three hours. Know that I have trust in you and I will recommend the Board look favorably on your request. But for the moment, I haven't failed to notice the incredible meal that is waiting for us. I suggest we do as so many have done in the past and take time to share bread and speak of family."

One hour later, as he walked toward the door, he again embraced the two petitioners saying, "May Allah be with you. I truly believe He has great plans for you, as do I."

As the door closed behind him, Ra'id and Mohammed turned and looked at each other for a moment. Then both clenched their fists, pulled their right arms back as do hockey players after scoring a goal, and yelled, "Yes!"

They did not have long to wait to celebrate. Two weeks later to the day, Ra'id received a letter through Fedex. Two short phone calls and twenty minutes later, Mohammed and Samihah were staring at the package in Ra'id's apartment.

With trembling hands, he slowly opened the envelope and began to read the letter aloud.

"Dear Mr. Al-Eissa:

Please be advised that the Board of Directors of the Foundation for the Promotion of Islamic Culture has studied your request for funding. The concept paper put forth has created much interest on our part and that of our partners. We are therefore pleased to inform you that your request has been approved.

The sums you have listed in Appendix C will be covered by our Foundation, as will any cost overrun you might incur, with prior approval by the Board. We recommend that any computer time required to complete your work be leased through an alternate provider, as we feel this would accelerate your timelines. We will provide you with details shortly and again, costs will be covered by the Foundation.

Congratulations on your project. We are proud to be of assistance to you and your colleague. Islam is made stronger by your contribution.
May Allah be with you."

The letter was signed by the Chair, Sheikh Wadi Al-Kabir.

Ra'id's legs were like jelly and he shook slightly. Mohammed's mouth was open, but no sound came from it. Samihah simply sat back onto the sofa, both hands covering her mouth, tears running down her cheeks.

Not quite understanding the full impact of the letter, they could but look at each other. Slowly the feeling of ecstasy began to rise from the pit of their stomachs, up through their throats, emerging in shrieks of joy. Mohammed danced around the room like a child. Ra'id grabbed Samihah and held her tightly. Two years of doubt and fatigue drained away. Only one thing more which could make it perfect: soon, he would have a question for Samihah.

*****

It took Ra'id a week to make all the arrangements. He wanted to propose in style and had come up with a unique way to do so, hoping to really impress Samihah. But could he pull it off?

He had confided in Mohammed, who was as elated with the news of the proposal, as he had been with the letter

43

from the Sheikh. The two had agreed on a plan, as well as who would do what.

The first task was to find a ring. On his meagre budget, Ra'id knew he couldn't afford one that would break the bank. After all, he had to think of the dowry as well. He did know, however, exactly where to go to find one. He headed to the MyZeil Shopping Center in the Innenstadt District, downtown Frankfurt. If he was to get the perfect ring, it would be there.

He loved the architecture of this one-of-a-kind shopping center. The exterior walls were made up of diamond-shaped glass panels, which wrapped around the entire building. Above the main entrance, however, the glass panes where shaped in triangles, allowing the architects to create an inward-flowing cone, much like that of an old-fashion gramophone, with the large end blending into the flat exterior glass wall and the funnel, flowing into the building and down to the center of the atrium, three floors lower. The ceiling was equally interesting! Made up of the same triangular glass panels, it swooped and flexed, much like a veil that had been tossed into the air and allowed to float to the ground, folding and curving into large, wave-like forms.

He spent a whole afternoon going from one jewellery store to another, comparing ring styles and prices. He finally found one that pleased him, and, he hoped it would also please Samihah. It was a yellow gold, solitaire ring, with a three-quarter carat brilliant diamond, supported by four gently curving claws. As he looked at it in the blue velvet case, he thought, "Simple, but with class!" Then he smiled.

Mohammed had the more difficult task to complete, that of getting permission to access the site for the proposal. Ra'id wanted to make that evening a memorable one. So he had decided that the only truly spectacular place to propose to Samihah, was high above the city, in the Europaturm Telecommunications Tower. This one-thousand-one-hundred-seven foot tower was the tallest structure in the city and would provide a breathtaking view. The one problem, however, was that the restaurant and disco, which were originally housed in the pod in the top portion of the tower, had closed to the public in 1999.

Mohammed, though, had a solution. He had befriended another student in one of his courses, whose father was a security guard looking after the tower. His friend had indicated that whenever he would like, Mohammed could be taken up to the top, to view the city, as long as it was when his father was on duty. Mohammed approached the friend with Ra'id's request and to his surprise, he returned the next day with his father's consent; but it had to be on the Monday night, three days hence. When told, Ra'id was giddy with delight at the thought of the plot unfolding as he had dreamed.

The next item on the agenda, was to rent the van that would take the table and chairs, the table settings, and the candles to the building. Mohammed would arrive a half-hour ahead of Ra'id and set everything up in the former restaurant area, next to a window overlooking the Frankfurt downtown. Since the room no longer revolved, it would be important to choose the best position to see the bright lights of the city.

Ra'id made arrangements with his and Samihah's favorite restaurant, to have the meal catered and delivered promptly at 8 p.m. They would start with a cream of mushroom soup, which would be followed by the main course, roast goose with seasonal vegetables and dill potatoes. Dessert would be apple strudel. Though Samihah rarely touched alcohol, he would have a nice bottle of Beaujolais to accompany the main course, and, depending on her answer, a bottle of chilled champagne. To top it off, Mohammed had volunteered to serve as waiter!

On the appointed day, Samihah sat in the apartment, waiting for Ra'id. He had told her he would be by at seven-fifteen, and true to his word, the taxi stopped at the front door of the apartment building at that precise moment. Ra'id hopped out and pressed the buzzer to her apartment. She let him in remotely and walked to the door to wait for him. When she opened the door, Ra'id stopped dead in his tracks. She looked so beautiful, with her dark eyes and sultry hair, wearing a simple black strapless silk dress, highlighted by a simple white pearl necklace. "You look incredible! Praise Allah for making me the luckiest man in the world." She simply smiled and wrapped a gray silk scarf around her neck and over the shoulders, and without a word, they headed for the taxi. Ra'id *was* speechless, but bursting with pride.

The ride took about a half-hour and she kept looking at him with a puzzled look, tinged with a smile. "Where *are* you taking me?"

"It's a surprise!" was all he would say. In fact, it was all he had said on the matter every time she had asked him the same question that week.

Arriving at the base of the Europaturm Tower, she looked at Ra'id and pointed to the top of the tower. "Are we going up *there*?"

"Yes we are! The surprise is up there."

Looking around, and seeing they were all alone, she said, "Is it OK for us to be here?"

"Perfectly fine. Arrangements have been made to get us up there."

Just as he spoke, a security guard came out to greet them. It was Mohammed's friend's father and he was smiling. He led them to the elevator, and pressing the correct floor level, he quickly stepped back out of the elevator and waved with a smile. "Lebewohl"

Ra'id made a mental note not to forget the bottle of cognac he had for the security guard, as thanks for the favor.

They were quickly whisked up to the top floor, where the doors opened into the empty restaurant area. There, in front of them, was Mohammed, dressed in a waiter's uniform, wearing a large grin on his face.

He played his part well, leading them to the table by the window, pulling out her chair and helping her sit. He then picked up the napkins and gently laid one on each of their lap and then said, "May I begin serving, sir?"

The meal went well, filled with conversation and jokes, often looking at the scene before them. When the moment to propose came, Ra'id began to perspire a little. He looked over to Mohammed who was standing a few feet away, and with a couple of flicks of his eyes, looking toward the elevator doors, he indicated it was time to leave. It was the signal they had agreed on.

No sooner had Mohammed left, than Ra'id leaned forward over the table and took Samihah's left hand. She stopped talking in mid-sentence, looking at him as if saying, "What?"

He cleared his throat and reached into the left pocket of his sport coat, pulling out the blue velvet box and placing it on the table in front of her. She looked at it and a slow realization of what was happening, set in. Putting both hands over her mouth to stifle any comment, her eyes grew wider.

"Samihah," began Ra'id, "I hope you know how much I love you and how hard I fell for you." Both chuckled at the obvious reference to when they first time met.

He continued, "From the first time I saw you, I knew that you would be the one and only love of my life."

By then, Samihah's eyes were misting up.

"I cannot see how I could ever go on without you in my life." Looking outside at the city lights, he continued, "I brought you here tonight because I thought it would show you how special you are to me. You need to know that there is nothing I would not do for you."

Clearing his throat once more and opening the box to show her the ring, he continued with a slightly hesitant voice,

47

"Would you consider becoming my wife and sharing your life with me? Grow old with me, knowing no one could love you more."

By then, the tears were flowing and though she still had her hands over her mouth, Ra'id could see the signs of a smile on her face. She nodded her head a few times and simply said, "Yes, yes, I will! I have never been happier!"

Ra'id rose from his chair and in an instant, he whisked her up into his arms. He gave her a long, passionate kiss. Reaching over to the box, still on the table, he removed the ring and gently fit it on her finger. They kissed again and held each other for a long time.

When Mohammed entered the room, some fifteen minutes later, carrying three champagne flutes in his hands, he found them standing side-by-side; Samihah's arms around Ra'id's waist with her head resting on his chest, his right arm over her shoulders, holding her tightly to him. They were looking down at the city, feeling the world was at their feet.

They were so engrossed in the moment, that they failed to realize that Mohammed had returned. The moment was *that* perfect!

Chapter 6

Samihah had graduated the previous May with a Master's in languages and translation. She had returned several times to Kuwait to see her family, in preparation for the wedding the two had scheduled for four months hence.

The plans were well on their way and though their courtship had been anything but traditional to date, they wanted to adhere to a few of their customs. Since some weddings could last a week, the two decided to follow Yemeni customs, in part because they would be familiar to Ra'id's family and friends, and because they could include only those customs the two could agree with, and reduce the length of the event to five days. The Ambassador had graciously consented to the changes the two proposed, seeing it as a coming of age issue for his daughter.

Ra'id had sent Mohammed as his intermediary to *negotiate* the official engagement and to get permission from Samihah's father to marry her. Umayr approved as well, but reluctantly, after suggesting only once, that the date might be delayed until after the research was complete. It was a foregone conclusion on Ra'id's part, that this would not happen!

As is traditional, Ra'id traveled to Kuwait to present the dowry to Samihah's family. The gold necklace, earrings and bracelets were as breathtaking as they were expensive. The twenty-two-karat-gold items had been purchased from a Kuwaiti jeweller known for the quality of his gold and his attention to detail. Ra'id had used a substantial portion of his inheritance to purchase them, but he knew he had to make a statement because of Samihah's station in life.

In turn, Samihah had to prepare for the wedding itself. There were a great many details to look after, not the least of which, looking after the guests over the five-day celebration. She could picture it all in her head!

On the first day, she and her girlfriends would go to a steam, or Turkish, bathhouse, specifically reserved for the wedding group. She would wear a necklace made of red onyx, believed to ward off the evil eye. Arrangements would have been made to have a female singer greet them; a cosmetic expert and hairdresser would also be present, to apply their makeup and to cover Samihah's head with a veil, once the bath was finished. Upon leaving the bathhouse, she would break an egg, again to ward off evil. Taken home in a limousine, the friends accompanying her would sing happy songs all the way.

On arrival, she would be greeted by her male relatives, who would shoot their guns in the air as a sign of celebration. Though this custom would traditionally happen often during the wedding, this was the one and only time Samihah had agreed to it being performed.

Entering her home, she would again break an egg and would they be escorted to her bedroom by the women in her family. Following this, there would be a feast for all their friends and relatives.

On the second day, called the *green day*, the bride would wear a long green dress with full sleeves and a sheer veil, secured by silver clasps, to cover her head. She would then be ushered by a female singer, singing traditional songs and accompanied by flutes and drums, from her bedroom to the room where the women would be waiting for her. Hot drinks like traditional coffee and white tea, as well as homemade cookies and biscuits, would then be served. Tradition would also have Ra'id come to her house to recite the *Fatiha*: the first chapter of the Holy Quran.

The third day of celebration, or the *colorful day,* Samihah would go to the hairdresser wearing a thick red dress with gold strings, similar to an Indian wedding dress. She would wear all the gold that she owns, as well as a gold-colored veil. The bride-to-be would be accompanied by a *Sana'ani* singer, who would lead her to her guests.

The following day would be dedicated to *henna.* She would have a henna artist decorate her arms, shoulders and legs. Samihah would get a special pattern, different from that given to her family and friends. She would also have Ra'id's name written inside a well-decorated heart to the left of her chest, as a dedication of her love.

Ra'id as well, would have his prenuptial *ceremonials.* He would be expected to go to the barber to be shaved and to have facial masks applied. He also, and his friends, would go to a Turkish bath, and when exiting the building, Samihah would have arranged to have a band playing traditional instruments to receive him. The band would continue to accompany him to his home, in this case, to one of the wings of the Ambassador's estate, where he would change his clothes in preparation for an afternoon session with male friends and guests.

The last of the five days is considered the wedding day. Samihah would be accompanied by a few of her friends back to the beautician, where her makeup would be applied and she would don her perfumed, white dress. The afternoon and evening would be spent with her female family members and friends, in one of the great rooms of her father's home, singing, listening to music and eating.

Ra'id would be kept busy by his male relatives and friends out on the street in front of the Ambassador's house, singing and listening to music from loudspeakers, set up especially for the occasion. A band, composed of flutists and drummers would play old and popular Sana'ani songs. At one point, the women would come out onto the balconies and the roof of the house, to observe the men and to trill.

At about midnight, Samihah would be escorted to the nuptial bedroom and prepared to receive her new husband. She had rehearsed this part in her head a hundred times: Ra'id would come to her, put his hand on her forehead and then remove her veil. He would then gently kiss her on the forehead and lead her to the bed. At this point, tradition would dictate, that the women in attendance would trill as a sign of congratulations, but, both Ra'id and Samihah had agreed that there would be no fanfare of this type.

The two had also discussed who would run their household, and the honor and responsibility had fallen into Samihah's hands. To demonstrate this, they would play out the ritual in her favor. On returning to Frankfurt and their new apartment, Ra'id and Samihah would stand before the front doorway and he would try to step on her foot. If she wanted to be subservient, she would allow him to do so. If not, she would withdraw her foot. Both knew which she would opt for!

"Yes," she thought to herself, "it is to be a beautiful wedding!"

*****

On her third trip home, she decided to fly to Gaza City to visit Amal al-Hamara. The two had been inseparable as children, both having gone to the same schools and prayed at the same mosques. Amal was the daughter of the personal assistant to Samihah's father. She had been introduced to Samihah and her family during an informal get-together at the Yemeni embassy where the two girls had bonded instantly.

She was of the Zaidi Tribe from the mountain region. Though her father was Shi'ite, he had been able to gain employment as a domestic in the ambassador's home. Over the years, the Ambassador, himself of the Shafii Tribe, grew to appreciate Asad's views on local and foreign issues, which gave some balance to his own Sunnite interpretations. It was not long before the ambassador decided to make Asad his personal aide and confidant. When the former was appointed to Kuwait, Asad and his family followed.

Their stay was to be a long one, lasting twelve years, giving the two girls the chance to grow together as sisters. But when Samihah's father started his own worldwind series of appointments, the two almost lost touch, meeting only a few times a year.

Amal returned home with her family when the ambassador retired. There she met a young Palestinian, fell in love and married. Because of her station, Samihah had not been invited officially, but had nevertheless gone to the wedding as a welcomed visitor. After the birth of their first child, a boy, Amal and her husband moved to Gaza to be close to his family, wanting to raise their child in the traditional ways.

Samihah and Amal corresponded at least once a month during the first two years, but letters between them became less frequent, with greater and greater intervals between them.

Because her wedding was fast approaching and she wanted Amal to be part of it, she decided to ask Salah, Amal's husband, to agree to bring his family to the wedding celebration and to permit her participation. This would complete the festivities. Samihah would bridge the gap between her past and present, while preparing her future with Ra'id.

*****

(Present day)

Brigadier General Tyson "Tyke" Kelly was scheduled to appear before the Senate subcommittee on military appropriations. He had flown into Washington D.C. on Sunday night, a day before the televised sessions were to take place. He had booked a room at the Watergate Hotel, thinking there was a bit of irony considering members of the subcommittee he was to face. The interrogators would be looking for *plumbers* in his testimony, as was the case in the famous Nixon scandal.

Rising at his usual six in the morning, late for the military, he ordered up breakfast for a half hour later. Retrieving the complimentary copy of the Washington Post he made his way to the washroom. After a shower and shave, he dressed just in time to answer the knock at the door, announcing his breakfast had arrived. Looking at his watch, he saw he had an hour to eat and relax before getting down to business.

As he was making the final adjustment to his tie and checking to make sure his uniform was just so, another knock came to the door. "Maid service!"

As he opened the door, he was met by a pretty, olive skinned young woman, in a slightly oversized maid's uniform. Though not tailor-made to fit, it could not fully hide the shape of her slim body.

"Maid service, sir. Is it convenient for me to begin now, or would you prefer I return later?"

"Maid service. I'd like to service you," he thought to himself. "No, no. I'm just leaving now. Please do what you need to do."

Stepping back to the closet he grabbed his cap and slipped by the young lady and her cart. Twenty-six years of marriage had trained him well: he could look but not touch. As he walked down the hallway to the elevator, he directed his attention to the more serious things he had to think about. As he entered the elevator and turned to face the door, he was already reviewing in his mind the dollar figures he would use in his presentation. "Two hundred forty million......"

Returning to his room after six hours of gruelling testimony and questioning, he was exhausted. He mused about how well it had gone for him that day and decided he would celebrate with an expensive dinner and good scotch.

He stepped into the washroom and noticed something was odd. "Damn it," he said to himself. Picking up the telephone to call the main desk, he could feel his blood start to boil.

"Concierge. How may I help you this evening General Kelly?"

"There are a few articles missing from my room. Everything else seems to be in place, but my tooth brush, comb and hair brush are missing from the counter in the washroom."

"Sir, is it possible you left them in your suitcase or on a dresser?"

"No it isn't. For thirty years I have religiously maintained a few quirky habits, among which are the placement of my personal things for ready use. I suggest they were taken by the maid."

"General, I find that difficult to believe. France Mueller, your maid, has been with us for seventeen years and never have we had a complaint."

"How could she be with you for seventeen years when she is barely twenty-one...." He thought again.

"Jesus Christ, man! That would mean the woman I saw was not the maid!"

"It would seem so, sir," was the concierge's response.

"Then you have a real problem on your hands. Your security sucks now as it did years ago! What I can't figure out is why someone would go through all of this for just a few personal items."

"Please accept our apologies. I will send security up to see you promptly and take your report. As well, room service will be up to replace the missing articles. Once again, please accept our deepest apologies. We will get down to the bottom of this. And it goes without saying that your stay here and any expenses will be covered by the management." He hung up.

Tyke slowly put the receiver back on the phone and returned into the washroom to make sure he hadn't been mistaken. Seeing he was right, he grunted to himself, feeling miffed that he had been robbed; but then he remembered the concierge's offer and thought the numbers were in his favor: approximately twenty dollars worth in return for about seven hundred in room and board. Not bad! And yet he was still seething. How could this have happened and why?

Chapter 7

"Doctor Al-Eissa…"

"Doctor Al-Eissa…" boomed the voice from the lab's P.A. system.

"Yes, what is it?" Ra'id responded while clicking on the response button of the intercom, frustration showing in his voice at being disturbed from his work. He had long asked to have the speaker disconnected. He had even done so himself, once, only to have maintenance reconnect it within two days.

"Sorry to interrupt you. But you have a guest and he is asking if it would be all right to see you. He says he is your uncle and his documentation would seem to be in order."

Ra'id unconsciously looked up at the disembodied voice. "Uncle Umayr? Yes, yes. Send him up. I'll wait by the door to let him in myself."

"Thank you doctor, I'm sending him up with security now." Security here was tighter than at his first laboratory. One of the suggestions the Sheikh had made was to have him move his project to another building on the campus. It was four times the size and occupied the entire second floor of the building.

Ra'id rose from his desk wondering what could be bringing his uncle to Frankfurt. Skirting the many half assembled masers and the rest of the paraphernalia strewn across the floor and counters, he walked gingerly toward the locked door to the lab. Opening the door, he watched down the long hallway for his guest. It took about five minutes, but finally he saw the familiar figure along with the security guard. His uncle's walk was certainly not as crisp as that of the tall blond guard. Reaching Ra'id, the guard seemingly anxious to discharge his duty, quickly and without a word, returned along the same hallway.

Ra'id embraced Umayr.

"Uncle, it is good to see you!"

"I apologize for not calling before to let you know I was on my way. I knew you would be here, hard at work. I thought I would surprise you."

"That you have! I am happy you have come. I have much to show you."

They walked back to the desk where he was working. "I've been able to move quickly on my research, especially with Samihah gone home to plan the wedding!" he said with a chuckle.

"It is good to hear you laugh. And, hopefully I can help keep that smile on your face."

Sporting a puzzled look, Ra'id said, "I'm not sure what you are getting at, but Uncle, you do not look well."

Seeming to ignore Ra'id, Umayr looked around the room at all the equipment. "In part, that is why I'm here. But for the moment, show me what you are working on."

Ra'id grinned and for a half hour, he proudly showed his uncle his 'toys'.

"… and so, when I've finished assembling this component, I'll be able to feed the computer program sequence through this port and the maser will reproduce the *notes* required to destroy the virus. This will be the only multi-frequency, broadband maser capable of producing the range of oscillations required to do the job. The computer I have been able to lease, thanks to the Foundation's contacts, has permitted me to identify the right sequences to reproduce in a matter of hours rather than days. It's a super computer capable of performing five hundred billion calculations a second!"

"Very impressive! Not that I truly understand how it works, but I know enough to trust you will succeed. When do you think you will be able to test it?"

"Well, I've been delayed somewhat. The broadband spectrometer I needed has been on back order from the company in France. I should be getting it within a few days. After that, I would say no more than three weeks."

"That is incredible! I am truly pleased for you. And it sounds as if my timing is right. I have a favor to ask of you."

Ra'id knew this was to be the real reason for his uncle's visit. He simply smiled and waited for the punch line.

"I am not well, as you perceived. My doctors want me to stop smoking and reduce my weight. I have not been able to keep up with the demands of your father's business, nor with the demands of my own."

"Well, I noticed you were having some trouble keeping up with the guard as you arrived. How serious is it? Is there something I can do to help?"

Umayr sidestepped the first question and moved on to the second. "As a matter of fact there is. I don't tolerate traveling long distances anymore. And at the moment, I need to run a few errands which would require my absence for a week or so in total. I was wondering if you might be interested in completing these tasks for me? It seems you might have a little time and where you would need to go would not be a hardship for you."

"Uncle, how can I refuse? You have been a surrogate father to me and Ali since our parents' death. What can I do for you?"

"Thank you. You know, growing old is not easy! In my line of work, I have need for bank accounts in various parts of the world. Often, I need to draw on these to purchase the autos for my clients on a moment's notice."

Ra'id nodded.

"Sometimes I need to deposit my commissions personally, without an electronic or paper trail. I was hoping you would do this for me. You are the only person I would trust other than myself."

Umayr sensed a little hesitation from Ra'id and quickly added, "What I am asking you to do is not illegal. It is just that I have found it less conspicuous to travel as a simple business man, drawing little attention from others."

"Where would I be going?"

"Georgetown, in the Cayman Islands. You'll love it, I guarantee!"

Three days later, Ra'id was on Air Lufthansa flight #LH9766 with a connecting flight on American Airlines flight #1113 to Owen Roberts International Airport in Georgetown. Other than the baggage he checked in, his only carry-on baggage was a locked briefcase and an affidavit for the customs officers confirming the one hundred thousand dollars he had with him.

Ra'id could not help but smile to himself as he sat back in his first-class seat, sipping on complimentary champagne, with the briefcase at his feet. He would take time to enjoy the sun and sand. Germany might have its history, but it was most often cold and damp. He was to arrive on Sunday and his appointment was scheduled for Monday, leaving him plenty of time to enjoy the island until his departure on Friday.

Arriving at the airport, he stepped off the airplane only to be hit by a blast of hot Caribbean air. What a great feeling, he thought to himself! Walking into the air-conditioned terminal he half heartedly felt like turning around and stepping out in the sunlight for a few more minutes. But there would be time for that. Instead, he walked up to the immigration officer at Customs and presented his credentials and passport. He was surprised that he was ushered through quickly and seamlessly. There wasn't as much as a raised eyebrow when the briefcase went through the security X-ray machine. There had been some consternation over the contents in New York. He had to think this was not the first time money was being brought into the country in this fashion.

He made arrangements for a private limousine to his hotel. Not wanting to chance a taxi, a limo would afford him more privacy and more security. He still was very nervous about the contents of the briefcase.

On his drive into the city, he was surprised to see all the signs hanging on the buildings: all signs announcing banks rather than the usual restaurants or businesses. Not that the buildings were skyscrapers as you would find in New York or other major financial centers, with the tallest being a mere six storeys high. Well, in Canada there are coffee shops on every corner; in the U.S. it's bars; in Georgetown, there are banks!

After settling into his room, Ra'id deposited the briefcase in the hotel safe, obtaining a receipt for the parcel left behind. Somewhat less apprehensive, he decided to take a walk and get his bearings. About a half block away he reached North Church Street, the main street leading to the center of Georgetown. Lined on one side with shops and boutiques, and the ocean on the other, he strolled among the many tourists that milled in and out of the tourist traps on the strip. Looking out at the bay he could see four cruise ships, all lined up offshore, forcing the passengers who wanted to visit the town to take shuttles to and from the dock. When he asked, he was told that the townspeople refused to build a dock capable of accommodating the large ships, because they wanted to protect the coral reefs in the harbor and provide more jobs for the locals, shuttling tourists to and from the docks. In any case, for an island whose total population was only thirty-two thousand people, these ships increased the

61

population of the capital alone by some eight to ten thousand each and every day.

He kept walking along the seaside walkway toward a red-roofed restaurant called the Paradise Bar and Grill. He realized he was thirsty and a bit hungry. Sitting at a table on the harbor-side terrace he ordered a Corona and lime, along with a plate of nachos; not quite Caribbean-like, but it seemed to suit his mood.

The view was gorgeous. From there, he could see the large cruise ships from an angle, moored in a picture perfect position, each bow protruding slightly ahead of the other. Sailboats and motorboats alike crisscrossed the harbor, dwarfed by the behemoths next to them. The water sparkled and, looking back toward the town, he marvelled at the buildings painted in hues of pastel beiges, pinks and blues.

Ra'id suddenly felt alone. He missed Samihah: he knew how she would have loved to be there and to witness the view with him. As much as these feelings of emptiness hurt, he tried to tell himself that they were a reflection of how much he loved her. He made himself a promise that within one year, he would return to this Caribbean paradise with her.

Four hours later, Ra'id was in his room sound asleep. Jet lag had hit him hard after his beer and he had to hail a taxi to get back to his hotel.

Bright and early the next morning, he was up, showered, shaved and had had by 9:00 a.m. His appointment at the Bank of Geneva was for ten and he did not plan to be late.

Mr. Hanif, the bank manager, was waiting for him in his office. Ra'id was somewhat surprised to find a Saudi managing a bank in the Cayman Islands. He realized it was probably one of the reasons his uncle had selected this particular bank to set up his account.

The procedure was quick and simple. Ra'id was to present his credentials along with a letter from his uncle giving the manager instructions for the money. Ra'id would also confirm the account number and the password he had memorized, in order to complete the transaction. Once done, he could simply leave the briefcase and enjoy the rest of the week.

Mr. Hanif thanked him profusely and asked that Ra'id bring his warmest regards to his uncle. Walking out of the bank into the heat, Ra'id thought this had been too easy. Hey, why not enjoy it!

Returning to his office, Mr. Hanif retrieved the sheet with the combination lock numbers. Opening the briefcase, he let out a quiet whistle. This was a lot of cash, he thought. Calling his assistant, he asked him to bring a money bag. He then gave him the account numbers the currency was to be deposited in and scooped it out of the case and into the bag. The assistant turned and walked to the vault, where the funds were safely stored. Satisfied everything was in order, Mr. Hanif went about his business as usual.

At four o'clock, his regular departure time, he took his hat and then reached down next to his desk to pick up a briefcase. It was the one used by Ra'id. He walked out of the bank and, rather than turn to his left as he always did, he headed to the right, walking up three streets and then to his left for two. He was in a residential area of modest but well-maintained homes, each painted in a different pastel color, with contrasting wood shutters. As he stepped up to the door of the third house on the right, he was met by a short stocky man in his forties. With one quick glance around to see that no one was paying attention to them, Mr. Hanif simply handed over the briefcase, turned and walked away.

The other man quickly retreated into the house and went to the kitchen table. There he proceeded to turn the briefcase over, taking a jeweller's screwdriver from his shirt pocket. He began to undo the small screws holding the four footrests. As he removed each in turn, he tipped its contents onto a black velvet cloth on the table. In the end, twelve flawless diamonds, measuring about twenty-four karats all together lay there, shimmering in the sunlight, for a total value of about six hundred thousand dollars. These would be sold to the wealthy tourists on those cruise ships looking for *bargains*, moreover the gems could be hidden from customs officers upon the tourists' return home.

*****

(Same day, BBC News at 6:00 p.m.)

"We have received a report from Israeli officials, that a raid on a home in Gaza City resulted in the death of several individuals. They would only say that, based on reliable informants, Sheikh Salek al-Mayden, spiritual leader of Hamas and one of Israel's most wanted for promoting and organizing suicide bombers against the state of Israel, was in hiding in the house. The owner is known to Israeli intelligence.

The home was surrounded about 5:00 p.m. today local time, by an Israeli platoon, supported by heavy artillery. Israeli officials indicate that the house was destroyed after repeated orders to evacuate were ignored. Palestinian officials deny this, indicating witnesses had told them shots had been heard from inside the home prior to the attack. Furthermore, they said the Israelis had given no warning, but had fired on the home in an unprovoked act of aggression.

The action is believed to be in response to a recent stepped-up campaign of suicide bombers by Hamas, sanctioned publicly by Sheikh al-Mayden. Four suicide bombers killed a total of twenty-seven Israelis in the past two weeks.

A forensic investigation will determine if al-Mayden was, indeed, in the house at the time. Two women and a child were also reputed to have been inside the house and to have been killed during the attack. Because neighbours are hesitant to volunteer information to Israeli officials, it could be some time before the identity of each victim is confirmed.

Hamas has issued a press release indicating that this act demonstrates Israel's real intent: that of the genocide of the Palestinian people. They also vow to take whatever retaliatory action necessary to counter the Israeli moves...."

One hour later, the telephone rang in Ra'id's room in Georgetown.

Chapter 8

Ra'id had been a guest in Samihah's father's home during the funeral and for the previous four days. Extremely depressed, he had become a recluse and, to the consternation of the ex-ambassador, he had eaten little and had said even less. Indeed, Mohammed, his closest friend had met with rejection when he tried to get Ra'id out for a walk.

An unexpected caller knocked on his door at about 2:00 p.m. Sheikh Wadi Al-Kabir was greeted by a Ra'id he barely recognized. It was apparent he had not shaved for the four days he had sequestered himself, evident from his black stubble. His clothing looked a little *baggier* than usual due to the eight pounds he had shed. His eyes had lost their sparkle, showing heavy red veining and dark circles around them.

"Ra'id, you look terrible!" Al-Kabir moved forward and embraced Ra'id, who responded without enthusiasm

"Sheikh al- Kabir, excuse me for my appearance. Please step in. And forgive the condition of my room. I have not been an attentive guest of Sami..." A pause. He cleared his throat and continued, ".. of Samihah's father."

His eyes began to moisten and he turned away, seemingly to make room for Al-Kabir to walk by. A quick wipe of his handkerchief... He gestured towards the chair next to the desk. "Please, take a seat and make yourself welcome."

Al-Kabir deposited himself in the upholstered chair and leaned forward, looking into Ra'id's eyes as he in turn sat on the edge of the bed.

"Ibn Imad, I have come to see if I could help you during this time of grief. My heart is full of sorrow for you. What should have been a time of joy and hope for you and

Samihah has become a time of desperation and tears. I want to share in your pain and lend you what support I can provide. When, and only when you are ready, I would like to talk to you."

"Ra'id's eyes moistened anew and before he could speak, he had to clear his throat. "I would like that very much."

Al-Kabir added, "I would like to invite you to my villa on the west coast of Italy; but only when you are ready. I think you will find the view amazing and the setting will help you heal."

They spoke for a few more minutes before the Sheikh rose and made his way to the door, followed by Ra'id.

Ra'id thanked his guest for his support and kindness, opened the door and Wadi Al-Kabir was gone. Alone again, the darkness in his soul set in once more.

He would meet with the Sheikh when the time was right, but he *knew* he needed to speak to Samihah's father. Why had the ex-ambassador not launched formal complaints, either with his own government or with the Israeli government? There was no way Samihah would associate with someone dealing with terrorists! Or could Amal or her husband be responsible? So many questions and so few answers.

He had to speak to the ambassador and find out why he wasn't acting like a father! "He must have as many questions as I have!" thought Ra'id as grief gave way to anger.

Part 2

Chapter 9

(Present day)

There was nothing unusual about the lecture room. Like many of the newer minimalist styles of construction, the plain concrete walls still had faint signs of the forms used to build this room, as well as the other ten in the biophysics building. Nor was there anything unusual about the two hundred fifty plastic formed seats, with pullout writing surfaces. The lighting was just bright enough to allow students to see what they were writing, but the main demonstration table at the front was brightly lit, forcing the audience to focus on the presenter. What *was* unusual was the fact that every seat was taken. Even more unusual for a physics class, was the fact that there were more women in the seats than men!

Though he had only two hundred eight officially registered students, another forty-two had opted to audit the course: most of these were third year female students with time on their hands, an interest in sitting up front to get a better view and hoping to find out if the rumors were true. Not a *Brad Pitt*, Sam Buckner was considered by the ladies population to be attractive in a tall, blond and brilliant way. He wasn't exactly the typical nerdy university professor. Even under his white lab coat, it wasn't too difficult to see that he was quite well built. At six foot one, with a perfect rack of white teeth, broad shoulders, it was no wonder this green-eyed blond, with wavy locks, would be considered quite the catch by members of the fairer sex! On several occasions, he had been seen out at coffee shops and concerts with some of the senior-year female students. It was a matter of getting noticed by him, or so they hoped.

As Sam paced back and forth in front of the table, he rarely looked at the students, much to the consternation of some. It wasn't that he was aloof or uninterested in their presence; rather, he was usually so engrossed in the topic, he would lose himself in his lecture. And the topic today was somewhat more fun than usual.

"Whether you know it or not, radiation is constantly bombarding us. Luckily for us, the earth has a protective layer of ozone which shields us from most of the damaging ultraviolet rays of the sun. Other particles, however, are not stopped by the ozone layer: neutrinos for example, are small, almost zero mass particles that interact with matter via the weak nuclear force. They literally find matter transparent and travel through it, us, the earth, as if none of it existed. On the contrary, other particles such as protons coming at us from the sun or the *billions and billions of stars*," said in a Carl Sagan voice and drawing a few chuckles, "do have mass and therefore will interact with matter. And that would include us!"

Looking up at the audience he raised a question: "How many of you here have ever seen a Wilson chamber or water vapour chamber?" One hand went up about ten rows up.

"And where was that?" Sam asked.

"Back home in Vancouver," was the response.

"Give the man ten thousand bonus points!" responded Sam.

"You're right! In the reception room at the TRIUMF cyclotron facility in Vancouver, you can find one. You might be thinking: *What's so great about that?* Well, nothing more than a demonstration of protons, neutrons or photons actually colliding with matter: in this case, super cooled, supersaturated water vapour. When the particles enter the chamber and interact with the medium, they leave behind the telltale trails of energy released by the collisions. It's quite

70

beautiful, actually. They show up, from ten to twenty hits per minute, as little bursts of gray contrails going in every which direction, or as small explosions about an inch or so in diameter. I stood there for two hours once, just peering into the sealed tank, until they threw me out." A few more chuckles came from the audience.

"Right, I know, I should get a life!" More chuckles! "In any case, it has a link with today's lecture." Again looking up, searching for just the right subject.

Pointing up at a well-tanned girl in the fourth row. "I see that you had fun in the sun during Reading Week." At first, there was a look of surprise and fear; then a smile came to the young woman's mouth and she nodded in the affirmative. "Well, this is one way to get noticed," she thought.

"The tan does look good on you, but you should try to refrain from doing it too often." The smile disappeared and a look of, *I know what is coming*, replaced it.

"Just as can be demonstrated in a vapour chamber, particles from above not only strike the earth but each and every one of us. Most of the time the body can withstand the rays and particles, leaving only nicely-tanned skin as a result."

He said this while looking up again at the young lady. "However, often the particles will strike genes within our DNA, damaging them and therefore weakening the genetic code in that double helix strand. Luckily for us, every cell of our body has the sum total of the same code. So a few hundred genes per day is not a big deal, you might think. But as more and more of these genes are damaged, the cells begin having problems performing. Damaged skin cells show up as dreaded wrinkles. And people, trust me. All those skin creams can't repair the damage to those genes! Thinking the cream molecule is capable of repairing the individual genes would be like having a great humpback whale try to feed a minnow!" There were some groans and moans from the audience.

As he quickly glanced at the clock on the wall, he concluded, "So, one could say that aging is not a factor of time but rather an accumulation of damaged genes! And that's the subject of next week's lecture!"

Through the rising noise of binders closing, writing shelves being put back in their resting positions, Sam could barely get the last word in. "And don't forget that your papers for this week's tutorials have to be in no later than Friday!"

Sam began storing his lecture papers in his briefcase and casually looked up again at the mass of students leaving through the four exits. He noticed three people staying put in their seats in the last row at the top of the room. Looking more carefully, he saw they were all dressed in dark suits. "OK, what the hell is going on now!" he thought to himself.

As if to answer his mental question, the third to the right stood and said with some air of authority. "Doctor Buckner, could we talk?"

It wasn't a question!

Chapter 10

As the three started to descend towards Sam, all he could think about was that this couldn't be good. These weren't *local yokels*, so they had to be Feds! "Then, what could it be about?" he thought to himself. "Wait! Cabo? So I raised a little Cain! Ok, so I was escorted from that bar to my hotel. Could that be it? No, don't be ridiculous! That can't be it!" He kept an eye on Curly, Larry and Moe until he realized they were Curly, Larry and Maureen!

Leading the pack was a tall, polished, agent type. Trimmed hair, crisp white shirt and shiny shoes, just as policy required. Following him was a much shorter and stockier man. From the tanned and leathery face, it was obvious this one was more at home in desert fatigues than in a suit. The third person bringing up the rear really surprised Sam.

At first he had thought another male agent, since the hair seemed as trim as the first agent, but what he could not see because of the distance and the dim light, was that she had her jet-black hair was pulled back into a ponytail, keeping the sides flat against her head. Her suit was black as well, but once she moved toward the short agent, there was no mistaking her for a man.

It would dawn on him about an hour after the three had left, why she looked so good: 1:2:5! These were the classic Greek proportions of the body as described by his former high school History teacher: one head, two heads to the waist and five heads to the floor. All clothing designers used these proportions to create their designs. At about five foot ten, she had those proportions, enhancing the way the black suit made her look, in contrast to her two male companions. He even noticed her slightly elevated heels, which he imagined gave her behind a nice sexy shape. Once Sam could actually see her face, he saw that she was a complete package! Not as tanned as the short agent, Sam realized she was a black woman, but with lighter skin. Her bone structure was striking: high pronounced cheekbones, perfectly straight nose and full lips. And then there were her eyes! He had never seen a black woman with bright blue eyes! Sam was taken aback by her beauty, so much so, that he barely tuned into what the first agent was saying.

"Doctor Buckner, I'm Agent O'Connor from the Canadian Security Intelligence Service." Pointing to the other male agent, "This is Agent Cohen from the Israeli Secret Service. And this," looking at the third individual, "is Agent Gordon from Homeland Security. We were wondering if we could have a word with you, in private."

"Ok!" he thought. "Not Cabo!"

"Would you mind telling me what this is all about? I'm not used to getting your type of visitor."

"It is a sensitive matter, but it's about some deaths I hope you might be able to help us with," responded agent O'Connor.

"But my area of expertise is genetic biology, not forensics. I could suggest someone else if you would like," Sam added, hoping to steer them elsewhere.

"Our friends at the Rockefeller Biological and Health Sciences Foundation strongly recommended you," interjected Agent Gordon in an icy voice, not meant to compliment but rather to control. "They indicated that you were probably the best qualified scientist for what we need to find out."

Looking at Agent Gordon, he said, "OK then, why don't we go to my lab where we can have some privacy and I can see what I can do for you."

Agent O'Connor stepped forward slightly. "Sounds like a plan. Please lead the way Doctor." As he started to follow Sam, he gave Agent Gordon a look that said clearly she should *butt out*: this was his backyard, so to speak, and he would lead the presentation. The slightest flinching of her blue eyes told O'Connor that she had understood but wasn't happy about it.

As they reached the exit door to the right, Sam gallantly opened it and stepped aside to allow the three agents through. He couldn't help but look down at Agent Gordon's backside as she passed. "Yep, I was right!" he thought to himself!

Chapter 11

Sam's lab was a foreign country as far as Agent O'Connor was concerned. He wasn't familiar or comfortable with the stark environment he and his colleagues had walked into: a black-tiled floor, black inert rubberized countertops, and white cupboards and walls everywhere else! Another thing he felt ill at ease with was Sam's mess: piles of paper reports; six, no, seven computers in different areas of the lab, and a huge garbage can full of empty McDonald hamburger boxes and coffee cups. Back at his own office, there was a place for everything and everything was in its place. The top of his desk was always tidy and cleared before he left every day. He thought, "How can this guy even think in such a mess?"

Seeming to sense the agents' thoughts, Sam pointed to one of the few empty tables saying, "I know its cliché, but sorry about the mess. It's the maid's day off! Grab a stool and make yourselves comfortable over there while I take off my lab coat."

As soon as they were all seated, Sam positioned himself next to the Israeli in order to get a better view of Agent Gordon across the counter. Agent O'Connor began. "Let me get to the point! Doctor Buckner, I assume you've heard of spontaneous human combustion."

Sam's head snapped from looking at Agent Gordon's face to O'Connor's, with a look of bewilderment molding his face: "Huh? Pardon me, but you came here to talk to me about the incident my partner mentioned a few weeks ago?"

Agent O'Connor repeated, "What can you tell me about spontaneous human combustion?"

Sam momentarily dropped his head and then looked up again. "What I can tell you is that it is incredibly rare. About two hundred alleged cases have been reported in the last three hundred years. There's a lot of speculation as to whether it is fact or fiction. No one has yet been able to adequately demonstrate how it would happen, if it were true, nor have they been able to provide definitive proof that it has happened. That is why I basically dismissed the supposed case Jalal mentioned to me."

Looking around the table at the lack of smiles and their intense eyes on him, he had to ask, "Are you trying to tell me otherwise?"

The three agents looked at each other briefly and Agent Cohen nodded slightly to O'Connor. Agent O'Connor turned to Sam and said, "We don't have one case. We now have six and all within the past month!"

Sam could not believe his ears. Six cases within one month would make the odds against such an occurrence some millions to one!

"You mean to tell me that you think these cases are true spontaneous human combustions?"

O'Connor responded, "What we are saying is that we have six cases in which individuals have burned totally, without any obvious external source of heat close by: no chemicals, no flames, no gases, nada!"

He looked for confirmation from Agent Cohen who nodded in the affirmative. O'Connor continued, "Each one of the bodies burned to a crisp without affecting anything else around them. Officials are at a loss to explain the phenomenon: hence our visit here today."

Sam sat back without saying anything. He had completely forgotten about Agent Gordon. His mind was racing to try to understand what he was being told, and even more so, how he could help. A hundred questions sped through his mind. Quickly, however, his scientific discipline began to categorize them in related groupings. Some needed answers now, others later, but all needed to be answered if he was to be of assistance.

"Ok," he said, "let's back up a moment!"

He looked briefly at the three of them. "If I'm to make some sense of all of this, I need to know why you three are here: a Canadian, an American and an Israeli. Let's start with that!"

O'Connor was the first to speak. "Good question. Agent Cohen can best answer that."

This was the first time Agent Cohen had opened his mouth, symptomatic of a well-seasoned agent who knew when to speak and when to listen. As short as his five-foot-six height was when standing, he seemed to be looking at each one around the table at almost the same eye level. He obviously could use some help with the 1:2:5 proportions where his legs were concerned. Too bad men didn't wear high heels: he could *really* benefit from a boost in height.

When he spoke, he could not hide his heavy Jewish accent. "The three of us are here because of the sequence of the events. What Agent O'Connor did not mention was that the six cases we have are all Israeli, all military, all in different locations and all dead through spontaneous human combustion."

Sam's eyes widened, his brief conversation with Jalal coming back to him!

Agent Cohen continued, seeing the effect his words were having on Sam, "We have yet to find how these six cases are related. We think it could have something to do with some of the missions they had been sent out on. So far, the trigger link evades us."

Sam interjected, "OK, let me guess. The math would indicate that this is no ordinary sequence of events. The probabilities of six deaths, all from one country and all military can be calculated. But add the way in which they died and the odds are astronomical! Therefore, we are not talking about a naturally-occurring event. So, you have surmised that this is a man-made event and that you are talking about a weapon of some type. Am I right?"

All three agents nodded at the same time without speaking.

"So the Israeli government thought this was too big to keep to itself and decided to involve the US government because it had no idea how this possible weapon worked. This would explain Agent Cohen's visit, as well as Agent Gordon's presence, but why are you here Agent O'Connor?"

O'Connor looked at Sam and with a glance at Agent Gordon, he said, "You're not the first scientist they have met with."

It was Agent Gordon's turn to speak. "He's correct. After being contacted by the Israelis, Homeland Security assigned me to scout out the scientist who could possibly help us with our investigation."

With a little smile she couldn't suppress, she continued, "Agent Cohen and I have interviewed twelve scientists who have been referred to us. You happen to be number thirteen." Sam's ego had just been dealt a severe blow and he knew she knew.

"The problem is that none could supply us with feasible or relevant information which could help us understand what is happening and how this is happening. We're running out of names. We came to you because we were told you could think out of the box. So when in Canada, CSIS had to be involved."

A quick nod from O'Connor.

"Do you think you can help us?"

Sam realized she really wasn't as secure and in control as she had tried to convey earlier and that he could still salvage his ego! It was his turn again. "If you've come to me, then you have determined the answers lie with the biology of the body. Again, I'm no forensic expert, but there are certain items that beg explanations. First, the simple fact that you have six victims removes any question spontaneous human combustion. Moreover, because there are six, we can assume that however it is done, whoever is responsible, has proven that they can do it over and over again, targeting different individuals. Now, there could be two ways this process can occur: the first is having the victim ingest something that is either the catalyst which would then cause the body to ignite. Or, whatever is ingested becomes the vehicle which is somehow ignited, spreads throughout the body and burns the victim."

Looking at Agent Cohen, he queried, "Have your scientists found any indication that such a chemical was used?"

Agent Cohen responded, "We have tried to find residue which could possibly tell us that this was how it was done, but to date, we have not been successful: perhaps because the bodies were so totally consumed."

Sam resumed his brainstorming. "Let's say this was not the means used. And by the way, it would be difficult to explain how it could be administered to so many, in some many different places, without any one of them being aware, or without anyone else accidentally ingesting the chemical agent."

Again, a nod of agreement from the trio. Sam was thinking maybe he could yet possibly impress Agent Gordon!

"So, if not a chemical taken internally, that leaves the cause of death by some external source. The only one that comes to mind would be something along the lines of microwaves. Somewhat like those you use daily when you use a microwave oven. But even this method presents issues that do not help explain what has happened. For example, consider how the microwave works: it excites the molecules to vibrate at very high rates, thereby producing the heat that actually cooks the food. The more water molecules present, the faster the process occurs."

The look of boredom on Agent O'Connor told Sam he might be giving him a Cooking 101 course. "Let me get to the point. Have you ever tried to microwave an egg in its shell?"

Agent O'Connor shook his head. "I wouldn't suggest it. You'll end up having to spend the day cleaning up the mess after the egg explodes all over the interior of the oven! If microwaves were used to kill the victims, I have no doubt they would have exploded much as the egg would. And, if the news report my partner Jalal shared with me is accurate, there were others present. With the microwave scenario, they would have been affected as well."

O'Connor responded, "Some of the other scientists we consulted believed it could have been done with highly directional microwaves. So you are saying that isn't what is responsible for the murder of the six soldiers?"

"I'm not saying that," responded Sam.

It was his turn to show a little smile curling the edge of his mouth.

"I truly believe microwaves were used, but not on the molecular level. Rather, it was done on a level much, much smaller than that: possibly at the genetic level. And it would have to simultaneously affect every cell the same way. In a microwave, the outside and the inside of the food do not cook at the same time, and with the different components of the body such as blood, bone and skin for example, I can't see them frying so quickly and homogeneously. But for now, I'm clueless as to how this could be done!"

Agent Cohen interjected, "Dr. Buckner, one of the reports we have mentions a colony of bats flying away. Does this mean anything to you?"

Sam thought for a second or two. "That would fit! As you know, bats target their prey using ultrasonic waves. If, as

I imagine, this weapon uses something along these lines, then, they could possibly be sensitive to the microwaves."

All three agents looked at each other. This time it was Agent Gordon who spoke. "I think I need to apologize for my comment about you not being our first choice."

Sam could see by the softening of her features that she was sincere and he felt his ego heal instantaneously. "I think my colleague from Israel will agree that we have gotten farther with you in less than fifteen minutes than we have in weeks of interviews." Sam acknowledged the comment gracefully.

She continued, "Your explanation does make some sense, but we are still a long way from being able to find who is responsible."

Sam jumped in. "Yes. However, if I could study the bodies or what's left of them, I might be able to confirm my suspicions. If I'm right, it could go a long way in helping me identify a *signature* that could direct you to the culprits. The principle on which this process works has to be highly structured and this means a telltale signature should reveal itself if we know what to look for. I would need to see any and all reports from bystanders and witnesses. There could be something in what they saw or heard that could help us narrow down what happened and how."

Agent Cohen interjected, "That's what we are hoping for." Looking briefly at Melinda and then back to Sam: "You say culprits! Does this mean you believe we are talking about more than one person?"

"Yes, we are talking about an incredibly sophisticated weapon. No one individual can finance and assemble something like this on his or her own, especially the finance portion."

Agent Cohen added, "I think you are on the right track. What is the saying, *follow the money*?" He was about to continue when his cell phone rang. He answered in

Hebrew, listened a few seconds and then turned it off. He raised his eyes to look at the other agents and said, "We have another victim: this time in Hebron!"

Again the agents did their ESP thing, looking at each other before turning to Sam. It was Agent Gordon who spoke first. "Dr. Buckner, feel like taking a trip?"

The comment caught him by surprise and he could only look back with his mouth wide open in an effort to say something, anything!

"Look, Dr. Buckner, I think I speak for the others as well: I believe you're our man on this mission. We need someone who will explain the science involved. Any information that can bring us closer to finding this weapon and destroying it is critical. Can you imagine if the Russians or the Chinese, or God forbid, the Iranians are involved!"

Sam finally regained his composure and replied, "It's not that I don't want to help, but what about my research?"

Agent O'Connor responded, "Before coming to meet with you, we took the liberty of contacting your department chair about the ramifications of you leaving your research at this stage. First, he assured us that we would have his and your full cooperation. Secondly, if my information is correct, I believe your lab partner is in a position to run this phase of your project on his own and that your presence will be required once the data you are looking for is available. Am I wrong?"

Sam frowned realizing they had done their homework and that they were correct. He wasn't needed here, at least not in the immediate future.

"OK, I'm in."

Chapter 12

Within two hours, they were on a flight to Tel Aviv.

Sam couldn't believe the sudden whirlwind he was living. The first thing he had done was to call Jalal to let him know he was leaving. He couldn't tell him why, yet, or for how long. He had been told that Jalal would be provided with a world cell phone number Sam could be reached at any time of the day or night. His only concern should be to get the computer program they had worked on started and debugged.

Next, he had thirty minutes to get some of the basics he would need from a few boutiques close to the lab: a carry-on bag, toothbrush, toothpaste, a couple of pairs of underwear, nightwear boxers and an extra shirt. The rest he could buy in Tel Aviv, all on Canadian government's credit card!

An hour before the flight, two black SUVs showed up just outside his lab. Agent O'Connor stepped out of the first and pointed the second vehicle to Sam. "You take a seat in that one. I won't be going with you to Israel, but you'll be in good company." He quickly got back into his vehicle. As Sam opened the rear door of the SUV, he found Agent Gordon in the other seat while Agent Cohen sat in the passenger side of the front seats, next to the driver. Without any warning, as soon as the door was closed, the rack of lights on the top of both SUVs was turned on and the cars squealed off in the direction of the Gardener Expressway, which would then take them on the highway links to Pearson Airport.

During the time Sam had shopped, Agent Cohen had already arranged for three tickets on El Al flight LY104 which was to take off at 1:30 p.m. and get them to their destination. It would be a long eleven hour flight. Though every seat had been pre-booked, with a little arm-twisting and the threat of getting his director to call to confirm the authenticity of the request, he had convinced the airline staff to find him three seats in first class. He didn't care what they had to say or offer the passengers: he just wanted those seats! He *knew* they would be available upon their arrival at the airport.

The roads were relatively congested, but the one thing they could count on was the courtesy of Canadian drivers. The traffic parted like the Red Sea when they saw the flashing lights above the SUVs. Sam did get a glimpse of his condo building by the lake as he was whisked by on the Gardiner Expressway. The trip took only thirty minutes and when the short convoy got to Terminal Three, instead of going to the entrance, the vehicles raced through several gates leading directly to the tarmac and the base of the already-running airplane. As Agent O'Connor waved goodbye to the individuals climbing the exterior steps to the gantry, he could only guess at what they might be getting themselves into. He would have given his right arm to go along with them!

Agent Cohen was the first to enter the plane and was greeted by the flight attendant. A few short words, this time in Hebrew, and the anxious steward led them personally to their seats as the plane's doors were closed and sealed. The last in line was Sam who was the only one of the three showing any expression on his face. As he looked around the cabin, he couldn't help but crack a smile of satisfaction. Trying not to say anything that would betray his amazement, he quickly sized up the first-class seats: large and made of leather, with legroom worthy of his six foot one stature. The seats were set five abreast, two on each side next to the windows and one in the center between the two aisles. Sam was particularly pleased that Agent Cohen was shown to seat 3C, a middle seat, and Agent Gordon and he were shown to seats 4A and 4B. He felt a little guilty until he saw Agent Cohen throw them a look of satisfaction for his lot. Sam could only assume it had something to do with providing Cohen with two ways out of his seat *if* an emergency presented itself. "Shades of James Bond" he thought.

The plane was already moving to the take-off runway when Sam let out a long slow breath. Agent Gordon turned her head and those blue eyes towards him and asked, "Are you OK?"

"Nothing a beer couldn't help."

She responded with a smile that wasn't as sarcastic as it was seductive. "I'll tell you what, if you don't request a beer during the flight, I'll buy the champagne."

Sam wasn't quite sure how to take it, but he said, "OK, you're on."

As soon as the plane had taken off and reached its flight altitude of thirty-five thousand feet, the attendant closed the curtains between the economy class and first class. Another was moving to the individual passengers, offering drinks and *nibblies,* that she would get and bring from the galley: no carts like Sam was used to in economy class. When it was Agent Cohen's turn, all he asked for was a glass of orange juice. When she finally reached Sam, he smiled at her and pointed to Melinda. "She's buying champagne for two." The attendant returned with the crystal glasses and champagne bottle and poured for both passengers and then left.

Sam raised his glass to Agent Gordon and said, "I've only known you for a few hours and after a few of these, you'll have me flying higher than a kite. Here's to you Agent

Gordon." She looked at him and smiled. "First things first. It's Melinda and you're welcome!"

Sam smiled and said, "Shut up! Like on the Ghost Whisperer. I love that TV series. A little out in left field, but I think it's based on some fact. You're putting me on, aren't you?"

"No, it's my real name and no, I don't talk to ghosts! But I get that all the time. You should have been there every time I made suggestions about different cases I've worked on. The comments I got from my male counterparts were hard to take. Their problem, though, is that I was more often right than wrong!"

Sam could tell that he had hit a nerve.

"OK, I promise I won't go there. I have to admit, I've had a hard time not asking you a personal question."

She cut him off quickly and said: "I know what you are curious about. It happens all the time as well and the answer is one I'm actually rather proud of. You want to know why an African American woman has blue eyes!"

Sam was shocked that she had guessed correctly and hesitantly responded, "Jesus, you do have ESP! Look, if you don't mind me saying, I realize how your obvious good looks and overall package could be used as an advantage in some situations. I also know that, like in the university system, it could be seen as a negative: all superficial and no depth. I can only imagine how it could be difficult for you in an organization where testosterone is so prevalent."

She looked at him and thought she might have misread this one.

"Now you're the one with ESP," she said softly. "I know I came on strong when we first met.."

Sam interjected sarcastically, "An understatement!"

She continued after a short hesitation which clearly meant *don't interrupt until I'm done*, "… it comes with the

87

territory. I've made it to where I am because I'm good at what I do. I would guess the same can be said for you?"

Sam responded in a self deprecating way. "I'm not quite there yet. I think my thesis will lead me to bigger and better things. However, let's get back to your blue eyes why don't we!"

He ordered more champagne and shifted his weight slightly to be better able to look at her without having to twist his neck sideways.

"Well, where do I start? Of my three siblings, I'm the only one with blue eyes. The reason we know it wasn't the milkman, is the fact there have been at least one, if not a couple per generation of my ancestors, all going back to the seventeen hundreds, who have had blue eyes. We've traced it to about 1794 and my great-great-great," she smiled and went on, "great-grandmother Murielle Montpetit in New Orleans. She didn't have blue eyes we've been told, but a rich Cajun, Jean Pelletier, did. It seems it was customary at the time for rich plantation owners to take on black mistresses, set them up in their own homes or apartments in the French Quarter where they would visit these women when in town on business for their plantations."

Sam leaned back a bit and hesitantly said, "She was a hooker?"

Instinctively, she slapped him on the shoulder. "No, not at all! At least it wasn't taken as such. Many of the *kept* women bore children who were actually raised with the man's last name and sometimes, even worked in the father's business. Not on the plantation, mind you! The wives would not take kindly to that. They tolerated the situation as long as the husband never appeared in public with them while the wife was in town. So Murielle had four children, three of whom had the father's eyes. It would seem that blue eyed blacks were in high demand. The children were given the best education available at the time and were considered quite cultured. Two of the girls with blue eyes ended up finding their own rich partners. It is one of them of whose lineage I am a descendant. That's it in a nutshell! I have to admit, as much as the story could be interpreted a somewhat unsavory, I take some pride in it. It gives me character, don't you think?" She smiled and cocked her head slightly, reinforcing her question.

"What a great story! Do you know what makes it even better?"

"No clue, what?" she responded.

"We could be related!" he said with a devilish smile on his lips. Now it was his turn to look for a reaction.

With an incredulous look on her face, she blurted out, "How the hell can that be?"

"Well, you know that at the beginning of the Seven Years War, England rounded up thousands of French citizens living in Acadia, now the Maritime Provinces in Canada. About one-third were deported, men in one direction, women and children in another."

Melinda interjected, "That's terrible! It really isn't much different from the slave trade."

"You're right, but that's another discussion. In any case, about a third ended up in Louisiana which was still French. Many disappeared into the swamp areas or *bayous*, which is what the English later called them because they couldn't pronounce the words *bas lieux* or lowlands! They couldn't pronounce *Acadien* either. That was butchered to *Cajun*. But you knew that, didn't you?"

Melinda stared him straight in the eyes and half sarcastically responded, "What do you think? Every self respecting Cajun would!"

"Ok, right!"

Sam continued, "Some Cajuns integrated in the business community and became relatively wealthy. That was the case with my ancestor: Jean Buchanier. Sometime with

89

the next generation or two, the name was anglicised to Buckner. One of the grandsons migrated back to Nova Scotia and the rest is history."

A curious look came to his face. "Wouldn't it be funny if somewhere in the past, we had a common ancestor?"

"I'd say it would be interesting but not likely," she responded, breaking off her stare and sitting back into her seat.

"Oops!" thought Sam, not too sure why the sudden chill.

Just then, the flight attendant came with the headsets for the video and audio system. Sam appreciated the break!

Both perused the available movies. They had just enough time to watch one before dinner was served. Sam chose James Cameron's *Avatar*, while Melinda selected, go figure, Guy Rithchie's *Sherlock Holmes*!

The stewardess was starting her dinner rounds. Melinda turned to Sam. "Hope you're up for a great Kosher meal!"

"I have to admit, it isn't a cuisine I've really tasted, but I'll try anything once!"

In turn, the meal was served one dish after the other: chicken Udon soup, sautéed chicken with olive tapenade, followed by lamb and spinach-stuffed onions and then soy spinach with sesame seeds; for dessert, a couple of pieces of chocolate Texas cheese cake with espresso coffee.

The attendant brought them their choice of after-dinner drinks. Sam selected a Courvoisier cognac, while Melinda stated she was partial to Grand Marnier.

As they both cupped their snifters, he opened up with, "I'd like to get back to a point you made during our talk in my lab."

Melinda leaned towards Sam and waited.

"OK, if my job is to look at the science to try to see *how* it's done and to try to narrow the field for you, how will you go about trying to find *who's* doing this?"

Melinda smiled. "Good question and one that I've been thinking about. We have several sources of information we can draw upon. For example, the Israelis are looking for the common element that links the victims. I don't think it will take long for them to come up with an answer.

Homeland Security can call on other police and intelligence organizations to look for *intel* that could give us some leads as to which country or group might have been involved in the type of research or project you tell us is at the bottom of this case."

Sam added, "Sure, no pressure? But I've been thinking about this as well. One area you haven't mentioned, involves the academic world."

Melinda gave him a quizzical look.

"Yes, if the weapon works the way I think it might, it could be the brainchild of some doctoral candidate or researcher somewhere in the world."

Melinda's eyebrows rose a little. "Yes, yes. I see what you are saying."

"Now if I could get some help from your computer geniuses, I might be able to look after that area of our search. I could start with the obvious universities in the US and Canada, and then, if I find nothing, I could branch out to Europe and Japan. China, I would imagine is out of my reach: that would then be up to your *spooks*! No offense meant!"

Melinda just shook her head. "None taken! But you may have a point. I'll make arrangements for you when we get back. Now, I don't know about you, but I wouldn't mind getting a little reading done before I try to get a few hours of sleep. You should too: we arrive at 7:35 a.m. and Agent Cohen has arranged for you to examine the victims at 9:00 a.m. You told him you needed an electron microscope, so we

91

will be going to the Wolfson Applied Materials Research Center at the Tel-Aviv University, once you've completed your work on what is left of the bodies at the university's medical center."

Sam couldn't help but frown. "I can't get over it. Like three first-class seats on a flight at only two hours' notice, a high-speed convoy down Toronto roads and overnight access to a piece of equipment that would take me weeks to get time on back home! I don't know how you do it, but you sure pull a whole lot more weight than I do!"

As he was saying it, he couldn't help but look her up and down quickly. She caught the look and while she pushed herself back into the reclining position in her seat, she said sternly, "I hope you were commenting on my clout and not my size?!" Then she smiled and opened her book.

Chapter 13

One month after Samihah's funeral, flying into Naples's Capodichino International Airport, the plane's glide path took Ra'id in from the north. As he looked out his window, there was no way he could miss seeing Mount Vesuvius looming off in the distance only six miles away. It was more than just impressive. It was actually frightening to see the very mountain that destroyed Pompeii and Herculaneum back in 79 AD and that could, by all accounts, erupt again at any time. He couldn't help but get a chill and to shiver a little at the thought.

It had only been one month since he had lost the love of his life. When he had received the Sheikh's invitation to visit him at his villa on Capri, he knew he could not refuse. He needed to speak to the Sheikh! He had had time to think things through and he knew the news he had to share would be difficult to say.

The plane touched down on schedule at 9 a.m. and within thirty-five minutes, Ra'id was walking through the exit doors of the terminal. Among the dozen or so limousine drivers standing with placards to draw the attention of their passengers, Ra'id saw his name being held up high by a tall, slim man dressed in a black suit, white shirt and black tie. Ra'id wasn't quite sure what to make of him. He had a long straight nose, caved-in cheeks and was white as a ghost. His slicked-back hair *a la Valentino*, gave him the sinister look of a vampire in those 60's movies. Not until the eye contact between them revealed who Ra'id was to the driver, did the blank look on his face transform into a wide grin. The driver came over to Ra'id, shook his hand in exaggerated motions and, in a thick Italian accent, introduced himself as Vincenzo

Provani. He immediately took the suitcase out of his passenger's hand and led Ra'id to the limo area. He pointed to a dove-gray convertible Ra'id recognized as a brand new Bentley Continental GTC. Sleek and sporty at the same time, it was almost sixty-four hundred pounds of sheer luxury. Vincenzo opened passenger door and dropped the front seat to let Ra'id step into the rear seat. Ra'id looked at him and asked if he could sit in the front. Vincenzo pushed the seat back into its initial position, smiled and waved Ra'id into his seat. Quickly depositing the suitcase in the rear seat, he hopped around the car and settled into the driver's seat.

Vincenzo was in his element. In a very thick Italian accent and almost impossible to decipher, he said, "I hope you are not in a great hurry to get to Capri? Sheikh Al-Kabir has ask me to show you my most beautiful city of Napoli."

What could Ra'id say? It was sunny, a warm breeze was blowing in from the bay and he was sitting in the incredibly soft leather seat of a Bentley with the top down. With one of the few smiles that had shaped his lips in a month and putting on his cool Versace sunglasses, he simply said, "Let's get out of here!"

With that, Vincenzo turned the ignition on, bringing the five hundred sixty seven horses to life. He could have shown off by pulling out quickly: the twelve cylinder, twin turbo vehicle could accelerate to sixty miles per hour in four point five seconds. He decided instead to impress Ra'id with the car's smooth ride rather than its brute force.

Vincenzo was to give Ra'id a roundabout drive through the city of Naples down to the dock area where they were to take the five o'clock ferry over to Capri. He headed down to the A56 which took them west of the main part of the city. As he pointed out different sites, he described them with all the panache of an Italian tour guide, arms flailing and almost yelling because of the noise of the wind and the traffic. He was loving it!

They passed over an intricate series of over and underpasses. He explained that the highway and bridges straddled the cliffs below them, were actually the interior walls of volcanic craters that pockmarked the landscape of Naples. This was due to the super volcano which lay dormant beneath the bay! Vesuvius was not the first, nor would it be the last the region would suffer. The landscape was not what Ra'id had envisioned as the interior of a volcano: there were trees, houses and streets covering every foot. Not the bleak rocky terrain of the documentaries on volcanoes he had seen on the Discovery Channel.

Exiting the highway, they drove eastward along Via Vicinale Cupa Cinitia, past the San Paolo stadium and towards another ridge. The road began to meander and zigzag upward through subdivisions of homes that clung tenaciously to the slope. Ra'id couldn't help but marvel at the nonchalant way they all seemed to ignore the frightening beast beneath them. Signs of down-to-earth living could be seen everywhere: brightly-painted houses in white, peach or yellow, with orange and lime trees growing in their small courtyards, and newly-washed clothing hanging from their upstairs balconies. He began to understand the Italian love of life, family and tradition. His heart saddened as he thought that these were all the things he had lost not long ago.

The Bentley reached the crest of the ancient caldera and slowly began its way down towards the bay. Ra'id sat up in his seat and marvelled at the view before him. It was spectacular! In the distance towards his left was the ever looming Vesuvius, with its perpetual hovering cloud. Before it, lay the bay of Naples, framed by the crescent shaped land on the one side and the expanse of the Western Mediterranean on the other. The water sparkled, reflecting the sunlight as millions of blue and white stars, while pleasure crafts, ferries and cruise ships criss-crossed its surface. Below them, revealing the rate of the precipitous slope, were the red terracotta roofs of the homes and *palazzos* of the markedly more affluent people who could afford the view. Following the serpentine streets leading down to the shoreline, they finally levelled out onto the Via Francesco Caraciolo.

In the distance Ra'id could see Ovo Castle. Standing defiantly on its own little islet, it evoked conflicting emotions in Ra'id. On the one hand, he was amused by its shape which reminded him of a child's attempt at building an imaginary castle using Lego blocks: a large, more or less rectangular base rising three storeys directly out of the Mediterranean and capped haphazardly with a half dozen oddly shaped rectangular towers, some thirty feet high, others forty feet. On the other hand, its age, size and stark architecture gave it a sinister look, created specifically to ward off would-be invaders of old. It had not, however, scared off the many pleasure-boat owners who docked their skiffs in the marina within its shadow.

Waking from his momentary day dream, Ra'id realized that Vincenzo was still jabbering about the sights, talking as they say, with his hands.

He turned inland on Via Cuma and zigzagged his way towards the Piazza di Plebiscito. As they rode along the piazza, he realized the square really wasn't square at all! The large open cobblestone area was shaped like a tea cup on its side. Half of it was framed on one side by a building similar to the Pantheon and a colonnade extending on either side, suggestive of Bernini's in St. Peter's Square. It was hard to tell if the large extended arms of the colonnade were there to warmly greet the tourists or to seduce them into getting closer, before scooping them up into a deadly embrace.

Shaking his head in an effort to dissipate the thought, Ra'id once more told himself to chill out and enjoy the sights.

The cup-shaped piazza was bordered on the opposite side by the Royal Palace. The large building was just one of four homes built by the ruling Bourbons in the 18th century and was typical of the architecture favored by them. Straddling the full width of the square, the three-storey edifice was aesthetically pleasing to the eyes, using balance, based on odd rather than even numbers. There were twenty-one, twenty-five foot-high arches, eleven of which allowed access into the palace, ten of which housed individual statues of the rulers of the Kingdom of Naples recessed into the openings. The narrower second and third floors each displayed twenty-one aligned windows with alternating peaked and rounded capitals.

Before Ra'id knew it, the car was turning right on Via Console Cesario, then made a hairpin turn onto Via Ammiraglio Ferdinando Acton, where it blended in with the non-stop stream of cars on the seashore avenue.

The flow of traffic slowly took them below and past the large elevated platform the palace was built on and down to the docks where cruise ships spewed their passengers out into Naples.

All of a sudden a mischievous smile came upon Vincenzo's face. He quickly took a look at his watch and then turned toward Ra'id. Trying hard to translate what he wanted to say in English, "How about I show you something amazing! And besides, the Sheikh will not get to the villa until late tonight."

With a grin on his face, he suggested they take the long way to Capri, via the Amalfi coast from Salerno to Sorrento. If he hopped to it, Vincenzo could make the six-thirty ferry from Sorrento to Capri and still have enough time to prepare Ra'id a gourmet meal before the Sheikh arrived. Vincenzo seemed to be trying to extend his drive in the Bentley as long as possible and since Ra'id subconsciously wanted to postpone sharing with the Sheikh the decision he had reached, they both agreed to head up the highway towards Salerno.

97

Approximately forty minutes later, the Bentley was exiting the highway and began to meander through the streets of Vietri sul Mare towards the famous coastal highway. It became immediately obvious that the fifty-mile drive was not for the faint of heart.

As Vincenzo began to expertly maneuver in and around the tight curves which hugged the sides of the cliffs that made up much of the Amalfi coast, Ra'id began to question his decision to go along with Vincenzo. Perched about seven hundred feet above sea level and some seven hundred feet below the clifftops, the highway could easily substitute for many of the more daring amusement park rides!

It took Ra'id a good half hour of white knuckle riding next to Vincenzo, before he finally began to relax enough to realize his driver was having the greatest time negotiating the never ending S curves, adeptly pulling his side-view mirror in and out in order to give the oncoming tour buses enough room to pass, sometimes, with only inches to spare. Ra'id also became aware that Vincenzo's breakneck speed around the corners was possible in part due to the parabolic mirrors strategically positioned on the outer railing, allowing him to see the traffic coming around the rock cliff to the right of them. Vincenzo had indicated that the car had all-wheel-drive, a specially-tuned suspension, making the ride both incredibly stable and safe. He had also pointed out the *infotainment* unit which included not only a high-end music system but a state of the art GPS unit. Beautifully framed in the burl-walnut consol, it allowed him the advantage of being able to see the curves ahead and make provisions for them with his driving. Ra'id realized that Vincenzo had probably taken this direction in order to make the ride a little less frightening, by driving on the inside lane of the highway.

About halfway to Sorrento, they came upon the town of Amalfi, namesake for the coastal drive and charmingly cradled in the V groove between two cliff walls.

Vincenzo suggested a late lunch. He brought Ra'id to a small restaurant in the Piazza Duomo, sheltered at the base of the steps leading up to the famous Saint Andrew's Cathedral.

While Vincenzo checked out all the female tourists walking by, Ra'id allowed himself to decompress while drinking his beer. As they waited for their meal, Ra'id unconsciously reached down to his right rear pants pocket, assuring himself that he had not lost the sheet of paper he had received by courier just a week before.

Looking at but not *seeing* the throng of people in the square, his mind was now in the past. After the Sheikh had left him following Samihah's funeral, Ra'id had indeed gone to confront her father to find out why a man of his stature and influence had not cried foul to high heaven. Considering his diplomatic status, should not the government of Yemen also have cried foul.

His meeting with the ambassador had been a sobering lesson in diplomatic considerations. The ambassador had indicated that he had expected Ra'id to come and question him about his lack of action concerning the death of his only daughter. In contrast to Ra'id's state of being, the ambassador seemed cool and detached while he described why he could not overreact to the event.

The Yemeni government had made it clear that, though they sincerely grieved with the ambassador for his loss, there was no way they could be dragged into a diplomatic clash with the Palestinians and the Israelis. As soon as they had been informed of the attack and the death of Samihah, inquiries had been launched to get to the bottom of the event. The ambassador's tone and eyes softened as he continued to explain the situation he was in.

He could potentially expose his government to irreparable damage for personal reasons, or, he could use his own resources to find out what had actually happened and develop a plan to satisfy his grief and that of Ra'id. Finally, through the first tears Ra'id had seen the ambassador shed, he was promised that nothing would stand in the way of their personal jihad.

Three weeks later, a courier had arrived at Ra'id's laboratory and hand-delivered an unmarked brown manila envelope. Inside was a single sheet of paper with eight names and addresses.

"Ciao, bella!"

Vincenzo leaned over to Ra'id and touched him on the arm closest to him and pointed to a tall model-like brunette *strutting her stuff* in her Prada stilettos and a classic Italian style chiffon dress, knowing she was the center of every man's attention.

"Beautiful, no?" he said to Ra'id. Shaken from his reverie and half hearing Vincenzo's comments, he smiled and nodded.

They soon finished their lunch and returned to the car. For the final leg to Sorrento and the docks, in spite of the harrowing route which mirrored the first leg, Ra'id was now impassive and unmoved by the spectacular scenery.

Chapter 14

Arriving at the Marina Grande on the Isle of Capri and having exited the ferry, Vincenzo smartly maneuvered the Bentley through the throng of tourists returning to the docks from Capri Town via the funicular. It linked the city center with the docks, saving the knees and hips of the thousands of elderly visitors to the jet-set island.

After working his way up to the town, Vincenzo aimed the car toward Via Giuseppe Orlandi, which would take them up to the top of the escarpment toward Anacapri.

Ra'id eyed the narrow road which meandered up and up, and realized that part of the road extended out from and around the cliff, suspended on nothing but tall concrete stilts! "What is it with Italians anyway?" he thought.

When they reached that spot along the narrow road, Vincenzo noticed that Ra'id was looking toward the sea beyond the cliff's edge. What he did not notice was that Ra'id's eyes were shut tight.

Reaching the top, the car moved away from the precipice, much to Ra'id's relief, past the Hotel Caesar Augustus on the right and then on for a few hundred yards before slowing and turning left through a stone gate onto a laneway. The lane curved slowly back toward the cliff, bringing chills to Ra'id's spine. Luckily, the high stone wall shouldering both sides of the lane, not only hid the other homes behind the wall, but any view of the cliff's edge Ra'id knew all too well was getting closer.

About three hundred feet farther, the car reached a solid metal gate which blocked any forward movement. Vincenzo leaned over to the glove compartment, opened it and pressed a button which triggered the gate opener. As the gate slowly slid sideways out of the way, Ra'id had his first view of the Sheikh's estate and his jaw dropped!

Beyond the gate was a large, pressed-concrete driveway, resembling an old Roman road. The driveway in front of the house was large enough to park some twenty cars. The house itself seemed to be an eclectic mixture of Roman and contemporary architecture. It stood three storeys high in the central portion, and was flanked by two, two-storey wings, angled slightly back toward the rear. It was massive with about forty to fifty thousand square feet of living space by Ra'id's best estimate!

The main entry was accessed through what looked like a semi-circular raised marble portico, framed by six Ionian columns. Protected within and to the rear, was a double wrought-iron gate leading into the area that served as the main entrance to the house. This part of the building had no windows to the outside and seemed to have a flat roof. The walls were built with red bricks which contrasted the white stucco walls of the main house.

The façade of the main building was almost windowless and looked a little like an old medieval castle with rampart walls around it.

Just as the sun was setting, Vincenzo brought the car around to the steps leading to the entrance and looked over at Ra'id. "Very nice! No?"

Ra'id responded, "Impressive, very impressive."

Vincenzo parked in front of the portico and jumped out of the car without opening the door, quickly grabbing Ra'id's suitcase. As they walked through the portico and into the room, Ra'id realized that it was a reproduction of a typical Roman villa and its *impluvium* or central pool of water, with a fountain in its center. Surrounding it was a series of Doric columns which supported what Ra'id had originally thought was a flat roof. In fact, the structure was a *compluvium* or inward slanted roof Romans used to capture water for their daily use. As they walked around the pool under the covered portion, he marvelled at the walls which were painted in the traditional red color of the times and were decorated with a series of authentic mosaics depicting all the Roman gods in different life situations: eating lavish meals, frolicking in the countryside, or ravishing human females.

Seeing the look on Ra'id's face, Vincenzo simply said, "The Sheikh wanted to have a peaceful entrance to his casa, where one could leave the problems of the world outside!"

On the opposite side of the room they came to two tall oak doors. Passing through the doorway and into the foyer was like walking into a Disney-like castle. The room had to have twenty-five hundred square feet of marble flooring. The three storeys high walls, also covered in white marble, were devoted to showcasing the double spiral staircase leading up to the second floor, where Ra'id assumed were the sleeping quarters on either side. The rear wall was an expanse of windows some fifty feet wide, from the ground floor to the full height of the room, allowing the walkway between the two wings and staircases to seemingly float in midair. He could not only see the patio, which was lit by a series of lampposts, but also the rear yard and a spectacular view of the Bay of Naples beyond.

During their drive here, Vincenzo had tried to describe the architecture of the house and the philosophy behind its design: few windows to the west, reducing the heat from the mid- and late-day sun, representing the harshness of life, while allowing the morning sun and the surrounding light to bathe the entire space with glorious light, signalling the Sheikh's belief in the promise of life.

Vincenzo gently put his hand on Ra'id's shoulder. "Come. Let me show you to your room and I will prepare for you a *delicioso* meal. You can relax at the pool," pointing to another double-door just off to the right in the atrium. "The

103

Sheikh will be back later tonight and you can see him in the morning."

Ra'id got shivers just thinking about someone driving up the side of that cliff at night!

His room was in the left wing of the house and would surpass that of any five-star hotel in Rome. Having changed into his bathing suit, he quickly skipped down the stairway two levels lower to the indoor pool room which was actually below the rear patio.

Again he was awed by the architecture of the room. It enclosed a thirty- by fifty-foot interior pool, surrounded by a deck decorated with mosaic motifs similar to those found in Pompeii and Herculaneum. Miniature palm trees and an assortment of local flowers dotted the area, with the whole of the exterior walls being made up of floor to ceiling windows. Recessed pot lights in the floor lit the walls, flooding the room in soft ambient light. Night had fallen and all he could see through the windows were the distant lights of Sorrento and off to the left, those of Naples.

The experience of the day and the surprise of the estate were starting to take their toll. Vincenzo came to fetch Ra'id about an hour later and led him to the kitchen to serve him his supper. He said the kitchen would be a less formal and cosier place to eat. Again not quite: the kitchen was as large as some of the professional kitchens in the great restaurants. And yet, Ra'id agreed, the table in the corner where they ate was indeed cosier than what he imagined the dining room would be.

He then retired to his room and, after finding the cognac the Sheikh had left for him, poured himself a drink, slid under the blankets and propped himself up against the pillow. He needed to rehearse what he had to tell the Sheikh in the morning. He turned the nightlight off and closed his eyes. Just as he was dozing off, he thought he heard the whoop-whoop sound of a helicopter coming closer and closer. "Wouldn't you know it! The Sheikh is arriving in style."

Ra'id woke up about 8:00 a.m. to the sight of a slim blade of bright sunlight slicing through a thin slit between the curtains. Walking over to the window and pulling the curtains apart, he caught the view of the Bay of Naples down beyond the edge of the escarpment, which was surprisingly close. He hadn't realized that the rear of the estate was actually only two hundred yards away and that the edge of the property was marked by a concrete newel fence, *a la Italiano*.

Close to the edge, but raised a few steps, was a twenty- by thirty-foot stone patio covered with what reminded Ra'id of a Bedouin tent made up of white linen sheets. Sitting at the marble pedestal table in the center, reading documents and having his morning coffee, was the Sheikh.

Chapter 15

In spite of the soft breeze flowing through the linen sheets of the gazebo, the Sheikh heard the footsteps in the grass behind him. Without hesitation, he looked up from the documents he was reading. "Good morning Ra'id," and only then did he turn to look. Ra'id hopped up the few steps and warmly embraced his patron.

"Before you sit, please, take a look at the scenery," he said as he walked with Ra'id, arm in arm, to the edge of the property behind the barrier.

He could feel Ra'id strain a little as they approached the edge, but then, the site of the town of Capri below and to their right, and the expanse of the bay ahead of them with a view of Vesuvius, was enough to enthral him if not relax him.

"Isn't it a glorious morning?" asked Al-Kabir.

Ra'id's smile dimmed a little. "I have things I need to discuss with you."

"I had a suspicion this was the case," responded the Sheikh. "Let's retire to the *tent* and talk as our ancestors once did."

By that time, Vincenzo had arrived at the gazebo with coffee and fresh-pressed orange juice. His demeanor was different however: stiffer and more formal than Ra'id had seen.

"Oh well, the boss was home," he thought.

After pouring the beverages, Vincenzo bowed slightly and left. When he was about twenty yards away, Ra'id turned to the Sheikh. "It was such a pleasure meeting Vincenzo and having him look after me yesterday. He is quite the character."

"Yes, that he is and more. He does so much for me as well," responded the Sheikh.

Ra'id leaned a little toward the Sheikh and began. "I'm not much for *beating around the bush* as they say. I have come to a decision. One you may not like."

The Sheikh simply sat, impassive, without an accusatory look.

"My life has not been the same since Samihah's death." His eyes misted a little, but his face took on a hard look.

"The last time we met, I wasn't in my right mind. I was conflicted, not knowing which way to go. The circumstances of her death did not make sense to me; yet, everyone around me acted as though it was an accident or mistake. I could not put my finger on the answer, so I went to see her father to confront him with my doubts."

The Sheikh stirred a little and brought his hands up to his lips, pressed together as if in prayer.

"A few weeks after her funeral, I received this."

He pulled out the folded sheet of paper and placed it on the table before the Sheikh. "I show you this because I believe you will understand *why* and *what* I must do."

The Sheikh reached for the paper and unfolded it. Looking at the content for but a moment, he put it back on the table and pushed it toward Ra'id without saying a word.

"I have come to you in order to let you know I need to leave my research for a short while. There are things I need to do in order to follow our holy commandments. I will need to take lives, but only in accordance with our belief of not taking lives unless it is to serve justice."

He stopped to see if the Sheikh would react. He saw no show of emotion, one way or another.

"The names on the list are those responsible for Samihah's death and I need to avenge it. She deserves justice. The soldiers involved will not only go unpunished for killing innocent people but will probably receive praise for their actions. I cannot allow this to happen. So, I have decided I need to track them down and kill them."

Still without saying a word, the Sheikh sat back in his chair, but this time there was a look of disapproval showing.

"I see you do not approve of my decision, but I am afraid it is non-negotiable. This is my personal jihad and I was hoping you would understand." He, too, sat back in his chair.

There were a few moments of silence before the Sheikh stirred. He looked directly into Ra'id's eyes and said, "First, let me commend you for your devotion to Samihah and to your beliefs. If I were in your shoes, I would wish to do the same!"

The surprised look on Ra'id's face did not go unnoticed by the Sheikh.

"Having said that, I need to ask you how you plan on completing your task. For example, the method you will use, how you plan on getting to each person on your list, or the fact that once you begin, how you will protect yourself from the Israelis who most certainly will be looking for you?"

Ra'id looked at him somewhat sheepishly. "I haven't worked out all the logistics, but I think I can put together a plan based on timing and stealth. Whether I use a gun or knives, I truly believe that with some patience, I will be able to find each one and dispatch them."

The Sheikh stood and slowly moved around the table without saying anything. He then turned to Ra'id. "Listen, my friend. We have invested an incredible amount of money into your concept. The potential for the world is truly unimaginable! There are a great many people who believe in you, and dare I suggest, Samihah was your greatest supporter."

Ra'id was stunned by the comment, which hinted at the direction in which this discussion was going.

"I do not take your wish for revenge lightly. On the contrary, some of my discussions with our specialists and consultants have raised sensitive questions and issues. I am, if nothing, an opportunist. In some circles, that would be considered a fault. In others, a quality which allows one to see potential and make things happen. The success of the Foundation is a result of this approach."

Ra'id didn't know what to make of this disclosure, but his curiosity was beginning to pique.

The Sheikh continued, "Tell me the truth please. How far away are you from completing your project and proving that you have a cure for HIV?"

"I would say a month to a month and a half at the most." was Ra'id's response.

The Sheikh looked down at the table for a moment, hesitated and then slowly looked up at Ra'id. "What I am going to suggest to you could be wrong and, I dare say, diabolical from the point of view of the Holy Quran."

Again he hesitated. "Theoretically speaking, could more of the DNA be destroyed by your procedure?"

Ra'id looked up at the Sheikh. "In theory, yes. If more of the DNA is factored into the formula, the equipment should be able to destroy much more of the cell material."

"Then I suggest to you that I would be willing to assist you in your quest by using our network to locate and collect samples of the DNA of these eight individuals for you to use."

When the full meaning of this offer sank in, Ra'id could not help but sit up in his chair.

"This will not happen however, until we know your process does work. Is that understood? This is why I suggest you put aside your jihad until you have results. Once completed, you will then be able to have your revenge, without putting your life in great jeopardy. You are too important to us to put your life on the line, without a plan and the proper equipment."

Ra'id stiffened in his seat and then slowly rose to his feet. He gave the Sheikh a slight bow as a sign of acceptance. The Sheikh approached him and gave him the traditional embrace he had once done when Ra'id had first described his concept.

The Sheikh stepped back and sat down as he gestured to Ra'id that he do the same.

"What would you need to do in order to make your system portable?"

Ra'id thought for a moment. "I believe I could reduce the size of the equipment to several components which could be moved in a small truck or van."

The Sheikh smiled for the first time and looked over to the patio at the rear of the house where Vincenzo waited. He waved him to come.

When he reached the gazebo, the Sheikh informed him that he was to take Ra'id to the airport the next day, but stop by on the way to visit his *cousin,* who could help select a vehicle which would be modified to Ra'id's specifications.

The Sheikh then ordered breakfast for himself and Ra'id.

Chapter 16

The rest of the day was spent determining what Ra'id would need to do to prepare the equipment to fit the van.

After breakfast the next morning, Vincenzo stood by the car waiting for Ra'id. He was wearing a limo driver's hat and quickly moved to take Ra'id's suitcase from his hands and opened the rear car door, all prim and proper.

The auto was not the Bentley they had driven the day before, rather an elegant but a nondescript black sedan. The look on Ra'id's face prompted Vincenzo to say, "Where we are to go, is not a good idea to have a *spensive* automobile."

When he finally sat in the driver's seat after putting the suitcase in the *boot*, Ra'id quizzed Vincenzo, "You don't seem to be in the same mood today."

Looking at Ra'id through the rear-view mirror. "Yesterday was a treat for me. This now, is my job and is what is *spected* of me!"

The only good thing about the drive down the escarpment was that the car was on the inside lane and that, other than the knowledge of the height they were at, there was some sense of security from the presence of the outside lane between them and space!

The ferry to Naples was on schedule and once they arrived at the port, they retraced their journey, using some of the roads they had taken into the city, but in reverse. They traveled along the waterfront and then up the bayside slope of the volcanic crater that had so mesmerized him on his arrival. Then they zigzagged down to the base of the interior of the crater toward the San Paolo Stadium; but, instead of turning right to the street leading to it, Vincenzo turned left. They soon found themselves driving along an access road to a train yard. Vincenzo stayed to the left of the train tracks, bringing him to a *Y* in the road: the right side continued onto the end of the yard, but the left branch led them to a gravel road, through the industrial part.

Ra'id had fleeting moments of trepidation, wondering where in the world they were going, especially when the gravel road turned into a dirt trail, closely shouldered by trees and bushes. He was about to question Vincenzo, when the car took a sharp left onto a short driveway leading to an opening through a ten-foot rusted privacy fence. The fence surrounded a large compound with a few buildings made of similar tin walls. Littered everywhere in the compound were hundreds of derelict automobiles of every shape and size.

Only then did Vincenzo turn to Ra'id. "Welcome to a my cousin's auto restoration business."

As the car slid to a stop, Vincenzo cautioned Ra'id to stay inside until he had a chance to locate his cousin and explain their purpose there. He would soon return to introduce him. Ra'id did not object, now understanding why the Sheikh had not sent them in his Bentley.

Within five minutes, Vincenzo returned with a stocky man he introduced, with a wink, as his cousin Hanz!

The man was all business! After a short, curt handshake and a nod. "I understand you need a special vehicle?"

Ra'id was confused at first. With a name like *Hanz* and a Bavarian accent, they could not possibly be related. Not wanting to look like a deer in the headlights, Ra'id tried to control his facial expression by thinking he would ask Vincenzo later.

"Yes, I do. I'm looking for something along the lines of a small cube van, with a box approximately three yards wide and five long."

"I don't believe I have such a vehicle on the lot, but we did get something in that might meet your needs. It is a

Mercedes Sprinter Cargo Van which is a little smaller than what you want. It was involved in an accident a week ago. The insurance company assessed it as a total write-off, but with some tender care, I can make it look brand new!" Turning around and looking from left to right, he spotted it in the far corner of the lot. Pointing to it, he started walking toward the wreck with Ra'id and Vincenzo in tow.

As they approached it, Ra'id surmised by the damage, that it had been quite the accident. The side of the cab had collapsed inward and the frame was bent by what must have been a powerful collision. Red stains on the window on the driver's side led him to think there had been a death involved.

He turned to Hanz and said, "Can you really restore this van to its original shape?"

Hanz gazed at him with the look of a man whose ego had been injured. "Not only will it look the same, but I'll also improve the engine's performance so it will give you an extra ten miles per gallon."

"Can the sides and top of the cab be made of acrylic?" asked Ra'id.

"That will cost you more and will require an additional month to complete," responded Hanz, confident he had a lucrative contract. "I'll deliver the vehicle in two months. I will contact Vincenzo to let him know where you can take delivery. Will that do?"

"Yes, quite well, but," handing Hanz a sheet of paper, "here are a few more modifications I would need."

Hanz took the sheet, looked it over and said, "No problem, but it will be another month and cost you even more!"

Without another word, Hanz simply turned around and walked away, leaving the other two standing by the van. Ra'id chuckled. "Not much of the social butterfly is he?"

Vincenzo smiled for the first time that day, shrugged his shoulders and waved Ra'id toward the limo. Forty minutes later, Ra'id was walking into the airport terminal for his return journey.

Chapter 17

Shortly after Ra'id left the estate, the Sheikh was on the telephone with the board members of the Foundation. The summons was simple. Be here in forty-eight hours!

Two days later, twelve limos crawled up the face of the escarpment toward the Sheikh's estate.

The board members all walked through the mock Roman villa, into the grand foyer and to the meeting room on the first floor of the Sheikh's wing.

The room had a medieval feel about it, in that the table around which thirteen chairs were set, was reminiscent of King Richard's fabled round table. The walls were faced with beautiful floor-to-ceiling walnut bookcases, filled with hundreds of leather-bound books, including a four hundred-year-old hand-written Quran and original manuscripts of Copernicus and Darwin.

When they were all seated, the Sheikh entered the room followed by Vincenzo who was carrying a tray with a pot of tea and traditional Arabic tea glasses, each decorated in gold motifs. Once all had been served, Vincenzo promptly left, closing the soundproof door behind him.

The Sheikh began, "I've called for this meeting because I have good news to share with you. I believe all of our planning will shortly come to fruition. My meeting with the young Al-Eissa yesterday has taken us to within one step of success. He has consented to complete his project and, in order to achieve his personal jihad, he has agreed to modify it to make it the weapon we have been hoping for, even though he is doing so in order to seek revenge for the death of his fiancée."

This brought about nods of approval from every member of the Board to the Sheikh, as well as to one another.

"He has estimated he would only need about one month or so to perfect and demonstrate his concept to eradicate HIV. I had to promise him that the Foundation would orchestrate the announcement of his project to the world. There is no doubt that he would receive the Nobel Prize for it. But he understands that this will happen only when he has completed his quest for revenge."

Again nods of approval as well as a cacophony of hands slapping on the table.

"We need to put into place our plan to take advantage of the new weapon and use it to help us bring about the creation of a United Islamic Federation. With this weapon, we will be able to direct the politics of the world to our advantage."

This time, there was a round of applause.

"We all know that the leverage we and our brothers have been using to influence world politics, will no longer exist before long. Both, the price of oil and alternative energies, will bring an end to much of the income of our future member states. With this weapon, our assets to destabilize the world scene will no longer be needed."

The Sheikh smiled a little and added, "Al Qaeda has proven to be an effective tool to keep the world's attention away from us and help focus American policies on their own war against terrorism. But I think you will agree, we need to reel the movement in somewhat, before it becomes too difficult to control. With the death of Osama bin Laden, this could be somewhat problematical, considering the egos of some of the fill-in leaders that have surfaced. Bin Laden was a useful pawn for us because we only needed to deal with one individual; now we are looking at trying to coordinate an ever-growing but fragmented group of followers, all trying to outdo one another."

116

One member of the Board raised a finger to get the Sheikh's attention, "What do you propose we should do at this point?"

"For one, we will reduce our funding to these radical groups and allow them to simply wither. We then can divert our investments toward the implementation of our master plan. For the moment, Ra'id still believes the weapon will only be used to eliminate the eight Israelis on his list. Once we have the technology, we will adapt it to our needs. Mustafa, are you still on track for acquiring the array of satellites we will need?"

"Yes! We should be in position to sign the leasing agreements in a week. Our cover story is that we are to launch a new worldwide Arabic virtual university."

"Good! Keep us informed of your progress," responded Al-Kabir.

"Our immediate concern is the need to gather DNA from the eight soldiers in order to provide Ra'id with the samples he will need. We must deliver on that promise. Ali, you coordinate our assets in Israel. I will give you a copy of the list and you will need to mobilize our people to get what we need. As for the rest of us, we have to go through our lists of priority targets and continue gathering DNA samples for phase two of our operation."

Another member caught the eye of the Sheikh. "And what of Ra'id?"

"As much as I like him, he will be expendable once we have the technology. We must be diligent however, never to allow him to know how we have manipulated his life to draw him into our midst: from orchestrating the death of his parents and sending him into the arms of our man, his uncle, to the disinformation provided to the Israelis, which led to the demise of his fiancée. It is too bad that he will never be known for his contribution to humanity. If his concept were ever made known, too many governments would realize its

117

potential as a weapon and want to use it as we will. No! We need to be discreet and use the weapon strategically in order to ensure none of our enemies ever think they can retaliate. We need only to make an example of one or two well-placed targets and they will all fall in line. If they think any one of them could be eliminated at will, who would dare challenge us?"

This brought more nods and table-stomping noise. With that, they all rose and were led to the main dining room for a grand lunch before their return to the port and then home, leaving the Sheikh sitting alone in his study, sipping on a Cognac.

Chapter 18

The Sheikh

He was close, very close to achieving his life's goal: being powerful and influential, well beyond anything his family could have hoped for or expected of him. True, it had taken a chance meeting with Umayr Al-Eissa and the story of a proud uncle concerning his brilliant nephew and the invention he had conceived. He had quickly realized the true potential of the invention and how he could possibly make use of it to change history, both his and the world's.

Sheikh Asim Wadi Al-Kabir downplayed his origins by using only part of his name when doing business. But everyone *in the know*, knew his complete name: Asim Wadi Al-Kabir Al-Sallah. His link to the Kuwaiti royal family had opened many doors for him and had also acted as a barrier, which he felt had prevented him from realizing his full potential.

The son of Salim Al-Mubarak Al-Sallah, brother of the future Emir of Kuwait, Mufti Al-Salim Al-Sallah, Asim had been born just after the end of the Second World War, a time of turmoil in the Middle East. It isn't known just how many wives his father had taken, but there were over thirty children, of which Asim was somewhere in the middle.

He, therefore, had little chance of moving up to the position of ruler of Kuwait, a fact that had always bothered him! As a child, he had lived a life of opulence and had taken on that air of importance, characteristic of great leaders.

Attending the best schools in the Middle East and then in Europe, he had demonstrated an above-average intellect, showing he could quickly grasp different concepts and expand them beyond their obvious meanings.

He was a *horizontal learner*, meaning he learned many things from a great many areas, but was able to see the links between them in ways *vertical learners* could not.

One event in particular had marked him and helped shape his future. When he was fifteen, Mufti Al-Salim Al-Sallah became the ruler of Kuwait. Mufti's tendencies were definitely less pro-Anglo and more pro-Arab. He moved quickly to end British control over his country and then signed up with the Arab League. At the same time, he wrote a new constitution and declared himself Emir instead of Sheikh.

Asim had been jolted from his predictable and posh lifestyle, and began formulating the stand he would take *if* he were ever called upon to assume a position of responsibility. He believed Mufti had moved in the right direction, just not far enough. Salim believed that the Arab world was too tribal and divided, and that it needed to rally around a higher cause or purpose: Islam! This would mean that existing national barriers would need to be torn down, including those of his cherished Kuwait. Members of the *new order* would also have to extend a hand to other non-Arab countries that embraced Islam as well.

He took on a more focused interest in Islam, not so much for its dogma; rather, because he realized that it could be a unifying tool for his people and for the other Arabic nations around him. Also, while at university, he concentrated on courses dealing with international diplomacy and finances, looking for models he could use to advance his dream.

After graduating, he worked for the family business, generating huge sums for the Al-Sallah coffers, with investments made mainly in the US. In fact, by 1991, after the Gulf War, the Al-Sallah families were worth ninety billion dollars according to *Time* magazine and within twenty years was estimated to have tripled or quadrupled! Asim, as

120

did many of the family members, earned a very comfortable monthly stipend, allowing him to concentrate on his work rather than on making ends meet. In fact, he had invested his personal income in the very same investments which were making the whole dynasty wealthy.

Over and above the money he was earning, his business ventures allowed him to make very important contacts everywhere around the world, especially in the Muslim world. Even at this early age, he had wisely decided to use just a part of his name, preferring to think he was *making it* on his own rather than on the merits of his family's name.

When he proposed and created the Foundation for the Promotion of Islam, he took on the honorific title of Sheikh. Though his title meant leader, he preferred to work from behind the scenes and in the wings of the theater of world politics and power.

Using the Foundation as a vehicle for his dream of a more unified and respected voice for Islamic countries on the diplomatic stage, he began grooming like-minded individuals. He would scout out, wine and dine, and *educate* promising young Muslim talent, enticing many of them with free tuition and board at the best universities or military colleges around the world.

He used his influence to help them find important positions in the political, diplomatic and military ranks of their respective countries. He needed enough of them placed in strategic positions, capable of influencing their nations in the direction of his dream of a unified Islamic Federation.

The twelve who had just left his villa in Capri were his generals: completely devoted to the cause and ready to work at removing the leaders of their countries. These leaders, they believed, were only interested in maintaining the status quo and enriching themselves to the detriment of their people.

He knew this would be a long venture, filled with possible obstacles, but he had many *pots on the burner*: plan upon plan that could accelerate the process. Then, the chance meeting with Umayr.

If this young Yemeni scientist could actually pull off the creation of his medical tool, Asim had been assured by some of his most trusted protégés, that such a weapon could revolutionize warfare. He quickly put a plan together to isolate the young Ra'id, while making him beholden to the Foundation for financing his research. The plan took a few years to mastermind and implement, but now he was so very close.

It would take all of his intellectual prowess to coordinate the coups which would take place across the Muslim world and also ensure that none of the Western powers, or those in Asia, would dare retaliate.

With the creation of the Islamic Federation, there would also be a need for the position of President of the Federation. Who better than himself? He had already decided that he would keep his title of Sheikh and not change it to Emir, both as a sign of humility and his deep belief in history and tradition.

Chapter 19

True to his word, Hanz contacted Vincenzo three months later, almost to the day. Ra'id was to take delivery of the van in a quaint hill town in central Greece. Arachova, on a Sunday morning, was simply charming! Families were out in force, local restaurant patios were packed, Orthodox priests walked on the main street with children surrounding them. Hanz was sitting at a secluded table on one of the patios, next to a group of loud French medical doctors on holiday.

The transaction was to be short, as expected of Hanz. Ra'id walked over to the table set for two, ducking slightly under the canopy of grapevines suspended on a wire mesh arbor. Hanz was nursing a glass of Uzo with water. He waved to the waiter to bring another, but Ra'id signalled that he was fine and did not want one. Then, sitting on the empty chair, he said, "Good morning, Hanz. I have been anxiously waiting for this day." Looking around and down along the narrow road beside them. "Where did you leave the van?"

Hans pointed to a street intersection about sixty yards to the left. "I parked it along that street. There was no place on the main road and I did not think you would want to make it obvious."

He quickly downed the rest of his Uzo and got up to go. "Come, I'll show you what I built for you. I think you will be pleased."

They walked away, leaving a few Euros on the table. As they turned the corner at the intersection, Ra'id saw the van.

"It looks beat up," Ra'id said and hesitated a moment for effect. "but it is perfect!"

123

As per specifications, Hanz had disguised the van to look much older and well-used. "I will tell you, that despite its outer shell, that vehicle is in perfect condition, as promised."

Ra'id took several minutes to inspect the van.

He smiled. "Yes, it is perfect."

Keys were exchanged for a manila envelope and Hanz was gone.

Fifteen minutes later, the black van negotiated a right turn onto the main road out of Arachova, heading down the mountain and on its way to Frankfurt.

Soon he would return to Greece, to spend another few days in Mykonos to rest before taking the ferry to Kusadasi in Turkey and his destiny. Perhaps he might meet that sweet young woman again? Perhaps…

Part 3

Chapter 20

(Present day)

The plane began its slow descent from thirty-five thousand feet. They were above the Alps and the sun was just peeking over the horizon. Lights were turned on and a flurry of activity began in the cabin, with curtains being drawn between first and economy class, carts being pushed along the aisle and passengers stirring from their sleep, to the smell of that great European coffee.

Sam drifted out of his dream, his head leaning on the window shade, his pillow crushed into the crook of his neck and a blanket covering his shoulders. He realized that he had a little drool dripping down the side of his chin. Quickly wiping it with his sleeve, he looked for Melinda. She was already busy working on her laptop, typing something into her word processor. Apparently, she hadn't noticed the drool!

Just then, the flight attendant leaned over to them to ask if they wanted coffee. Shortly after, their breakfasts were brought, forcing Melinda to store her computer away below her seat. The food trays were deposited on their small fold-down tables and Sam decided to put off a visit to the washroom until after they ate.

Still trying to wake up, and between mouthfuls of croissants with butter, cold cuts and Brie, Sam was hoping to keep the discussion light.

Melinda would have nothing of it!

"Tell me, just what will you be looking for when we get to the bodies?"

Without blinking, Sam came back. "Well OK, enough of the small talk!"

"I have a hunch I want to play with. If you'll remember our discussion at my lab yesterday, I mentioned I thought whatever had happened to the victims had possibly happened at the genetic level. So I got to thinking: what would I need to see in order to prove my hypothesis or to indicate I was *barking up the wrong tree*, so to speak."

Melinda listened intently while taking her turn at her breakfast.

"I thought I might take a sample of the bodies to analyse. In order to be as respectful as possible, I would only take a cross section of their small toe at one of the joints."

Only the slightest hint of a frown showed on Melinda's face, like a mental *Eww*!

"I know it sounds a little gruesome. But I will also need to sample an organ in the middle of each of the torsos. These should show me if every part of the bodies was affected in the same way. I'm hoping the electron microscope will allow me to see some evidence of the pattern of destruction. I assume the DNA of each cell might be damaged too severely to locate which part of the cells was affected, but the pattern around the cells will tell me a lot. If I'm right, there should be a consistent pattern around each cell, whether it is bone, blood or cartilage."

"And that will tell you what?"

"That will give me some proof that the frequency used by this weapon is incredibly high. In fact, if I can find some DNA which isn't completely cooked, I should be able to calculate whether or not individual RNA or strands of RNA were targeted. This would give me an idea of the frequency used."

Melinda had stopped eating. It occurred to Sam that she was just now starting to understand how complex the weapon was. He hoped as well that she might be impressed by his theory, by him!

With a warm smile, she looked at him. "I guess we do have the right man. Just amazing!" she said!

"Bingo!" he thought as he smiled back at her.

*****

An hour later, the plane was making its final approach to Ben Gurion International Airport. The drive to the university wasn't as hectic or as much fun as the one in Toronto, but they made good time.

Sam spent about an hour retrieving the samples he needed and they took them to analyze under the electron microscope. As Sam peered at the screen on the microscope monitor, Agent Cohen was on the telephone with his operations center. Folding his worldphone and putting it into his inside coat pocket, he walked over to Melinda and quietly spoke to her, ensuring they weren't disturbing Sam.

Sam sat back in his chair, folded arms on his chest and uttered a long, quiet 'Yes!' After about ten seconds, he looked over at the two agents and waved them over.

They came to where he was at and he simply pointed to the screen. They stood behind his chair in order to get a good view.

"Now, do you see those little dark spots spread out throughout the image?" he asked.

Both agents nodded, with only Agent Cohen responding with a 'Yes'.

"What you are looking at is what is left of the RNA within the DNA of one of the victims. Now, the particles aren't what is interesting. Notice the spacing between the particles of RNA."

It was Melinda who spoke up, having been privy to their discussion on the plane. "OK, right! It looks like each particle is equidistant from the other!"

"In fact," said Sam, "in every sample I have analyzed, the pattern is the same whether it is bone or another tissue sample. We are definitely dealing with an extremely high frequency. I'll be able to calculate this or rather, these frequencies when I get back to my lab."

"What do you mean frequencies?" blurted Melinda.

"The fact that each particle is spaced equally, no matter what type of tissue, would mean that multiple frequencies, all in the same high range have been used: one for each type, that is, for each chemical composition of RNA. This is just mind boggling!"

Agent Cohen spoke up. "Quite interesting, but what does that tell us about who is responsible? I have murders I need to solve!"

"Good point!" responded Sam. "First, you are definitely looking at a theoretical genius. This weapon has to have some basis in research somewhere. As I said yesterday, we should be able to scope-out all the doctoral which use microwaves in a similar manner. That should give us some leads. Secondly, this weapon is way more difficult to create than I first guessed. It would mean a tremendous amount of money would be required for the equipment. As well, the equipment would be highly specialized."

"Hence a money trail," said Melinda.

"Right! Thirdly, I suspect the computational power needed to calculate the correct frequency would necessarily be equal to some of the most powerful computers in the world, and consequently more leads to the source!"

"This is good! Now we are getting somewhere," said Agent Cohen.

Melinda put her hand gently on Sam's shoulder. "Is there anything else these results can tell us?"

"For the moment, I'm afraid not! But I think that with the help of a few friends in the Physics department, the results of my calculations could help us identify some of the required equipment," responded Sam.

"OK then," her hand still on Sam's shoulder and looking down pensively. "we can take each of these lines of investigation and see if we can find the culprit or culprits. As well, Agent Cohen just informed me that his people have analyzed the events common among the victims. They were all involved in covert action in some thirteen missions. However, the last victim was only involved in three of them. Though we don't know how many more victims will surface, we now have some commonality and a manageable number of permutations to at least find out *why* they were targeted and with that, possibly *who* is responsible!"

Chapter 21

Ra'id and Mohammed had been traveling in Israel for a month, crossing to and from the West Bank using different border checkpoints. The Sheikh had provided them with a series of safe houses in the West Bank, as well as other areas within Israel, all of which had shelters large enough for the van.

They had planned to do *the deed*, as they called it, quickly enough to keep the authorities from figuring out what was happening. They had to keep on the move most days, staking out their victims and deciding the best position for them to take, while allowing for good exit strategies.

After Ra'id left Mykonos on the ferry to Kusadasi, where he met up with Mohammed, the two of them drove to Israel by way of circuitous and dusty roads in Turkey, Syria and then Jordan. Visas and passports had been forged by the experts at the Foundation and would provide easy access to each country. A family history had been fabricated and any computer search at the border points would lead to dummy sites set up to show a thriving local business in Irbid, Jordan. Ra'id was the son of the aging owner and Mohammed was the help, and they were making deliveries to Israeli customers.

The Mercedes van had, indeed, served its purpose. Hanz had done a good job of fabricating an acrylic body, eliminating all large metal pieces above the frame other than the wall behind the front seats. Only when they reached Irbid in Jordan, however, did they have the black acrylic side panels painted with Ra'id's alibi for his movements in Israel. Both sides had large motifs of old furniture painted on them, with the company's name. "Mustafa's Pre-Owned Furniture", written in Hebrew in the upper-left corner, and somewhat smaller, in Arabic in the lower-right corner of the signs. A few scratches and dents on the bumpers and sides completed the look of a well-traveled vehicle. The four rear tires, two on either side, seemed to show the stress of the vehicle's weight. In fact, the tires were rated for the additional two thousand five hundred pounds of lithium-ion batteries hidden between the floor and undercarriage of the vehicle.

The interior of the rear cab was just large enough for an assortment of old pieces: two antique tube-type radios; an Art Deco Grunow World Cruiser Tombstone radio and a larger floor model antique Philco AM Radio. Both were secured by bungee cords to the front wall. There was a single bed with box-spring and mattress lying flat on the floor to one side, and an assortment of crates piled on top. An antique Louis XV armoire stood against the right-side wall, next to an old Crystal Ice Box from Freemont, Nebraska. There was barely enough room for anyone to move within.

Ra'id and Mohammed did not need to step into the rear to accomplish their task. Protected from possible radiation by the metal wall behind their seat, they could operate the weapon from the front. The truck's radio functioned as the control unit for the equipment in the rear, a fact that made the drive to their destination feel that much longer without music. Cleverly hidden within the furniture in the rear were the different components of the weapon. The two radios had working dials and control knobs, but hidden inside the speaker cavities, the oscillators and capacitors for the maser were crammed tightly. In a false back at the rear of the armoire were hidden the components for the computer which coordinated the process. The spring assembly in the box spring below the mattress was actually the antenna array. The maser which created the microwaves was itself in parts, hidden inside the walls of the old metal icebox. As for the crates on the mattress, they were filled with old dishes, pots and pans.

The equipment had worked flawlessly eight times, producing only a quiet, low hum when first turned on and quickly rising in pitch to the ultrasonic range when the full power was unleashed. Both Ra'id and Mohammed felt that each time they used the weapon, the experience was truly surreal! In those moments of silence, when they knew the weapon was working, it was as though they were gods, simply willing Death to visit their victims.

Now that he had accomplished what he had set out to do, Ra'id thought he could return to normality. Well, if not normality, perhaps recognition for saving lives rather than taking them. He felt no remorse for the deaths of the eight soldiers he had dispatched, but hidden within his subconscious, was an awareness that he had caused pain for their loved ones. Hopefully, he could atone for that pain by relieving disease-related pain in the future.

Ra'id turned the van south toward the Wadi Araba crossing, not far from the port of Aqaba in Jordan. From there, he and Mohammed would board a ferry which would take them down the Red Sea, around the tip of Saudi Arabia and back up through the Gulf of Suez and the canal, and, finally, into the Mediterranean to Athens.

They would return to Frankfurt to resume their work in preparation for the grand announcement, but not before making two phone calls. The first was to Samihah's father to let him know that he had not put his faith in him in vain. His daughter's death had been avenged and in doing so, Ra'id hoped he had earned the ambassador's respect. The second call would be to the Sheikh to thank him for his understanding and all the help he provided in order to give his soul, and Samihah's, some peace.

Chapter 22

Sam had taken the flight back to Toronto alone. He was still seated in the first-class section, but the flight without Melinda just wasn't what the first on had been. Arriving at his condo by taxi, he decided that after such a long trek, he needed a shower and then a run along the lake to help clear the cobwebs.

He felt privileged to be able to own a condo in such a beautiful setting. His meagre salary as a university lecturer would normally not allow him such luxury. But it had been a wise investment, made possible by his inheritance when his mother had passed away, ten years before. He had held back spending the money his mother had planned for him, but then the opportunity presented itself, he didn't hesitate. The one-bedroom apartment was being sold privately and for a song. He paid two hundred seventy-five thousand, however, he knew he could easily turn it over now for about a half a million.

His dad had died from cancer when he was only eleven and his mother had raised him on her own, moving them from Moncton to Toronto, just before he started university. She held two jobs as a waitress in a couple of the swankier restaurants and was able to put Sam through the first two years of university.

All the while, Sam had started to save his own money back in Moncton with his part-time job selling popsicles and ice cream from a vending trike. When they moved, he was able to get a job with the same company, whose head office, was located in Toronto. By the time his mother passed on during his last year as an undergraduate, he had moved up from the streets to the office, as manager of the trike division.

Though he didn't miss the sweating while riding the trike on his route from subdivision to subdivision, he did miss the open air, the smiles on the kids' faces and the exercise it provided. The shape he was in now was largely due to the summers he had spent pushing several hundred pounds of frozen goodies for ten hours a day.

The condo stood next to the entrance to the Humber River, not quite in town but close enough to get a great view of the skyline featuring the CN Tower. When it was built in 1976, the tower was the tallest in the world at eighteen hundred fifteen feet, and boasted a great revolving restaurant and the famous Sky Pod, with its glass floor: not a good idea for people with vertigo.

His building had an unusual shape in that the corner facing the lake was curved, allowing the architects to design balconies that wrapped around the outside, permitting the occupants to exit through sliding glass doors, both from the bedroom and the dining room. At night, Sam could pull back the curtains in his bedroom to see the romantic Toronto skyline from his bed or sit at the patio table on his balcony off the dining room to take in the morning sun at breakfast and gaze upon the lake, usually dotted with hundreds of small sailing skips.

For today's run, he started by crossing the graceful Humber River Bridge with its double tub arches, supporting the pedestrian deck with a series of harp-like cables. He normally ran five miles, giving him enough time to work out issues in his mind: from planning his lectures to solving problems with his project with Jalal. Today, however, there was only one issue he contemplated: *what* could he glean from the evidence he had on the case? *What* tidbit of information could bring him closer to knowing how the weapon worked and who could be responsible for the eight murders?

135

He knew for certain was that it somehow involved some type of frequency emitter and a process that affected almost every cell in the body. In spite of the afternoon sun, he shivered at the thought!

As he ran, he went through the steps he needed to take to help the investigation. Melinda had agreed to head up the search for the doctoral theses dealing with the methodology or technology Sam had suggested would be required in such a weapon. Agent Cohen would follow up on the money trail and also pinpoint the links between the missions the eight soldiers had been involved in. Sam would concentrate on trying to confirm his theory on how the weapon could work.

He felt as if he somehow needed to label the weapon: it had to be the teacher in him. And then it struck him! What created vibrations? Well, instruments such as guitars. That was it: strings! And the purpose or objective was *death*. What would represent death?

He stopped running, bent over and breathed heavily. As he straightened, he stretched backward and briefly looked up toward the sun. The name of Ra came to mind. No! That wouldn't work! But Osiris, the Egyptian god of the dead, would! He would call the weapon *The Osiris String*.

Chapter 23

Things began to move quickly.

Agent Cohen and Israeli intelligence had pieced together the one common link between all eight victims: a mission in Gaza City in which a major target had been eliminated. There were also a few collateral victims. One in particular, the daughter of a former Yemeni ambassador, was of major interest.

But the money trail was still dry.

Sam had pulled together a team of physicists and biologists from the university to discuss the concept of the possible effects of extremely high harmonics on living cells. They had agreed *not* to ask why! They also had come to the conclusion that the concept Sam's hypothesis could produce the type of results the sample images he provided them of the dead soldiers' cell structure. Moreover, they had postulated the frequency ranges required to do so and the type of equipment that would be needed to produce the said frequencies.

However, no word from Melinda, until several days later.

Sam's phone rang at three on that Sunday afternoon. After his daily run, he had taken a shower and decided to treat himself to a power nap. It was a short one.

As he rolled over in his bed, groping for the telephone, he halfheartedly groaned a few chosen explicitives.

"Umph… Yeah."

"We know who it is!" was the reply.

A short sniffle, blinking his eyes open and clearing his throat. "Melinda? What was that?"

"Sam, we think we know who created the weapon!"

That was enough to fully waken Sam.

"OK, I'm listening."

"We think it's a young Yemeni physicist working out of Germany: more specifically at the University of Frankfurt. His name is Ra'id Al-Eissa. Intel has traced applications on his part for some funding for research on HIV prevention, or rather, a possible cure. Sam, you were right. And it seems the research was based on some kind of vibration that could *zap* that part of the cell to be destroyed, without affecting the rest."

"OK, but how does this relate to the victims?"

"Agent Cohen has put two and two together, and found that one of the victims in the single common incident linking the eight soldiers, happens to be the dead fiancée of Al-Eissa."

"Holy shit!" was all Sam could say!

"Sam, we need you to take another trip. I'm actually in Berlin and we are working with the German government to put together a SWAT team to secure the technology and take him down. But we need someone to help us look at whatever technology we find. We, no, *I* need you to get to the airport for a flight leaving at 18:00 hours, your time, to meet me in Frankfurt."

Sam was still trying to process what he was hearing, but one thing was clear: the rush he was feeling was partly due to the news Melinda had relayed and partly due to the fact that *they* had connected.

"We'll have a CSIS agent waiting for you with your tickets. Go to the Lufthansa desk. By the time you get to Frankfurt, it will be early morning, so I'll meet you at the mission launch site: your driver will have instructions. Agent Cohen will be there as well. We plan to move on the target relatively early tomorrow morning, German time."

"OK, I'm there for you. I'll pack a few items and head to the airport. Really looking forward to seeing you! Talk you soon!"

Chapter 24

Sam was met at his gate by airport security and quickly escorted through customs to the terminal exit by a *man in black*. He was whisked away to a hangar at the south end of the airport.

As the large doors opened to allow their SUV to enter, he saw an additional four SUVs parked side by side, and members of the SWAT team huddled around a table off to the right side.

As he got out of the vehicle, he noticed from the corner of his eye, someone in a black flak suit coming toward him. As he turned his head to look, he realized it was Melinda who was walking over to him with a mug of coffee in her hand. "Here, I thought you might need this after your flight!"

As she turned and walked toward the SWAT team, she looked back at Sam and smiled. "You look awful by the way."

All of this had happened within but a few seconds, taking Sam by surprise. He couldn't even respond with a good come back.

He followed Melinda and was introduced to the team leader, Commander Heinz, and the rest of the group. As promised, Agent Cohen was there, dressed for the *take down,* but conspicuously dwarfed by the other members of the team.

The commander shook Sam's hand. "Welcome to Frankfurt. I understand you have been brought in to assess any information or equipment we may find in the lab."

Sam nodded.

"That is fine, but you will have to stay at the rear of operation, as will agents Gordon and Cohen, until we have secured the facility." He looked at each one of them, as if to reinforce the order.

"We have just received *intel* that the target is at the university." He turned on his iPhone and flicked on a slightly grainy picture of a man standing in line at a cafeteria, pushing a tray toward the cash register with what looked like two take out cups of coffee and a couple of Danish muffins.

Melinda responded, "Yes, that does look like a picture of Al-Eissa, but older than the undergraduate picture we pulled up."

The commander looked slightly uneasy. "Unfortunately, our man has lost contact with the target. We assume he has headed to his lab."

The look on Sam's face was more one of concern. "I'm worried about what you call *collateral damage*. Wouldn't there be a large number of students running about?"

Commander Heinz seemed to appreciate the chance to respond to a question he could answer, "We have factored that in and we can contain the possible danger to the staff and students."

Looking at his watch. "First, it is 07:30 hours and there are few students about. Most classes do not start until nine hundred hours. It will take us no more than thirty minutes to get to the site and set up the perimeter. The lab is not at the main campus in the center of the city, but rather at the Riedberg campus, north of the city. The layout of the campus is more spread out and only houses about six or so departments. So, as you can see on the map of the campus," pointing down to the table, "there is still a fair amount of construction going on and the existing buildings are fairly well spaced. It would have been a completely different if the lab had been at the downtown location!"

He glanced at Sam and got a look of what was either one of satisfaction or of resignation. At this point, it didn't matter. Time was passing.

Checking his watch again, the commander surveyed his team. "You understand what we need to do. We have rehearsed this and each one of you knows his job. Let's go! Schnell!"

"You three," he emphasized, looking at Sam and the two agents, "are with me. I'll continue briefing you as we travel."

Not waiting for a response, he headed to the first black SUV and got in front to ride *shotgun*. The other three had to crowd into the rear seat, but Sam didn't mind. Melinda sat next to him in the middle.

In spite of the butterflies in his stomach, worrying about what he had gotten himself into, Sam had a bit of a smile on his face as they drove out of the hangar.

Chapter 25

The convoy of five SUV's, led by the commander's vehicle, raced along the express highways leading from the airport, over the River Main and into the city proper. From there, they drove along Highway 5 to route 66, and then on the Rosa-Luxembourg Strasse, where Sam spotted the Europaturm Tower off to his left. He didn't say a word, but thought to himself, "Look at that. A Mini-Me CN Tower!" He looked at it more closely. "Looks as if the upper pod is upside down, with the roof facing the ground." He turned away, to look forward in the direction they were going.

They had their emergency lights flashing as they sped in the left lane. Typical of German drivers, all the vehicles moved over to the right lanes, when they saw cars barrelling down on them from the rear, flashing their headlights. Today, it was the fleet of Mercedes and fast-moving BMW's, which made way for large North American-style SUVs.

As they approached the exit to Marie-Curie Strasse, the commander gave the order to turn off the lights.

From the main drive onto the university campus, the convoy detoured into a driveway leading to one of the construction sites on the south side of the grounds. From there, they drove onto a gravel work road which circled the campus from the west, leading them to the most Northern side.

The commander had shared the fact that a lab had been occupied by Al-Eissa in the building housing the Biomolecular Nuclear Magnetic Resonance department, on the north side, and that the records showed his modest rent was still being paid.

143

The university's satellite campus was indeed small, and Sam was rather surprised at the fact that, in a city as old as Frankfurt, the buildings were new and modern in juxtaposition to the buildings in the rest of the city. Sam turned to look at the faces of the passengers with him, hoping to see some sign of the tension he was feeling. Nothing!

"Well, OK," he thought. "I just need to put my faith in these professionals."

Chapter 26

Ra'id and Mohammed were just finishing their breakfast and discussing the design of the *tool*, no longer called the *weapon*.

The problem at hand was to take the schematics of all the components and assemble them into a design that looked *sexy* for the purpose of the demonstration, but was functional as well. They would need to separate the internal components of the equipment, those connected to the mainframe computer which produced the required frequencies, from the radiation antenna which would be housed in the chamber in which the patients would receive their treatment.

"As futuristic as aluminium casings might look, if we used black acrylic, I think it would have a retro look about it, don't you think?"

Mohammed thought for a second or two. "I agree, and it might also convey the impression of *mystery*!"

"I think we also need to give them a *Feng Shui* look by keeping all the corners curved...."

Chapter 27

The SUVs converged on the Biophysics building on Max-von-Laue Strasse: the commander's vehicle stopped at the main entrance in the center of the complex while the other four split in two, heading to either end of the building.

The team of sixteen spread out in specific formation: one from each vehicle positioned himself at one of the four corner entrances. The other twelve quickly went into the building in groups of three, weapons at the ready, through each of the entrances. As they encountered wandering students and professors, the SWAT team would immediately usher them to the exits, and then rapidly regroup with the members converging on the leader's position.

The commander had moved quickly to the rear of the complex through the central hallway from the front doorway, followed by his three *guests*.

The laboratory they were looking for was number 129, at the rear. Within two minutes of arriving, all the members of the SWAT team had met up with the team leader just around the corner from the door of the laboratory.

The commander turned to the three foreign agents, alerting them to stay put. He then signalled the others to take up positions on either side of the opening to the lab.

Quietly moving to the door to verify that it was locked. He found it was! His choices were either to simply to knock on the door or to blow it.

Chapter 28

"Even though the chamber has to be a glass enclosure for the purposes of our demonstration, most hospitals will simply use an existing room which has been retrofitted with our radiation antenna. The rest of the equipment will be in another room nearby. I can't see the need for any type of shielding since the odds of anyone having a compatible DNA sequence with the patient is next to zero."

Ra'id and Mohammed were at the point of discussing some of the selling features of their system and how the presentation would differ from the actual implementation in hospitals around the world.

Though this conversation had nothing to do with the preparations for the demonstration and the Nobel Prize, which was certain to follow, they found that discussions about the application and the implications of their invention, provided a great stress relief.

There was a knock on the door!

Chapter 29

Three muffled thuds preceded the loud crash as the metal door slammed onto the hallway floor. The SWAT member closest to the opening simply twisted, lobbing a stun grenade into the room and twisted back out of the way of the repercussion. As soon as the boom subsided, one by one the team members entered, their Heckler and Koch MP7A1 machine guns pointing their laser tracers toward the unseen enemy in the smoke.

By the time the leader entered the room, it was clear that the room was empty!

Chapter 30

"Yes, what is it?" Ra'id responded.

"Doctor Al-Eissa, you asked me to bring you your cappuccinos when my shift changed." It was Franc, the day security guard who was just now starting his day's duties.

"OK, give me a second!" Ra'id opened the lock as he looked out into the hallway at Franc through the small glass window in the door.

"Thank you, Franc. We can really use the extra caffeine jolt. And, would it be asking too much for a couple of espressos sometime mid-afternoon?"

Franc smiled. "Not a problem sir. I'll make them doubles?"

Franc really didn't mind getting the coffee for the two scientists. His days were rather boring and it gave him an excuse to leave the building and take a walk outside in the open air. The change of venue would be godsend. As he walked down the stairwell next to the lab, he couldn't help but think how sad his life was if getting coffee could be considered the highlight of his day!

Chapter 31

"Where is he?" was all agent Cohen could say as he walked into the lab and realized it was empty.

"Obviously not here!" was Commander Heinz's response. Though his face looked impassive, the vein in the center of his forehead was visible, his cheeks were flushed and his clenched knuckles were white. There was no mistaking the inner rage he was feeling.

As Sam and Melinda entered, agent Cohen quickly gestured to them not to react or say anything.

Commander Heinz was on his wrist intercom, spouting out what could only be curses and questions in German, and in a manner only Germans could express them. It was clear to Sam that the commander was pissed off in the extreme. He moved away from the group, obviously not wanting them in the conversation he was having with his people at central command.

Meanwhile, Sam huddled with Melinda and agent Cohen, trying to make sense of the blunder which could have a major impact on their search for Ra'id Al-Eissa.

Where was he? Would he find out about the raid on this lab and decide to go underground?

Agent Cohen was the first to offer an opinion. In his heavy Hebrew accent, "It is probable that Al-Eissa is somewhere on this campus. The picture taken of him an hour ago is proof. I would suggest there has to be another laboratory. We need to find it."

"That would make sense." added Sam. "Once you train at an institution, you tend to develop some loyalty to it. Al-Eissa probably feels comfortable with the environment and possibly has maintained some of his contacts in the various departments related to his field."

It was Melinda's turn. "OK, assuming all that is accurate, then why would he not be using the lab were the rent is still being paid for? And if he moved, I assume it would be because the other lab is better for some reason or has some advantage for him."

"That's it!" Sam blurted out. "Why didn't I think of it before?"

This was more of a statement than a question.

"Look around. This lab is like the type a *frosh* or freshman might want to use. The power outlets are not heavy-duty, and look, there are just a few Ethernet outlets for Internet access, but nothing to meet the type of computer requirements he would need to run his weapon. No, what you are looking for would be a laboratory with a hefty power supply, state-of-the-art fibre optics and room for a powerful mainframe, one that would probably need refrigeration to keep it at the proper operating temperature."

Melinda was deep in thought as well. She looked up at Sam. "I think we are getting close. This would also indicate that we *are* talking big money, wouldn't it?"

Sam nodded.

"Then, if Al-Eissa is linked to this lab, we can bet the other lab is assigned to another person or group. If we can find the lab, we might be able to determine who is behind the funding."

Agent Cohen stepped in, "I see the commander is off his *com*. I'll get him over here and you can inform him of your suspicions."

As soon as the team leader reached them, Sam and Melinda filled him in on the conclusions they had reached and what the German Central Command had to look for with the help of their contacts at the university. No sooner done, the leader was back on his wrist communication device.

Sixty seconds later, he simply signalled the SWAT team, by hand gestures, to wrap things up and leave.

He turned to Melinda and her two partners. "I think we need to leave as quickly and as quietly as possible. We've probably already stirred up the curiosity of the few students and professors we had to evacuate. Word will spread, but hopefully will not reach the target and scare him off. We'll move off the premises and wait to see if we can finally locate him. The one thing I do know is that we need to find him today, or we won't find him at all. There is too much at stake. I will deploy part of the team at the major exits of the campus, just in case Al-Eissa does try to leave the grounds."

With that, he pointed toward the opening where the door used to be and they left the building, leaving the mess behind for the caretakers to clean up! The university would be well compensated for the damage.

The team leader decided to regroup the team just a few miles away at the Müllheizkraftwerk, or waste-to-power plant, which would give them easy access to the on and off ramps of the Rose-Luxemburg Strasse back to the campus. They could be there within ten minutes of getting word about the new lab site. Here, they would draw little attention while they waited within the plant complex.

Chapter 32

It was two in the afternoon when the team leader was contacted. Sam had been dozing off it off on the rear seat of the SUV in order to compensate for his sleep disturbance due to he onset of jet lag. The rest of the team calmly waited, playing cards, solitaire or exchanging stories of previous operations.

Central Command had finally identified where the new lab was. It had taken them a couple of hours to track down the occupants of each of the eighty-nine research labs and confirm who they were. Unfortunately none of the labs turned out to be the one Al-Eissa could be linked to.

The problem was that the investigators were thinking within the box. One finally checked his notes and reread the information relayed concerning Sam's suspicions. It was only then that he decided to expand his search to include not only laboratories, but also buildings which might fit the scenario.

And there it was! A two-story building on the south-eastern corner of the campus, built to house a series of generators to be use for the early part of the construction period at the new location.

At the time, the campus was located out in the middle of nowhere and they felt that by supplying their own power, construction of the other buildings could move more rapidly, at least until the entire city services were provided.

The contact at the university's rental office had indicated that about a year and a half before, they had been contacted by a mid-eastern call-center to see if there was any interest in renting the facility as a temporary relay center. Since it had been decommissioned and was to be demolished to make way for a green space next to the future Earth Sciences building, they saw it as a cash cow, inasmuch as the call-center required no retrofitting.

The building's blueprints were being scanned and sent to the SWAT team as they mustered. The commander did not want to leave until the group had analysed the situation and determined the best course of action: he refused to have a second blunder on his record.

Chapter 33

Franc was just returning to Ra'id's lab, carrying the espressos they had requested. He didn't bother to call up on the intercom from his office. He was expected. So he simply walked the long hallway from the main entrance on the east side of the building to the far west stairwell leading to the second floor hallway and to Ra'id's lab.

He did not dare just enter, but keeping to his station, he respectfully knocked. Mohammed was the one who answered this time.

"Hello Franc. Is it break time already?"

Franc simply smiled and raised the coffee cups up for Mohammed.

As he was about to leave, he turned back toward the two and, peeking over his shoulder at Ra'id, he added, "Thought you might want to hear about the excitement on campus this morning! Though I couldn't get all the details, it seems the police came looking for someone. Rumor has it in the security department that they were looking for some terrorist!"

Mohammed chuckled, turned to Ra'id, the smile now gone from his face, and then back to Franc smiling once more. "Really. Who could they possibly be looking for? Did they find a cache of machine guns or dynamite?"

"No, I don't think so. They say that no sooner did they get here, they were gone! Can you believe it, I have been here six years now, and when there is finally some action, I'm sitting in my office reading a girly magazine."

With that, he turned to leave. "Auf Weidersehen."

Once Franc had left, Mohammed walked over to the small glass pane in the door to make sure he had gone and turned to Ra'id. "What do you think? They are looking for us?"

"I don't know. It is possible. Franc didn't say where they were looking, but it certainly is disconcerting. I can't think of anything that could lead them to us here at the university and we are so close to our goal. I don't want to overreact, especially since the police have left. Just in case, however, let us initiate the precautions we have put in place. You know what to do."

Chapter 34

The convoy was just approaching the exit to the Marie-Curie Strasse and was within three minutes of the old power building. Commander Heinz had instructed the four members of the SWAT team keeping an eye on the exit points from the campus to regroup on the Southwest corner of the building and wait for the rest of the group to arrive.

He didn't worry that they would be seen since the only windows in the entire building were at the main entrance on the east side, by the security guard's office.

The seventy-eight by two hundred seventy-five foot building had been erected more as a utilitarian style warehouse than a school structure. The exterior was walled in simple dark brown bricks, the only concession to aesthetics the university was willing to pay. Windows were not needed since that would mean additional maintenance costs and it only housed generators and a guard room; the second floor was mainly used as storage space.

Safety was not a high priority other than the sprinkler system. There were only three ways in or out of the building: the main entrance, an exterior exit on the second floor at the Northwest end, which led out of Ra'id's lab, and, finally, a utility elevator on the east side by the front entrance.

The blueprints also displayed a circular metal silo about fifty feet from the north side of the building, which was connected by a tunnel housing the pipes leading from the silo to the inside of the building. This structure had been used as an oil tank to fuel the generators.

The commander had decided to send three members of the team up the outside stairway leading to the metal door at the top. The door could only be opened from the inside, but anyone trying to escape from the second floor this way would be cut off.

Three men would be positioned by the door at the base of the elevator in order to cover that possible exit point. The others on the team, followed by Agent Cohen, Melinda and Sam, would enter the main entrance, seek out the guard on duty, extricate him, then head down the hallway to the stairwell on the west side.

The rest of the operation would simply require classic seek and apprehend techniques the team had used over and over again in simulations and real-life situations. All the instructions had been relayed to the team in the few minutes before the convoy turned left on the main drive and onto the campus.

A right, then on for a few hundred yards and they were on the lane leading to the target building. The vehicles came to a halt on the lane and into the small parking lot just opposite the main entrance.

Guns at the ready, moving quickly and purposely in slightly crouched position, each member of the team found his assigned location. One last look around and the team leader whispered the *all go* into his *com*.

Sam had seen them in action that morning, but he was impressed with the professionalism this team demonstrated. Within twenty seconds, Franc in a daze, was being escorted at gunpoint out to the stoop at the main entrance.

A few quick questions were thrown at the still bewildered guard . They learned that there were only two individuals in the building and where they could be found. One team member stayed to guard Franc, who was holding his hands behind his head. The rest started down the hallway and in spite of the assurances they had, they quickly checked the generator room, just in case.

Reaching the stairwell, the group moved quietly up the steps, hugging the inside wall. Quickly checking for the obvious security cameras and not finding any, they continued to the second floor.

The hallway was relatively short, only about thirty feet. There was one door at the very end and through the small glass panel, they could see the room was dark. However, through the glass panel on the other door, which was about halfway down the hall, they could see the lights were definitely on.

Again using hand gestures, the commander pointed to two of the team, and had them duck and move to the other side of the door. When they were in position, he gestured to the soldier next to him to carefully look into the room to confirm the targets were there.

He slowly moved his back to the wall and hesitantly peeked, pulled back, peeked again and pulled back once more. He gestured to the commander that he had seen one person and that it was a positive match.

The leader then gestured to him to try the door handle to see if it was locked. It was. Ok, not a problem: they would blow the door in the same way they had done that morning. One of the soldiers on the far side of the door applied two small Semtex charges to the hinges, while the third soldier applied one to the door handle.

Just as he was crouching in front of the door, applying the explosive, all hell broke loose, but in slow motion!

There was a flash of light and the door blew away from its casing, crashing into the SWAT team member, throwing him backward and pinning him against the opposite wall, instantly killing him. Part of the door casing blew apart and struck both soldiers on the other side of the opening as well and the leader. They were hit by concrete shrapnel and the percussion wave, and were launched several yards away. Sam and Melinda had moved up to about the fifth position behind the commander, but even at that distance, they found themselves flying backward, falling dangerously close to the edge of the stairs.

The outside door had blown outward as well, not quite flying off its hinges, but nevertheless catching the closest SWAT team member and tossing him off the second-storey platform to the grass below. The other two were knocked off their feet as well and rolled down the metal steps. The soldier on the ground would be found with a broken back, while the other two would have to nurse cuts and bruises for the next week or two.

It may have felt like minutes, but it was only about ten seconds before the dust began to thin out and the SWAT training started to take over.

The commander struggled to get up, and though he was shaken and could not hear a thing other than ringing in his ears, he immediately took charge, gesturing to some of the team to look after those who had fallen. The rest needed to enter the lab and secure it.

Still trying to focus on what was happening, he staggered to the soldier who had received the worst of the explosion, felt his neck for a pulse and realized nothing could be done. He looked over at his three guests and seeing them slowly getting up off the ground, none the worse for wear, he rose to his feet and moved through the door opening into the lab to assess what was left.

And there was indeed little left!

He was expecting to find blood and body parts all over the lab. But all he could see were splintered stools, lab counters and dust: lots of dust everywhere. But no blood or any sign anyone had been killed in the explosion.

His mind was starting to clear, but that only meant he would start formulating all the questions he was now beginning to dread! Had the targets committed suicide? The fact there was no blood discounted that possibility. He knew the explosion had not been caused by the team, so that would leave but one answer. It was caused by the scientist to destroy any evidence and give them cover to escape.

Sam, Melinda and Agent Cohen finally entered the lab, obviously not badly hurt. Melinda's posterior took most of the impact of her fall to the floor, but she had instinctively protected her head due to her martial arts training. Sam wasn't as lucky, as was evidenced by the fact that he was holding his head and wincing. Agent Cohen had been lucky and had not been affected at all. So he took the lead trying to determine what had happened.

Chapter 35

Ra'id and Mohammed were cautiously but casually making their way from the trap door at the rear of the silo, moving toward the bus stop next to the Biophysics building. They seemed like just two other students going to class, carrying their computer cases and briefcases. They, unlike many more students and security guards, were walking away from the explosion.

After Franc had delivered the espressos and relayed the story of the morning raid, Ra'id and Mohammed had implemented the security protocol the Sheikh had insisted upon when they moved from the first lab to this one.

Among the precautions put in place were surveillance cameras hidden in the ceiling in the hallway, close to Franc's office, and activated by motion sensors. Their laptops were wired to automatically flip to the image of anyone coming into the lower area, giving them a minute or two to implement the rest of the plan.

Another camera was actually positioned, unseen, well behind the door at the end of the upstairs hallway, focusing through the glass panel and giving them a rather good view of area leading to the lab. This allowed them to see expected and unexpected visitors alike.

More important, the Sheikh had insisted on installing a personal elevator that connected the rear of the lab to the generator room below. From there, they had easy access to the tunnel leading to the silo. What the building schematics did not show was that the silo was double-hulled: an inner tank which acted as an oil reservoir, and an outer cavity about a yard or so wider, which allowed access to workers in case there was a need for repairs or as containment in case of a breach.

When Franc left the lab, Ra'id and Mohammed had begun to put together the important papers and gather the laptops with the data they had developed for their tool, or weapon. When the SWAT team entered the building, Ra'id's laptop switched over to the visual mode, showing the *invasion* underway.

Mohammed picked up most of the materials they needed to save and headed down to the first floor by way of the private elevator, and then sent it back up. He was to wait for Ra'id, who would watch for the soldiers to move up to the second storey. Knowing they would want to look into the lab to confirm it was occupied, he stood by the lab counter next to the closet door which hid the elevator, looking down at his computer display. He saw them sneak up and look in. That's when he knew he had to move quickly.

He got into the elevator, pushed the down button and then the trigger button which began the ten-second timer that would detonate the explosives.

He was already running toward Mohammed by the tunnel entrance when he heard the explosion. The whole building shook, causing loose dust, that had accumulated for years, to fall off the ceiling rafters, down, onto and into the to the generators feeding the mainframe computers above, effectively short-circuiting them.

A minute later, the two were at the door that led out of the silo. As expected, all of the SWAT team had run into the building to back the rest of the group, leaving the way out clear for the two of them.

Chapter 36

An hour later, Sam, Melinda and Agent Cohen were delivered to their hotel. There was nothing they could do back at the lab and the commander seemed relieved to see them leave. He had been subjected to two huge blows to his ego and his record. Worse, he had essentially lost two team members. He would be at the lab until the forensic investigators were done sifting through all the debris to try to find any lead to Al-Eissa.

Agent Cohen was riding shotgun and was the first to get out of the SUV. Melinda followed close behind from the rear seat. Sam was a little slower to get out. He ached all over. He glanced over at the two agents and gave himself an up and down look; he chuckled to himself, remembering his description of the three agents when they first visited him in his lecture room: Curly, Larry and Moe.

Now, including Sam, they must have looked like the comedy trio, all dressed similarly in black combat boots, black pants and black T-shirts. More precisely, the T-shirts were black; of them, including their hair, faces and arms were covered in dust and soot. They had left their flak jackets, which had protected their T-shirts, back with the SWAT team at the lab.

It was only then that Sam noticed the hotel where their rooms had been reserved. Melinda had mentioned the fact that it was her favorite hotel in Frankfurt: intimate and elegant, was all she had said. The Villa Kennedy was that and quite a bit more. It looked a little like a castle, including a medieval-style tower on the left. The large stone covered entrance led to the spacious main foyer and reception area. As beautiful as it was, Sam could only think of a long hot shower and an hour or two of sleep. He shared the group's deep state of depression because of the setback, and he was still feeling the effects of jetlag. Melinda took care of the registration process and handed each of the other two their keys.

Right now, Sam would be ecstatic with a room the size of a closet, but when he walked into the space he was really impressed. Though it wasn't the largest of the hundred sixty-three rooms and suites, it was warm and inviting. An oak floor hallway led to the living room, and next to it, the bedroom. The living room had a large French door opening out onto a French-style balcony overlooking the beautiful private courtyard.

As he looked down at the outside patio and the garden area, with its wicker chairs and tables, protected from the sun by linen parasols, he glanced over to his right. Melinda occupied the room next to his and had also come out to view the garden area.

She smiled at him. "Nice isn't it! It helps me decompress."

Sam smiled as well. It was the first time this day. "You sure know how to pick them."

Melinda continued, "I've taken the liberty of reserving a table for three at twenty hundred hours. Sorry, 8:00 p.m., if that's ok?"

"Sounds perfect. I have to clean up and it will give me time to rest a bit."

Melinda hesitated a bit. "I also took the liberty to having some clothing brought up to your room. I didn't know if you had packed for every occasion!" She smiled and walked back into her suite.

Sam stood there a little dumbfounded and walked back into his bedroom and to the closet. There, neatly hung was a pair of black linen slacks, a black form-fitting V-neck T-shirt and a long-sleeve beige linen overshirt. On the bed,

165

there was a black leather belt, and resting on a towel, a pair of black leather Italian slip-on shoes.

For a split second, Sam felt like a kept man, but after verifying that all the sizes were correct, he realized that Melinda had simply done her homework and had anticipated one of his weaknesses. He had only packed a pair of jeans, a pair of beige polyester pants, a couple of shirts and a Roots sweatshirt. OK, OK! At least he had included a pair of black leather Geox Respira shoes and, though they were running shoes, they were really nice *dressy* running shoes. Looking back at the new outfit, he thought, "She has taste, and she must likes me!"

Two hours later, after a twenty-minute steamy shower and a ninety-minutes snooze, he felt refreshed. Looking at himself in the mirror, he believed the outfit would not have been his first choice, but that wasn't a bad thing. He did look European. Besides being beautiful, tough and intelligent, she had taste.

Arriving at exactly 8:00 p.m., Sam looked around the elegant dining area and spotted Melinda sitting by herself next to the windows by the outside patio. His heart literally skipped a beat! Highlighted by the candlelight in front of her, she was stunning!

She wore a simple black silk dress with spaghetti straps holding a deep plunging bodice, revealing perfect cleavage. Her only jewellery was a simple diamond pendant on a gold chain. Her best feature, though, was her smile when she saw Sam walking toward her.

Sam's mind went to mush and all he could do was mimic Billy Crystal imitating Ricardo Montalban saying, "You look marvelous!"

As he said it, he realized he had dug himself a very deep hole. "OK, not exactly what I wanted to say. Let me start again. You *do* look amazing tonight. And, would you mind if I sat with you?"

She smiled and graciously gestured to him to take the seat opposite her. Then she chuckled a little. "And you don't look too shabby yourself."

"Touché! I have to thank you for thinking of getting me the threads. You wouldn't be impressed by what *I* brought to wear."

The waiter came to the table to take their drink order. Both asked for Vodka Martinis, straight up, Melinda with a twist, and Sam's with olives. Neither suggested whether they wanted them shaken or stirred."

As the waiter left, Sam looked around and then turned back to Melinda. "When is Agent Cohen meeting us?"

"He was called to the Israeli Embassy in Berlin. He sends his apologies."

Still with a smile on his face. "That's too bad." He was actually thinking *great*!

Then his smile faded and a troubled look replaced it. "He's gone for good isn't he?"

Melinda looked back in bewilderment. "Agent Cohen?"

"No, Al-Eissa. He got away and will probably go so deep underground we'll never find him or the weapon. I feel it's partly my fault."

"Why would you say that?" Melinda responded.

"If I had only thought it through earlier, we might have had him this morning and maybe caught him off guard."

Melinda shook her head and in a calm and reassuring voice said, "No, you can't think that way. I doubt anything would have been different this morning or yesterday. Already the investigators have ascertained that the building was so well-wired as to give him enough warning time to make his escape. The real problem is that we all underestimated him or rather, the money behind him."

Sam looked up at her. "What do you mean?"

167

"The monitoring system could have bee installed by almost anyone. The explosives were planned and placed by experts in order to thoroughly destroy the evidence. And the room next door, where the computers were refrigerated, are proof that a few bucks were invested there too! The personal elevator Al-Eissa used to escape was something you would see on the Starship Enterprise! That's just a start. So, yes, you might be right that he'll go into hiding, but we have so much more to work with now."

"Such as what?" Sam questioned.

Before Melinda could answer, they were interrupted by the waiter bringing them their Martinis.

Taking a small sip, Melinda resumed, "Remember the money trail I spoke about?"

Sam nodded and then his eyes lit up, "OK, don't tell me. Now we have specialized items you can source out to see if you can find any lead."

"Now you're talking my language. The mainframe computers were not totally destroyed. We have enough parts left over that we can determine exactly what make and model they were. There can only be a few manufacturers in the world that sell computers of this caliber and these companies would have client lists. Same with the elevator. And our terrorist analysts can determine the explosive signature and probably come up with some of the who's who of demolition experts, who might have been involved. So, in spite of today's failure to apprehend Al-Eissa, we are actually farther ahead than we were yesterday in finding out those who are behind the weapon. And, when we do find them, we probably will find Al-Eissa."

Sam sat back in his chair, looking down at the table before finally eyeing at Melinda. "That takes a huge weight off my shoulders. All of a sudden, I feel hungry. I just realized we haven't had much to eat today."

Melinda waved to the waiter standing not far away. He quickly fetched two menus and returned to their table.

Opening her leather-bound menu, Melinda said, "If you're not insulted, may I make some suggestions?"

"You did well with the clothing! What would you suggest?"

"How about," and speaking with a perfect Italian accent, "Carpaccio di Manzo con Crema di Parmigiano e Insalata d'Erbe?"

"OK, that was…"

"It's Beef Carpaccio with Cream of Parmesan and Herb Salad. I would suggest we then follow with Forest Mushroom Risotto with Taleggio."

Sam smiled. "I'm impressed."

Melinda continued, "Do you prefer fish or meat?"

"I'm partial to meat: I see they have a Rack of Lamb."

"OK, and I'll have the King Prawns. And to finish, I'm thinking of the Apricot Tiramisu with Yogurt Ice Cream that is to die for!"

Sam insisted on ordering the wine and in staying with the Italian theme, he selected a bottle 1999 Brunello di Montalcino. But with dessert, he ordered two glasses of Peller Estate Ice Wine from the Niagara Region in Canada.

While they were finishing the meal with an espresso, Melinda could see Sam was a little uneasy. She reached across the table to take his hand. He almost pulled it back out of a nervous reaction. He felt that he had screwed up his opportunities with her.

"Listen," Melinda said softly, "I like you very much and I think you like me. Tell you what, give me fifteen minutes and if you choose to do so, come to my room. I'll have two cognacs waiting and we can have a nightcap on my balcony."

Fifteen minutes later, Sam was in front of the entrance to her room, his forehead leaning against the door, his heart

169

beating fifty miles an hour and his hand steadying itself to announce his arrival. He hoped it would be more than just a nightcap.

When Melinda answered his knock and let him in, she reached up to kiss him and then slowly closed the door behind him.

Part 4

Chapter 37

Carl Broom, Secretary of Homeland Security, was sitting on one of the sofas in the Oval Office. He had been sent in a few minutes before, called to a meeting by President Alexander. As he sat waiting for the President to come into the room, he mulled over how he would describe the incidents and especially how the team had botched the mission. He decided he would simply follow the President's cues and questions.

At five foot eight, weighing a mere one hundred sixty pounds, he was usually dwarfed by the people he commanded. In spite of that, his non-designer black suit seemed to fit well due to the workout he did every morning between five and six. He didn't smoke, didn't drink alcohol and he ate healthily. He was what others would describe as *a lean, mean, fighting machine*.

Unofficially, his subordinates nicknamed him *Cool Hand Luke*. He never showed stress or impatience. Even now, there wasn't a drop of perspiration on his brow. They knew better than not meet his expectations. Those who did, usually found themselves looking for new jobs. His ruthlessness was one of the reasons he had been appointed by Felix Alexander. The President wanted someone who could deal with the pressure of the job and be uncompromising in getting it done. Broom just wasn't a *nice* guy. But the President didn't care about that: his only concern was whether or not he could be counted on. Broom was aware of that, which is why the next ten minutes would be that much more difficult.

Broom stood as the Alexander entered from his private office and walked over to him to shake his hand.

Alexander gestured to him to sit, undid the button on his suit jacket as he positioned himself on the sofa opposite Broom. "Mr. President, the report on the murders of the Israeli soldiers is on your desk."

"Thanks, I'll get to the full report a little later. I only have a few minutes, so can you summarize the mission for me."

Broom did so for the next five minutes, describing succinctly the team's composition, the diplomatic tug-of-war that had taken place behind the scenes and eventually the details of the assault on the lab at the university. He held nothing back concerning Homeland Security's mistake, therefore his, of underestimating the situation. They, *he*, had been caught off guard by the extent of the preparations put in place by Al-Eissa.

Once he had ended, he sat upright, waiting for more questions or the request for his resignation. Still no sweat.

Alexander was silent, looking at Broom but not quite focusing on him.

After a moment, the President seemed to return to earth. "OK, so we screwed up! Since the lab was destroyed, does this mean the danger is contained? What is your assessment of where we stand now?"

Broom's shoulders relaxed slightly. "Well, on the surface it would seem it is. As you'll read in the report, there were only eight soldiers involved in the raid on the home where Al-Eissa's fiancée happened to be. We have eight bodies, or at least what is left of them. So if it was an act of vengeance, it would seem to be over. The weapon had to be transportable in order to reach the soldiers and we believe the components had to be transferred to the new lab and super-sized. With the lab destroyed, along with the supercomputers, we feel the weapon is no longer a threat."

President Alexander sat back and crossed his arms on his chest and now looked at Broom for the catch.

173

Broom hesitated for a moment. "… but, *I* have reason to believe that is not the case."

He then leaned forward. "Based on some of the conclusions expressed by Dr. Buckner and our agent, Melinda Gordon, I think this is just the tip of the iceberg. This weapon and the technology behind it are something else. This whole story is still way under the radar of most heads of state, but because it has been tested and proven to be possible, someone, somewhere will put two and two together and want to duplicate it. Along with Israel, we are ahead of anyone else working at finding out who funded the physicist."

"I agree with your assessment. What are your recommendations for the next step?"

Broom sat back. "We have a lot of resources working on identifying the manufacturers of the equipment in the lab. They should lead us to the buyer and therefore the money."

"I'd like to create a new team to head up the search for Al-Eissa himself. He's gone underground, but eventually he'll resurface. We'll open channels beyond Interpol and Israeli intelligence to all of our allies' secret services. We'll pass him off as an important al-Qaeda asset, so as not to raise too many suspicions."

It was President Alexander's turn to lean forward. "OK. But I want to meet the original team. I'd like to get their personal impressions of what has gone on. A report doesn't give you all the information you might need. What they said, and maybe more importantly, what they did not say is critical. I want to see their body language. Then I'll decide if we should go with a new team or not. It would seem they did a good job in getting as far as they did. After all, the assault team that screwed up was not American."

Broom sat quietly, knowing the President had just wrapped him on the knuckles. He also knew that his strong point was his uncanny ability to read people. He knew he had just been *read* and that the President wanted to do the same with the three agents involved before moving forward.

"Yes sir. I'll arrange it with your secretary at your earliest convenience."

With that, the two stood, shook hands once more and Broom left.

President Alexander walked over to his desk, sat down and picked up the telephone. He dialled his personal secretary. "Mildred, can you get me the British and Canadian Prime Ministers, the German Chancellor and then, the French President."

Chapter 38

The phone rang on Sheikh Al-Kabir's desk.

Glancing at the display, he saw it was from an *unknown caller*.

It rang a second time and then a third before he picked up the receiver. "Yes?"

"Sheikh Al-Kabir, it is Ra'id."

The Sheikh hesitated briefly. "Are you using the cellphone I gave you?"

"Yes sir. I made sure it was in the encrypted mode before calling you."

The Sheikh relaxed slightly. "Where are you?"

"I am in Jordan, in one of the safe houses you provided us when we came for the soldiers. I used the same passports and came by the same direction we did previously."

"Good thinking. The authorities would not think you would ever return to the area," responded Al-Kabir.

"Sir, I can't begin to express my sorrow and shame for what has happened. Because of my laxness, we have lost everything!"

"Nonsense my boy! We knew something like this could happen, which is why we prepared as well as we did in order to protect you. The fact that it has, does however create a sense of urgency for our plans. Tell me, do you still have the basic research with you?"

Ra'id was somewhat confused. "Yes, I do. We saved all of our research on the laptops we escaped with."

"Good! Now, here is what I want you to do."

Chapter 39

Ra'id stepped off the World War II DC-3 plane, onto the baking tarmac followed by Mohammed. The temperature was nearly one hundred ten degrees and Ra'id instinctively raised his left arm to shield his eyes from the sun with his hand as he glanced up.

And yet he was smiling. "I am home!" he said turning to Mohammed.

Ra'id and Mohammed had flown by jet airline from Amman Jordan to the Hodeida International Airport in Al Hudaydah Yemen, only to be quickly shuttled over to the cargo area of the airport to take the DC-3 on to Kamaran Island. The Sheikh had instructed them to make haste in order to get ahead of anyone in authority who might somehow link them to the incident in Frankfurt.

Ra'id thought Kamaran Island was a strange destination. The thirty-seven square mile island sat off the west coast of Yemen, not far from Al Hudaydah, the fourth largest city in the country. With a total population of between four and five thousand, the island was essentially devoid of people.

Though it had been settled as far back as the time of the Persians, and perhaps before, it had fallen into the hands of the Ottomans and was used as a sanitary quarantine center for pilgrims coming from all over the world heading to the Hajj at the Kaaba of Mecca. However, their defeat in the World War I, the island fell to the British to administer. Rows of barrack-like sleeping quarters were built, along with the disinfectant factory. They even had an ice plant built in order to provide for some air conditioning, in what many thought was a Godforsaken place.

However, in order to take advantage of the lucrative returns from the ever-growing number of pilgrims going to Mecca, the Saudi Arabian government built its own center and Kamaran Island was largely abandoned.

Or so it was, until recently! A few years before, the Foundation for the Promotion of Islamic Culture had purchased the rights to set up a new tourist attraction: an island camp where one could live in huts built using traditional methods, partake in traditional music and food, and enjoy some of the best diving and snorkelling in the Red Sea. Tourists could take guided tours to see the tropical fish, the delicate corals, the mangrove areas and the bird life.

Ra'id knew the history of the island, but as he walked toward the terminal carrying his duffle bag and computer case, he noticed that the old hangar off to the left was in remarkable condition. Looking back at the landing strip, he realized that it had been repaved and extended to accommodate even larger planes than the one he had taken. The terminal windows were closed and he could hear the drone of the compressor on the roof, powering the air-conditioning unit.

As he entered through the main entrance of the small, one-room one-storey stone building, he immediately sensed the twenty-five-degree drop in temperature, and as good as the air felt, the sweat that soaked his shirt caused him to shiver a little, as it rapidly cooled and dried.

As he approached the counter just ahead of him, he noticed that the décor of the room was not that of a small airport terminal but rather of a Yemeni home with its Persian-style rug, blue ceramic wainscoting and bamboo fan hanging from the ceiling.

Behind the counter stood a man of indeterminate age, dressed in Yemeni-style garb, sporting a light gray suit with a Nehru-style button shirt. He was also wearing the traditional headscarf with the tail draped over his right shoulder down to

178

an ornate leather belt. Tucked between the belt and his fat stomach, was a ceremonial *jambiya* or double-blade dagger, with its unique hilt identifying the man's caste and tribe. It wasn't difficult for Ra'id to note that the hilt was not made of rhino horn or giraffe, as was tradition, but of plastic, probably made cheaply in China. A true *jambiya* would cost several thousand dollars, as did the one his father had owned.

"Welcome to the Kamaran Island Resort Camp," said the man.

Ra'id responded, "Thank you. We have reservations under the names of Mustafa and Hadir, gesturing toward Mohammed. How far is the camp from here?"

"It is about a fifteen minute drive and a shuttle is waiting at the side of the building. The driver will take you there along with your baggage."

After signing the register, the two picked up their belongings and walked back out into the inferno to the parking area at the side of the building. There, two vehicles sat: a jeep-style shuttle bus and a white Mercedes SUV.

As they approached, the driver's door of the SUV opened and Vincenzo stepped out. He waved Ra'id and Mohammed over and opened the rear door to allow them to enter. As they did, they handed Vincenzo their duffle bags which he deposited in the rear of the vehicle. They kept their computer cases with them.

As they settled into the vehicle, someone on the front passenger side turned and leaned slightly between the bucket seats toward them. It was Sheikh Al-Kabir. "Welcome gentlemen," he said with a smile. "I hope your flight was pleasant."

"Good afternoon, sir," said Ra'id. "Though the departure time was very early this morning, the flights themselves were uneventful, thanks be to Allah."

The Sheikh resumed his position in the front and spoke to them while looking back in the visor mirror. "I

179

thought I would come to greet you personally. There are issues we need to talk about."

"We are honored you would come here in person." said Ra'id. "We know how busy you are and especially after the Frankfurt incident and the destruction of the lab, we are at a loss."

"As I said to you before, I need you to believe me, that we do not assign any blame to you. On the contrary, we feel we must bear the blame for not finding a truly invisible site for you to work. However, before I say more, I will show you something that I want you to see." With that he flipped the visor up, closed his eyes and propped his head back on the headrest.

The vehicle pulled out of the airport driveway and onto the crushed-stone road, headed northeast toward the resort and away from the airport and Kamaran City just beyond. The car sped along, trailed by a tunnel of road dust and the crunch of stones beneath the tires.

They drove for about five minutes, both Mohammed and Ra'id looking in silence at the sterile landscape. Off to their left, they could see the first of the series of long ridges of weathered stone, the leftovers of the long-eroded uplifted bedrock. To their right toward the sea was nothing but flat barren terrain of sand and rocks, punctuated by the odd palm tree.

Before long, they noticed in the distance to the left, an old and unkempt stone fence set back from the road about two hundred yards. Behind this barrier, an eight-foot chain-link fence ran parallel to the other. Beyond and enclosed by the fence, was a small village of dilapidated, long stone barrack-like structures, lined up in military fashion. Front and center were several buildings that looked as if they had served as reception offices. At the rear, two very large Quonset huts towered over the one-storey barracks and beyond that, several low shrub-covered ridges served as a backdrop.

The vehicle slowed as it reached a driveway which led to a gate in the fence just in front of the stone reception center. As Vincenzo turned up the lane, the Sheikh reached for a button in the glove compartment and the gate door slid back, leaving a wide gap through which the SUV entered.

"Is this the resort camp?" asked a confused Ra'id.

The Sheikh responded, "No, that is about ten more minutes down the road. This is really what I wanted to show you."

As they drove around the stone reception area and along the road between the old barracks, the Sheikh smiled at the troubled look on Ra'id's face, while Mohammed's remained blank as usual. "Do not let the appearance of the buildings deceive you. They are not what they look like. Do you see the large vaulted ones over there?" pointing to the Quonset huts.

"Yes. They seem rather new compared to the other structures in this compound."

"They are. The one on the right is the desalination plant which was commissioned and never completed by the contractor. We took over the contract and now it is fully functional. The one on the left covers the original ice-making plant, which is now a refurbished power generation plant, fuelled by a natural gas well we discovered about a quarter of a mile away."

Ra'id still had somewhat of a puzzled look on his face. "You've done all of this for a resort camp?"

"Yes and no. You see, the camp is legitimate and fulfills our foundation's mandate. We needed both plants for the camp, but we did build them to overcapacity for other purposes."

181

At that point, Vincenzo turned the car into a small laneway between two barracks of the four or five buildings that still had roofs.

The car stopped and everyone exited the vehicle. The Sheikh walked back to the front of the building, waving to the others to follow. Arriving at the door, he turned and nodded to Vincenzo. He reached over to a panel on the side of the door, lifted the cover and entered a series of numbers on the keypad. A click was heard and Vincenzo opened the door, then stepped back to allow the others through.

As the Sheikh entered, he flipped the light switch to the *on* position, bringing the fluorescent lights to full power.

Ra'id and Mohammed entered and what they saw absolutely shocked them. Though it was perhaps in some slightly different configuration, they were looking at their lab in Frankfurt! Speechless, Ra'id looked at the Sheikh, not quite fully comprehending what he was witnessing.

"I can see I have surprised you," the Sheikh said with a chuckle. "Simply put, when you sent me the list of items you needed to create your invention, I merely ordered two of everything. Then, while you were completing your family jihad, I had a team of engineers record and duplicate your equipment in Frankfurt here in this facility."

"This is absolutely amazing!" Ra'id was finally able to say. "Does this mean I can continue my work?"

"I thought that would be evident." said the Sheikh.

Mohammed finally spoke, "And the supercomputers?"

"They are in the refrigerated barrack next to this one. And next to that one are your quarters with all the amenities. We have invested much in the two of you and there is no question that, in spite of Frankfurt, you need to continue."

The Sheikh turned to Vincenzo. "Please show them to their quarters and familiarize them with the compound."

Turning back to Ra'id. "I'm sure you will understand that until we are done, you will need to stay in the compound. We have provided a chef and attendants to look after you. The fence around the compound should keep the tourists out and if other more suspicious types decide to come looking, the perimeter will be protected by surveillance cameras and guards, twenty-four hours a day. We cannot take the chance you will be seen and recognized."

Ra'id nodded. "Yes, I do understand. I need to express my gratitude for everything you have done for me and Mohammed. We will not fail you."

The Sheikh smiled. "Good, that is the attitude we will need. Now, I have work to do. I will return in time to dine with you as we still have much to talk about."

With that, he turned and walked out into the heat to the SUV.

Chapter 40

The flight back from Frankfurt was seemingly shorter for Sam than the flight over. His night together with Melinda was now a fond memory and any tension between them was now gone.

Melinda took the second leg of the trip to Washington from New York, while Sam reluctantly flew to Toronto to meet with Jalal to discuss their research.

He so wanted to tell Jalal all about his adventures, the intrigue, Melinda… He knew he wasn't authorized to do so, not until and perhaps not even then, there was a final solution to the mission.

The good news was that the computer simulation Jalal had created was working flawlessly, recreating the celestial movement of the stars in our quadrant of the galaxy to about fifteen million years.

The heavy work for Sam would be dating the genetic mutations in as many species as possible, to identify biological patterns and correlating the position and alignment of the stars and nebulae. This could take years, but he knew he was on the right path. He could prove his thesis by concentrating for the time being, on human evolution. So, why could he not say the same thing concerning The Osiris String?

Sam had been at his apartment for barely an hour when he received a phone call from Melinda, telling him a private charter jet was being sent to pick him up at the Island Airport, downtown Toronto! The President wanted to meet the team, ASAP!

Chapter 41

True to his word, the Sheikh returned in time to dine with Ra'id and Mohammed. Dinner was filled with small talk about anything and everything not concerned with the project. This only heightened Ra'id's suspicions that the important part of the evening was yet to come.

The barrack which housed the dining area was also set up as a small library, with several comfortable leather high-back chairs placed to face the bookcases which shouldered the only window in the room. They were filled with scientific journals dealing with microwaves, the biology of HIV and Aids. One shelf however, held some twenty adventure novels. The window opened up to an unobstructed view of the hills behind the compound, creating both a peaceful setting, as well as one of isolation.

After they had finished their dessert of *Crêpes suzette flambées à l'orange*, the Sheikh invited both Ra'id and Mohammed to sit in the leather chairs, turning them in to face each other. The chef served them espressos and left them to continue their discussion. Vincenzo remained seated at the dining table, patiently waiting for further instructions.

The Sheikh looked at Mohammed. "I have chosen to include you in this discussion because I believe you have earned that right. As well, what we are about to discuss will profoundly affect your life as well as Ra'id's. And for that reason, the two of you will need to agree or not agree."

Mohammed looked briefly at Ra'id and then again at the Sheikh. "Please understand that whatever Ra'id decides to do, I will be his shadow. We are like brothers! When he began his research, I was there to support him. When he decided to avenge Samihah's death, I was there for him as family."

Ra'id was moved to lean over and briefly put his hand on Mohammed's arm in a gesture of thanks.

"Very well then," continued the Sheikh.

"I will be direct and blunt with the two of you. You must by now understand that your private jihad has altered your situations. The raid on the laboratory in Frankfurt can only mean that they know who you are and you can be sure they will continue to look for you."

Both Ra'id and Mohammed nodded without a word.

"You also must be aware that, though your research into the cure for HIV is successful, your quest for the Nobel Prize is no longer feasible!"

Again, both simply nodded.

"So if that is the case, why do you believe we have done all of this for you?"

Ra'id spoke up, "The question had crossed my mind."

The Sheikh held back for almost ten seconds before hesitantly continuing. "I believe you still have a place in destiny. What if I were to tell you that the foundation has been deeply involved in promoting, not only the Islamic culture, but also Islamic unity."

Ra'id sat back in the chair, waiting for the revelation.

"Yes," continued the Sheikh. "The Muslim world has until now, been held captive by the Western world, dependent on commodities such as oil and the pyramids to bring in the money to feed our people. Though oil has been leveraged to gain some influence on world politics, with most of the Western countries now strategizing on how to reduce their dependency on petroleum, and therefore us, we can foresee a dramatic reduction in our influence. As for tourism, that has dropped significantly as well, due to recent incidences across the Arab world."

186

The Sheikh stopped for a few moments, letting what he had just said sink in a little. "What if I were to tell you that your invention could reverse this trend and make Muslims masters of our own fate, unfettered by Western control and interests?"

The Sheikh waited for a response.

"Sir, I know that my invention can be an effective weapon. We," gesturing to Mohammed and himself, "have used it and understand its power. But, in spite of the satisfaction of avenging Samihah, I am saddened by the death of the soldiers involved. To use the invention to kill others, not connected to my grief would worry me."

The Sheikh responded, "I understand your concerns, but let me assure you that what I am proposing would take them into consideration. We are not in the business of death. The Foundation is in the business of the glory of Islam and of its disciples. Though there may be some casualties, we believe your invention would so frighten world leaders that they would soon come to understand that they finally need to see us as equals! Ultimately, we would like to see an Islamic Federation, united in the glory of Allah, feared and respected by all. You and your invention are the key, young *ibn Imad*. Will you finish connecting the equipment we have set up for you and link it to your software?"

Ra'id was taken aback somewhat. He turned to Mohammed with a quizzical look, getting a nod of approval in return.

"I would imagine our options are limited, and if my invention could bring about such a change for the betterment of our people, it would be selfish of me not to agree. I am a little confused, however, about how we could influence so many individuals all over the world with our van? Even if we had a fleet of them, would there not be too many obstacles?"

The Sheikh smiled. "Please leave that to me. I will have something to show you in the morning before I return to Capri. For the moment, I want the two of you to contemplate the honor Allah has bestowed upon you and know that history has changed tonight. My confidence in you has been rewarded a thousand fold."

The Sheikh stood, followed by Ra'id and Mohammed, whom he embraced. He walked over to the door where Vincenzo was waiting. He whispered something in his ear and then turned to wave to Ra'id and Mohammed. "Sleep well and I will see you first thing in the morning. Vincenzo will be staying with you to ensure your well-being and look after your needs."

Chapter 42

The next morning the Sheikh arrived about ten to find Ra'id and Mohammed hard at work in the new laboratory. "Good morning."

"Oh, good morning to you, sir."

"I see you have committed to my proposal. It pleases me. As I told you last night, I have one more thing to show you. Please come with me."

The three exited the barrack and walked silently toward the one closest to the Quonset huts at the rear of the compound. As they approached the building, nothing seemed to be out of the ordinary, but instead of finding a darkened room when they entered through the keyed door, they were hit by a brightly-lit area. A huge section of the roof was missing and in the center of the otherwise empty room, were three satellite dishes, each aimed at a different spot in space.

"Last night you were wondering how we could reach the individuals that need to be targeted. Well, now you know. The equipment in the new lab is linked to a powerful transmitter which connects these dishes to a series of geosynchronous satellites we have leased for our purposes."

Ra'id quietly walked around the array of dishes, now and then running his hands over their bases, as if to make sure he wasn't imagining them. "Why would I have questioned you sir?"

Smiling in triumph, the Sheikh walked over to Ra'id and put his arm around his shoulders. "I'm sorry I had to be so secretive, but I could not include you in the complete story without knowing you were committed. Now, I need to leave you once more, this time to put into motion the great movement you are making possible."

The three left the antenna-array building, heading back to the barrack housing the laboratory.

Approaching the SUV they had used the day before, the Sheikh added, "Vincenzo is driving me to the airport, but he will return to help you."

Opening the passenger door himself, the Sheikh turned to Ra'id. "You cannot understand the degree to which I am proud of you. Can you tell me how long it will take you to complete your work?"

Ra'id looked at Mohammed and as if they could communicate telepathically, the two turned to the Sheikh and Ra'id said, "I would say we will need a few days to connect the system and test it."

"Wonderful."

The Sheikh sat in the vehicle, closed the door and waved goodbye to the two scientists.

Chapter 43

"OK, what do I do when I meet him?" asked Sam. "I know I don't bow! Hell, I wouldn't even bow for the Queen!"

"Don't be silly, but wait until he addresses you. Then, just be yourself! This is my first time in the Oval Room as well," responded Melinda.

The pair were sitting on a two-person cushioned stool in the hallway just outside one of the several entrances to the Oval Office. Security agents stood at the intersections of the hallways leading to the area. Employees carrying what looked like large reports paraded back and forth, ignoring the couple sitting nervously. A few minutes passed and a familiar shape came around the corner. It was Agent Cohen, along with another person. Melinda gently elbowed Sam and whispered, "That's my boss, Carl Broom."

She stood, as did Sam, and waited for Broom and Cohen to reach them. Quick introductions followed and Broom said, "He's waiting for us!"

He promptly knocked on the door, opened it and walked in. From his vantage point at the rear and framed by the opening to the room, Sam could see the President sitting behind the famous presidential desk.

Built from the timbers of the British Arctic Exploration ship *Resolute*, it had been given as a gift to President Hayes by Queen Victoria in 1880. Since then, it had rarely left the White House other than after the assassination of President Kennedy, when President Johnson sent it on tour as a traveling exhibition with the Kennedy Presidential Library, followed by a short stint at the Smithsonian.

President Alexander stood at once and walked around the desk to greet his guests. As he shook each one's hand, the President looked directly into their eyes and delayed the release of their handshake in order to convey his pleasure at meeting the team, immediately putting them at ease. Showing them to the two cushioned sofas, he sat in one of the two silk-upholstered chairs, positioned to allow him to look at all his guests, with his back to the desk and windows.

"First, let me congratulate you on your mission."

Agent Cohen was the first to respond, "But, we failed to apprehend the target."

"Nonsense, your team has accomplished much. You know who is responsible for the deaths of your countrymen, you've located his laboratory and destroyed his equipment and we hope, have ended the murders. And, based on reports from Mr. Broom, it would seem you are getting much closer to the source of the funding for the weapon, which should help us identify who is actually behind all of this. I would not call that a failure!"

Broom interjected, "Sir, we do have more information on that subject."

"Yes, go ahead," responded Alexander.

"We have tracked down the suppliers of the computer equipment that was used to power up the weapon. As you are aware, these were incredibly fast mainframe computers: expensive and cutting-edge technology."

"Let me stop you there!" interjected the President. "Did you say *they*?"

"Yes sir, I was just getting to that."

As if on cue, the three agents turned their heads toward Broom, each with a questioning look of their face.

Broom resumed, "We have located the providers of the computers and have debriefed them. We did not find anything to indicate that they were involved, other than selling the equipment. However, when we estimated the number of units which were destroyed in Frankfurt, we realized that we accounted for only half of the computers purchased."

Shock seemed to hit the three agents as the reality of the situation sank in.

The President didn't flinch. "So we aren't done yet. Is that what you are saying?"

"It would seem so, Mr. President," said Broom, still cool as a cucumber.

"So perhaps we *have* failed." said Agent Cohen.

The President looked up at Cohen, but it was Sam who spoke up. "Sir, if I may?"

"Please, Dr. Buckner."

"Well, unless I'm mistaken, we may have destroyed one laboratory, leaving the potential for another elsewhere. If I had to guess, the second *is* the backup! And as such, we can be relatively certain there isn't a third."

Broom responded, "Good analysis. That is precisely the conclusion we have came up with. Still frightening as a scenario, but at least we believe we know what we are up against and what we aren't. We have already started following the delivery route for the computers sent to Frankfurt as well as the other set of computers, to see if we can find some commonalities and determine where the second lab is."

"Good," said the President. "I want to be kept informed on any progress you make!"

"Yes sir!" said Broom.

Turning to Sam and Melinda, the President continued, "OK, assuming the other lab is operational, can you come up with what we can expect next?"

Melinda briefly looked at Broom who nodded, signalling to her to go ahead. "Well, we believe the deaths of the eight soldiers was an encapsulated event, spurred by a brilliant scientist wanting to avenge his fiancée's death. It would seem evident with this most recent information, that this is only the beginning. And we don't believe it will remain local, so to speak. Too much money and too much secrecy are involved to end there. If I had to guess, this is going international."

The President turned to Sam. "Would you agree?"

Hesitantly, Sam said, "Yes sir, I do!   What will probably come next has to be on a much larger scale. They know we are on to them and I think they will be desperate to put the weapon back into operation. However, this raises a few red flags in my mind."

This time, the gaze of everyone was squarely on Sam.

"We still don't know the delivery method which was used to kill the eight soldiers, but it would seem to me that it was land based, probably a vehicle of some sort." Nods of approval all around.

"But if they are to go to the next level, that delivery method needs to be much more sophisticated and more far-reaching."

Broom responded, "Any suggestions?"

"I can only think of one: a satellite network capable of transmitting a broad range of microwaves."

"That is a very frightening thought," responded the President. "Anything else?"

"Yes, just one more. Considering how the individuals are killed and the vehicle by which the microwaves are transmitted, and finally the need for computers of such speed, I can only surmise the weapon works on the level of the DNA molecule. They must be targeting the individual's own DNA, different for each one of them, disrupting enough of the genes to destroy each and every cell. The way the soldiers died had to be truly horrible."

Broom interjected, "So what are you saying?"

Turning toward the President, Sam continued, "Sir, have you been in hospital lately?"

194

Stunned, Alexander said, "Only for my yearly checkups. Oh yes, last year for a toothache. They removed a molar. Why?"

"Sir, what happened to the tooth?"

"Why, I don't quite know! Broom, would you have a clue?"

"Not off-hand, but I'll have someone look into that."

Sam continued, "Sir, what I'm getting at is that, if my suspicions are correct, and they have another lab set up, a delivery system in place and possible access to *your* DNA, you could be the next target."

"My God man, I would hate to have you as my enemy if you had the means," Alexander partly said to Sam, partly talking to himself.

The President sat silent, mimicked by everyone in the room. Then he looked up at Broom. "Carl, I know you suggested this could be bigger than we first estimated and that you wanted a more experienced team to head the mission."

Sam, Melinda and Agent Cohen momentarily looked at each other, somewhat surprised at the President's candor.

"But," continued the President, "considering this discussion and what I have just heard, we don't have the luxury of briefing a new team. I want you to oversee this mission personally, and I think we need these three on the team."

"Yes, Mr. President. Do you have preferences as to who does what?" Alexander knew this wasn't Broom's style, but considering it was his head on the block, the President responded, "No, I'm not going to tell you how to do your job, but I will suggest you need to put this into high gear. If I could be a potential target, we have to assume other heads of state could be in the same position. I'll take care of contacting our allies and inform them of these developments without giving them too much info on the *how*. I really don't like the looks of this."

Alexander stood up. "Gentlemen and Miss Gordon, good job." Everyone stood as well, except for Sam. He remained seated, looking at the carpet with the large presidential seal. A look of surprise could be seen on Melinda's face, as well as on Agent Cohen's.

Calmly, the President said, "Dr. Buckner, do you have more to say?"

Sam looked up at the President. "I'm sorry, but there is something I think we are all overlooking."

Alexander gestured to the others to sit once more, and still standing, asked, "And what would that be, son?"

"Well, I can't help but think about Al-Eissa's original thesis for the cure of HIV. I know the weapon he has created poses an incredible threat. But his initial invention to cure HIV could have and still could be, a remarkable advance for humanity."

"And so you are suggesting we do what?" said Alexander.

"I don't know. I'm struggling with the danger of the technology on the one hand, and the benefit of it on the other. I'm struggling with the need to stop the man and the need to salvage the good he could have done. I guess what I'm really saying, is that we're more or less in the same position you Americans were at the end of the Second World War, when there was a need to stop Hitler's V-1 and V-2 programs and a desire to take possession of the science. Didn't the authorities at the time decide that the rocket technology was best taken over rather than destroyed? You captured the scientists involved in the project and gave them asylum here in the US. Ultimately, these scientists launched your space program."

The President looked at Broom and then at Agent Cohen. "You know, that does make sense."

196

Turning to Sam. "So what are you suggesting?" Only then did he sit down in his chair.

"I'm not sure, sir. I'm trying to think as a scientist and a man. Until the death of Al-Eissa's fiancée, he was on the verge of one of history's great discoveries; well at least, in the modern day. Instead of trying to kill him to stop this insanity, could we not try to *bring him in* so to speak. That would have the same effect as taking him out by force, while assuring that the world would not lose this technology."

The President waited a few moments. "I see what you are proposing. How would you suggest we do that?"

"I don't know, but, if I could reach out to him, scientist to scientist, I could possibly reason with him and ensure we don't lose this opportunity. If we could contact him, let's say by Internet, we could send him a message of some sort. I know that he is probably monitoring what is happening over the Internet, as we all are!"

Alexander frowned a little and looked over to Broom. "What do you think?"

"Either way, he needs to be taken out of the equation."

It was then that Melinda said, "Sir, I think we could have a way of communicating with Al-Eissa."

"Really!"

"I'm aware that we at Homeland Security have the capability to *blitz* the Internet. Whether or not the message would reach Al-Eissa is problematic, but it could be worth the effort. We actually have a computer program that can come up with thousands of e-mail address combinations and we send a message that only he would recognize. We need to provide the programers with all the information we have on him."

"That would make sense," Sam responded. "Any scientist worth his salt would be online, monitoring anything connected to him on the Internet!"

Looking again at Broom, the President seemed to get that the head of Homeland Security was onside with the suggestion. "OK, I believe we have very little time to end this crisis, but assuming we are capable of doing so, I will give you one week to pull it off. Otherwise, Secretary Broom is authorized to move *without prejudice.*"

Sam looked at the President. "Thank you. We'll do what we can."

"Ok then, I think we have a plan. I suggest we get to work on this!"

He stood again and shook the three agents' hands. When it was Broom's turn, the President said, "Carl, can I have another moment with you?"

When the trio had entered the outer hallway and the door was shut, the President turned to Broom. "Carl, give me your honest opinion on Buckner's request."

"Sir, I thought you had agreed to take Al-Eissa in and let him develop his invention?"

"I know what I said. But I think you realize, as I do, how dangerous this weapon is. It has the potential to make *all* other weapons obsolete. On the one hand, it could revolutionize world politics and ensure our supremacy; on the other, perhaps in the hands of, let's say an unscrupulous president, it could bring about the *Brave New World*."

"Sir, these are issues only you and your counterparts around the world can deal with: it's above my pay scale. My job is to keep the US homeland safe and that includes keeping you alive. I think Al-Eissa can out into the open, he needs to be eliminated. We now know this thing can work, both as a weapon and as a medical marvel. With the insight we have on the technology, we have people who can duplicate it and we can keep it entirely *in-house*. We don't need Al-Eissa. If at risk, you could be targeted in five minutes, five days or five weeks. We just don't know where they are with this second lab. I can't chance it and by eliminating Al-Eissa, we remove a critical component to their program."

"OK, I understand," said Alexander. "Keep me informed on your progress and please come up with the plan for an operation to do it."

"Will do, Mr. President."

"Thanks, Carl. We will also need to make sure this doesn't leak out. I assume each member of the team has signed a letter of confidentiality?"

"Yes sir. It was the first thing we did when they agreed to participate."

"Good. Thank you."

Broom left the Oval Room and met the others waiting in the hallway.

The President looked at his watch and saw that it was five-fifteen. He walked over to the access door of the reception room and looked in for his personal assistant.

"Mildred, I hope you don't have anything on your agenda for this evening."

Chapter 44

"Members of the Board, I welcome you once more. I can now inform you that your destinies will change, beginning tomorrow."

Sheikh Al-Kabir was standing before the twelve members of the foundation's board of directors. Each had been personally chosen and approached by the Sheikh. Each had come from one of Mid-Eastern Muslim-dominated countries: Egypt, Lebanon, Iran, Iraq, Saudi Arabia, the United Arab Emirates, Libya, Yemen, Turkey, Somalia, Sudan and Syria. Each held a relatively high position in the government or the military of their country. And each one believed passionately in the concept of a United Islamic Federation.

"In spite of the assault by the Germans and Americans in Frankfurt, our security precautions saved young Al-Eissa and his colleague, Mohammed. As well, our precautions in duplicating the laboratory have demonstrated to be wise. And above all, Ra'id has agreed to support our cause!" This was followed by a round of applause and nods of approval.

The Sheikh continued, "The pilot project to kill the Israeli soldiers proved to be a complete success and now we can move on with our agenda. Young Ra'id has been working for the past few days connecting all the components of the weapon. He has assured me that tomorrow he will be able to run a full test of the system. We have selected one target which will serve as an example of our capabilities of reaching anyone, anywhere." The Sheikh smiled as he saw the agitated mood of the Board members.

"Please, let me continue." Quiet returned to the room.

"We will be sending anonymous messages to heads of state of America, France, Germany, Great Britain, Russia and China begin to let them know they should be on the lookout for the event."

The member from Saudi Arabia asked, "May we know the target?"

"Certainly." responded the Sheikh. "We are starting with the top general in Egypt: Bashir." A smile came to the face of the member from Egypt.

"Within the next few days, we should have eliminated all the individuals from each of your countries, who stand in your way of becoming the leaders all will turn to. Your efforts to collect samples of their DNA will pay dividends very soon!"

"As we have agreed, we need to position you *before* we move to the following step: that is, to make an example of the President of the United States." The tapping of the hands on the table lasted a full minute before the Sheikh could regain control again.

"Yes, yes gentlemen. I will take that as a vote of confidence!"

"Now, before that step, you will all be invited to the compound to witness the operation. In spite of the turmoil you will be dealing with, I would suggest you leave your schedule relatively free. I have planned a special event for you."

"Then, the day we take care of the President will be a day long remembered as the one on which our people were set free. No other head of state will dare oppose our demands. And if they do, we will be ready for them as well."

With a look of satisfaction on his face, the Sheikh suggested each member return to their respective homes to prepare.

He then retired to his private office, picked up the telephone to call Ra'id and tell him which sample number he needed to encode and prepare for the transmitter.

Chapter 45

Seven-thirty the next morning, the phone on the *Resolute* desk rang. "Mr. President."

It was Carl Broom.

"Yes, Carl."

"Sir, I have two bits of information: neither is good."

President Alexander sat back and waited.

"The first deals with the tooth which they extracted last year. Our investigation has determined it is missing! It was never disposed of by anyone of the attending staff. We therefore need to assume you *are* at risk."

Alexander closed his eyes. "And the second *bit* of information?"

"We received a message from *them*! It came through our embassy in Paris."

Still with his eyes closed. "And the message says…"

"We should look to Egypt for proof. That was all the message said, sir."

The President leaned forward, putting his elbows on the desk, rubbing his forehead with his free hand. "Ok, thanks Carl. I'll get in touch with the Secretary of State. We'll be contacting our people in Cairo. Keep me informed. And, any word from Dr. Buckner?"

"Not yet."

Chapter 46

Seven time zones away, it was two-thirty in the afternoon on Kamaran Island and both Ra'id and Mohammed were busy finishing the preparations to trigger the weapon.

Ra'id turned to Vincenzo.

"You may advise the Sheikh that we are ready."

Vincenzo switched on his world telephone and dialled. Within two rings, the call was answered.

"They are ready."

Vincenzo looked up at Ra'id. "Proceed."

Ra'id turned, hunched over his laptop, looked at Mohammed on the other side of the counter, raised his right eyebrow and pressed the *Enter* key. Even from the barrack where they were, they could hear the tremendous increase in activity in the computer room. Then, the deep hum which was emanating from the maser in the Quonset hut next to it, increased dramatically. High in space, unseen by the three, a transmission satellite was turning to point at the serenely beautiful image of planet Earth below. About twenty seconds later, the decibel level of the maser dropped and then stopped.

Ra'id looked at Vincenzo: "It is done!"

Vincenzo returned to the voice on the other end of the line. "Done." He then flipped the telephone closed. "They are calling our contact in Cairo as we speak. We should know soon."

One minute later, his phone rang and Vincenzo picked up the call, listening without speaking. He flipped it shut once more and smiled. "It was a success."

Ra'id and Mohammed gave each other a *high five* but Ra'id's smile soon left him. Though he understood the importance of what he was doing, he drew no pleasure or satisfaction from it. He thought it must be the type of feeling he had heard bomber pilots experienced when dropping bombs on their targets from high up, never seeing the victims.

He was troubled, both by this lack of interest over his mission and by the constant reminder of a strange email message on his computer the day before. No one knew his personal email address, rasam@gmail.com, short for Ra'id *and* Samihah, except for Mohammed.

The message was cryptic: "They found you once and they can find you again. But as a fellow scientist and researcher, I understand the importance of your work for the good of mankind. In spite of what you have done, we feel you can redeem yourself. I propose meeting you at a time and place of your choosing. I will be alone and unarmed. If yes, email me at the following address: sbuckner@yahoo.ca. To learn about me and my research, go to www.sbuckner/UofT.on.ca."

At first he thought it was a crackpot, but no such person could possibly know about Frankfurt, his research *and* his email address. He deleted the message and tried to put it out of his mind.

Vincenzo's telephone rang once more and he took the call. When he hung up, he said, "The Sheikh sends his *complimenti*. But, there is problem. It is your uncle."

Thirty minutes later, he and Mohammed were being driven to the island airport to fly to Sana'a, Yemen's capital. Landing an hour and a half later at the El Rahaba Airport, they took a taxi to the Saudi German Hospital on Sixty Meter Road, just a few miles from the airport.

Ra'id checked at the reception desk and was told his uncle was in a private room on the third floor. He stepped out of the elevator and looked both left and right. There was Ali,

205

Ra'id's brother, sitting on a chair outside a room about halfway down the hallway. Ra'id pointed Ali out to Mohammed who, as usual, was trailing just behind.

Ali jumped up when he saw Ra'id and walked quickly to meet him. They embraced warmly, patting each other on the back and giving each other the triple-cheek kiss.

"How is he?" asked Ra'id, finally releasing his brother.

"The doctor is with him now. He shouldn't be long. But it does not look good. His cancer has spread from his lungs to his liver and spine. They do not hold much hope that he will last the night!" Tears welled up in his eyes.

"Why was I not told sooner?" asked Ra'id.

"What do you mean? Where have you been for the last while? No contact other than word from Sheikh Al-Kabir that you were on some important quest, and that you were fine."

Ra'id looked down, shook his head gently.

"Yes, you are right! I'm sorry I was cross with you, but you are right. I have been so involved with my project that I failed to think of you and Uncle. Some day I will be allowed to tell you about it and you will understand."

The doctor came out of the room and seeing Ali talking to the two strangers, he walked over to them. Ali quickly introduced Ra'id as his brother.

"Your uncle is not well, as I assume your brother has informed you."

Ra'id looked at the doctor.

"How much time does he have?"

The doctor shook his head.

"Earlier, I would have said two or three weeks. Now, I would estimate two or three days. I'm sorry." The doctor left the three standing in the middle of the hallway.

"Go to him Ra'id. I think he has been holding out until your arrival."

Ra'id walked to the door leading into the room. There were butterflies in his stomach, the blood drained from his face and his hands were shaking. He sat on the chair next to the bed and whispered, "Uncle. Uncle, it's Ra'id."

Nothing for some time but then Umayr stirred and his eyes opened. Blinking and looking around, it took him a moment to focus on the source of the voice.

"Ra'id, finally you are here. Thank you. I've been waiting. We need to talk."

His voice was weak and raspy, but his words were clear and on the mark. It was typical of his uncle to get to the point and not resort to the Yemeni tradition of *small talk* before saying what he really wanted to convey.

He coughed painfully. "How have you been?" seemingly not concerned by the fact that he was dying.

"I've been well, but busy, Uncle. The Sheikh has been looking after me and has given me a purpose in life."

Umayr's eyes widened slightly, but before he could speak, he had another coughing fit. When he was finally able to relax, he put his hand on Ra'id's forearm. "Ra'id, you should be wary of the Sheikh."

Ra'id reacted with some surprise. "What do you mean? He has been nothing but supportive and there when I needed him."

Wheezing and trying to catch his breath, Umayr shook his head slowly from side to side. "There is more, much more to him than you know. I know."

Ra'id was taken aback. "Uncle, let's not talk about that for the moment. I came to see you, not to talk about other issues."

"No," responded Umayr. "Before I die, I need to speak to you about my shame. I could not meet Allah without baring my soul to you."

Ra'id felt the pain of his uncle's voice and covered the hand resting on his forearm with his own. "All right, uncle, I am here for you. What is troubling you so?"

Ra'id leaned closer to his uncle and listened. Umyr spoke of his association with the Sheikh, the circumstances around both Ra'id's parents' and Samihah's deaths... Everything!

From the hallway, Ali and Mohammed were looking in. They could see Ra'id still leaning over toward his uncle, his shoulders heaving slowly, obviously crying. They were touched by Ra'id's display of emotions.

Ten minutes later, Ra'id walked out of the room, tears in his eyes. "He is sleeping peacefully now."

Ali looked at Ra'id, concern registered on his face. "Is he dead?"

"No, he is just sleeping."

Looking at Mohammed. "Could I speak to you a moment?"

The two walked a few feet away and Ra'id put his arm over Mohammed's shoulders. "If anything were to happen to me, I need you to do something for me." They walked down the hallway and then back, talking in a whisper.

Ali could tell that both Ra'id and Mohammed were deeply affected by Umayr's situation. "Ra'id, don't blame yourself for your absence. Just being here for him now seems to have been what he wanted."

Ra'id looked at Ali and then embraced him once more. "It would seem your presence is more calming for him than mine. I, unfortunately, need to return to my work, but I will be back in a day or two. Can you let Uncle know?"

"Yes, yes I will. I understand you can't tell me what is happening yet, but I hope some day you can confide in your brother. I envy Mohammed."

Ra'id was shocked but his face softened. "Ali, I love you more than anyone in my life. True, Mohammed and I are very close, but I have only one brother and that is you."

This time it was Ali's turn to be misty-eyed, but he said nothing more. He only smiled through his tears and watched the two head to the elevator.

Chapter 47

When they returned to the compound, it was late. The sun had set hours before and the air was chilly. It had dropped from well over one hundred degrees to seventy-five degrees Fahrenheit.

Ra'id had remained quiet and pensive the whole trip back, Mohammed as well. As they got out of the white SUV, Ra'id noticed that the light in Vincenzo's barrack was still on. He wasn't in the mood to talk, so he decided to head to the lab to do a bit of work. He waved goodbye to Mohammed and headed off.

He keyed in the pass code and entered. Looking around, he thought everything seemed to be as he had left it, except for his laptop. He couldn't remember whether or not he had closed the lid. At the moment, it was closed. No, nothing to worry about. He shrugged it off. In any case, the computer was biometrically protected, needing his fingerprint to let him access the programs.

However, next to the laptop was a sheet of paper. On it was a message and twenty-seven numbers. The message stated, "The Sheikh would like you to program the DNA codes for the following targets. He would like to have all of them ready within a few days for rapid-sequence firing during one session."

Ra'id stood there for a full minute, not taking his gaze off the message and the numbers identifying the DNA *donors*.

He picked up his laptop, walked to the door, turned off the lights and left, heading to his and Mohammed's barrack. This one had been sectioned off into three large rooms, connected by a central hallway. At the end of it were the washroom and shower facilities, to the left Mohammed's bedroom and to the right, his own. He noticed that there was no light escaping from the bottom of Mohammed's door, so he must have already gone to bed. "Good," Ra'id thought, "I need a little time to myself."

Entering his room, he undressed, wrapped a towel around his waist and headed for the shower stall. Ten minutes later, he was in his PJ's, a pair of boxer shorts and a T-shirt, sitting under the covers with his laptop.

He slid his finger over the sensor and the computer booted up. Quickly going to his email program, he opened his *Deleted* directory and found the strange, mysterious message he had seen a few days before.

He opened it and read it again. He decided to go to the website provided in order to get a better idea of the sender if, indeed, it did come from him. He spent about a half hour checking and double-checking the information provided for Dr. Samuel Buckner, a researcher at the University of Toronto. He looked up the names of the research staff on the university's official website. He hunted down possible news articles about him in local newspapers, as well as some of the better-known scientific journals, all in order to confirm the doctor's credentials. They all seemed to be authentic.

He finally turned his web browser off and returned to the email. He brought his cursor over the address Dr. Buckner had provided and hesitated. He looked at the link for a full forty-five seconds; but, instead of clicking it to open a new outgoing email, he turned his program off, and then, the computer. Leaning over to the night stand, he turned the light off.

211

Chapter 48

The next morning, Ra'id was joined by Mohammed in the dining barrack for breakfast. He filled Mohammed in on the task that the Sheikh had given them and suggested they get to it immediately after they ate. It would take them all morning to get through half the list and the rest of the day to complete it.

As they worked on decoding the targets' DNA and converting the sequences into harmonic wavelengths that would trigger the high-speed vibrations, which would in turn, *cook* every cell in the targets' bodies at the same time, Ra'id was more intent and quiet than usual.

The two broke for lunch at one-fifteen in the afternoon. Ra'id told Mohammed to head off to the lunchroom and that he would follow shortly: he needed to do a verification of the software which controlled the transmitter.

Once Mohammed had left, Ra'id turned to his laptop and toggled his email program on. Within five minutes, he had opened the link to Dr. Buckner's email address, typed a short message and sent it. He disconnected from the wireless Internet network and went for lunch.

Chapter 49

It was six-thirty in the morning and Sam was just waking up. Melinda was already in the shower getting ready for work.

Homeland Security had provided Sam with a temporary apartment, ironically, in the Watergate Hotel. It had been fully renovated a few years back, and though the rooms were stunning, he couldn't the feeling he was being watched and listened to. Were the renovations for updating just the décor or to allow them to install new *bugs*? "So be it," he thought. "Let them have fun peeking in on us."

Melinda's apartment was in the Naylor Gardens area of Washington. She preferred to rent, because she never knew if she would be transferred to another city or even another country. Though small, the apartment was clean and not too expensive. Mostly, though, it was handy. She could easily get to her office in the US Department of Homeland Security's building at 7th and D street, two blocks south of the National Mall, by using the Suitland Parkway to South Capital Street, then on to the Southwest Freeway to the exit which brought her to E Street, a block away from work.

Because of the opulence of Sam's apartment, she had opted to stay there with him for a few days. The fact that the Watergate was on Virginia Street, somewhat closer to both work and the White House than her apartment, was a bonus.

Sam rolled over and reached for his cell phone. He turned it on and saw that he had six unread messages: three from travel agencies, two from local vineyards marketing their wines, and the last from a rasam@gmail.com. He rubbed his eyes to better focus: yes, he had read correctly!

"Holy shit!" was all he could say as he jumped out of bed. "Melinda!" He responded, "He emailed back!"

Melinda was in her bra and panties, drying her hair with her towel as she came running into the bedroom. "You're kidding!"

"Nope, seems our plan worked and he wants to talk. He says he hasn't made any decision yet, but that he is willing to talk."

Melinda was already reaching for her phone to speed-dial her boss.

Chapter 50

An hour later, they were sitting in Carl Broom's office. "So he says he wants to meet with you tomorrow, poolside at the Taj Sheba Hotel in Sana'a. At what time?"

Sam checked the display on his phone. "He says he'll try to be there at eleven in the morning, Yemeni time."

Broom took a moment to calculate. "OK, that would mean about nineteen or so hours from now. That will work!"

He turned to Melinda. "I need you to get the lay of the land there. I suggest you contact and work with the staff at our embassy in Sana'a. I want to know every nook and cranny within a quarter mile of the hotel." She nodded in the affirmative.

Reaching for the intercom, "Johnson, get a hold of the team we put together and tell them *wheels up* in two hours." He hung up the receiver, walked around his desk and sat on the edge of it.

"What team is that, sir?" asked Sam.

"It's the extraction team I'm sending along with you to look after the operation, assuming Al-Eissa agrees to cross over."

"Never thought of that. Not that I really thought much about what would happen if I *could* convince him to come back with me. I guess we just couldn't take a taxi to the airport and leave. OK. Just remember, I promised I wouldn't be armed."

"And you won't be. That's part of the extraction team's job and to keep you alive as well. Now, I would suggest you get your gear and be back here in an hour. You will all be driven to Andrews Air Force Base where you'll pick up your ride. We have a C-17 Globemaster on the ground as we speak, loaded with food negotiated in a bi-lateral agreement with Yemen. It will take you to your destination and then the plane will then fly on to our naval base in Bahrain, minus your team. The return flight won't be as spectacular however. We want to keep that one *under the radar*."

Broom continued, "On the matter of your specific role, Agent Gordon will have plenty of time to fill you in on the finer points of the *spy work* during the flight and on what will be expected of you whichever way this goes down." He stopped, looked at each person. "Any questions?" Seeing there were none coming, he raised himself from the edge of the desk and gave the signal it was time to move.

After everyone had left, Broom called the President. "Sir, the operation is launched!"

Chapter 51

The next morning at the compound on Kamaran Island, Vincenzo's telephone rang. He picked up the call. "Good morning sir!"

It was the Sheikh. "Is Ra'id there?"

"No, he went to see his uncle. His brother phoned and he said the time is here!"

"That is troubling. As you know, we monitor the Internet traffic of all the Foundations' protégés. I just received a call from our analysts that they have followed his last correspondences: a few from his brother and one to a university professor in Canada. It seems he has made an appointment to meet with this professor in Sana'a. I can assure you this is not good. Tell me, is the demonstration for this afternoon still ready to go?"

"Yes it is. Ra'id told me that Mohammed was fully capable of running it if he was delayed."

"Good. Then *you* need to deal with Ra'id. Now! I'm sending you a copy of the arrangements he made. I will be heading to the laboratory in time to greet our guests."

"I *capisce.*"

Chapter 52

"Thanks be to Allah, you are here! And just in time." It was Ali meeting Ra'id at their uncle's hospital room door.

"How is he doing?" whispered Ra'id as they entered the room.

"Not well. He lapsed into a coma about an hour ago. I doubt he will know we are here or that he will wake up."

Ra'id pulled up a second chair to the bedside, leaned over and placed his hand on his uncle's forehead. He sat down and took his uncle's hand, saying nothing for almost a minute. He then turned toward Ali who was sitting to his left, closer to the foot of the bed. "In spite of his past, he did do a good job in taking care of you."

Ali looked at his brother with a questioning look.

Ra'id simply shook his head. "I know you don't understand. Soon, very soon, I will be in a position to tell you all."

The two sat remained silent for about twenty-five minutes, listening to the beeping of the monitoring machine attached to Umayr and watching the up-and-down movement of his chest. The sound of his labored breathing suddenly stopped and was replaced by an ongoing beep emanating from the monitor.

Before the brothers could register what was happening, they heard scurrying in the hallway and within a moment the attending nurse was bursting into the room, followed by an orderly. The time of death was logged as 9:12 a.m. Ra'id and Ali were ushered out of the room for a few minutes and then invited back in, once the body had been disconnected from the monitors.

They sat on either side of their uncle and prayed for at least half an hour.

Ra'id then checked his watch. "Ali, I hope you can forgive me, but I must leave for a short while. I will return in a few hours and we will claim the body and bring him to his home here in Sana'a, in order to complete the burial rituals. While I am gone, could you purchase the oils and the shroud we will need to prepare the body?"

Ali nodded.

Ra'id hesitated a moment, then reached into his jacket's inner pocket. "Ali, if for whatever reason I do not return by three o'clock, you will need to take the body and complete the rituals without me."

Ali looked surprised. "Why would you think you might not return?"

"This envelope contains all the information you will need to understand what I have been doing and why I have been so secretive. It also has specific instructions for you to follow, *to the letter*! I am sorry to say that, whether or not I return, your life will be in danger and this information will help get you where you will be safe, with enough money in it to get you there. You will find further instructions that will allow you to disappear entirely, and with the means to live well."

Ali started to say, "But…"

Ra'id cut him off. "No time to argue! I should be back and we will then have a plan B to follow, which will ensure both our futures."

With that, Ra'id got up off the chair, took Ali's head in his hands and bent over to kiss the top of his brother's head. Then, he departed leaving Ali totally bewildered.

219

Chapter 53

Sana'a was very much that: a sauna. Sam couldn't believe the heat. Up until the taxi had dropped him and Melinda off at the Taj Sheba Hotel, in the banking district of the capital, he had been sheltered in an air-conditioned terminal and an air-conditioned vehicle. Now, even the short walk to the entrance of the hotel lobby had him breaking a sweat. Briefly looking up, he saw the two seven-story wings of the hotel, separated by a nine-story tower in the center.

Melinda took one look at him and smirked. "Wimp."

Sam shrugged, fully appreciating the wall of *cool,* as he walked through it entering the lobby.

Melinda glanced around carefully and seeing the windowless van arriving with the rest of the team, said, "OK, it looks secure. You know the plan?"

"Yes."

"We'll have our eyes on you and Al-Eissa. When he agrees to our conditions, you need only to shake his hand and we'll be there immediately to extract him. If not, don't try to stop him. Allow him to leave and we'll take it from there."

With that, Sam turned to find his way to the pool area, as instructed by Ra'id. Finding the table which was reserved with a tag displaying his name, he took a chair and sat down.

Amazingly, he wasn't sweating. He looked up to see that the parasol not only shaded him but was hooked up to a vent that blew out cooled air from a shaft connected from above to the building some fifteen feet away. As he looked around, he noticed that all the outside tables were set under similar parasols around the L-shaped pool area, and all in turn connected to the hotel with the air-conditioning ducts.

The circular pool was protected by the hotel on two sides and by a tall privacy hedge on the other two.

Looking up, he saw the tower in the crook of the *L*, the southern wing of the hotel and behind him, a single-storey conference and banquet area.

He kept looking at his surroundings, hoping to see Al-Eissa. The only people were a couple of women nicely clad in bikinis and a waiter in a white jacket walking with a beverage of some sort on a tray - no one else! He tried to find the team members, Melinda in particular, but could not see any of them.

The waiter walked over to him and asked if he would like to order something. Sam ordered a glass of ice water.

It was five minutes to eleven and Sam waited until the assigned time; then, five more minutes and then another five. He was beginning to think he had been set up by Al-Eissa.

While Sam was slowly scrutinizing the grounds, another waiter came out from the restaurant and walked by his table, then returned and sat down on one of the other chairs. "Dr. Buckner, I am Ra'id Al-Eissa."

Sam had been caught off guard. He quickly regained his full composure. "Please, call me Sam."

"And I, Ra'id."

"I was beginning to worry you wouldn't come," admitted Sam.

Ra'id looked at Sam intently. "Please believe, that thought has been with me since I sent you the email. There have been incidents which have made me question that wisdom. I am willing to listen to your proposal. Before we begin, are you wired for sound?"

Sam shook his head and started to unbutton his shirt Ra'id put his hand up and gestured *no*. "I trust you! I am here, am I not?"

* * * * *

Back in the War Room beneath the White House, Carl Broom picked up the direct line to the Oval Office. "Sir, it's time for you to come down. We're ready!"

* * * * *

Sam began, "Here is what I have been authorized to offer you…."

Chapter 54

Broom was standing in front of one of the large-screen television monitors in the War Room, hands on his hips and speaking into his wireless earphone microphone when the President walked in, nodded to his head of staff and to General George Murdock, the chairman of the Joint Chief of Staff. Broom looked at Alexander and then back at the screen. The President sat in his seat, at the head of the boardroom table. "What are we looking at, Carl?"

"Our man is on the roof of a four-storey building across the street from the target."

In fact, they were looking at Sam and Ra'id through a circular lens fitted with the traditional cross hairs of a sniper's scope. This one, however, was special!

The scope was actually a television camera which could capture and display the scene for the shooter and also for simultaneous playback or recording elsewhere. The ultrahigh resolution screen within the telescopic housing could display the image before them, along with important information such as wind velocity, temperature and precise distances related to whatever the shooter was looking at. The scene was going from Sam to Al-Eissa and back, with the telemetry information changing with each movement.

"One moment sir, let me put him on speaker." Gesturing to some invisible person behind a one-way smoked window, a voice, whispering, suddenly materialized over the sound system. "…and they have been at it for about eight minutes."

"Soldier, you're on audio with the President. Could you repeat your status?"

"Yes, sir. I set up here once I saw where Dr. Buckner was sitting. My position allows me to see both individuals. I can confirm the second person is, I repeat, *is* the target."

* * * * *

"Knowing the value of your invention for mankind, why would you weaponize it and kill those eight soldiers?"

Ra'id looked miffed. "I did it because it was required of me. I did it because I had, or was provided, the means to do so. I did it because beloved Samihah's death was so unnecessary. How can you understand? You Canadians are so protected and stiff, much like your British ancestors. I cannot and will not apologize for what I did. Because of information that I have recently become aware, I know I need to take responsibility and atone for my actions."

"Ra'id, I'm really not here to chastise you, nor am I here to judge you. My sole interest is to make your invention available to the world. We need to ensure your safety, along with your technology, and we also need to destroy the weapon."

Ra'id said nothing, but a slight nod told Sam he understood and seemed to agree.

"We are aware this new weapon works. Word has reached us about an Egyptian general who has died in the same fashion as did the Israeli soldiers."

"Yes," responded Ra'id, "we did test the weapon with a specific target. However, I was not made privy to the target's identity. That was left to others to decide."

"Well, you can understand, then, that the American President, and I would say any of the world leaders who might be aware of the technology, would take this as a personal threat."

"Therefore, if you decide to cooperate with us, we will need to know where your backup laboratory is."

Ra'id hesitated. "It is on an island, Kamaran Island, not far from here. I, too, have some conditions…"

* * * * *

"Sir, I need to know what my orders are."

Broom turned to the President.

Alexander looked down at the table before him, drummed his fingers on it and then looked up at Broom. "Do it."

Broom instinctively turned to the screen, as if to look at the sniper. "It's a go. Take the target out when you are set."

"Copy that." responded the sniper, still in a whisper. The image with the cross hairs shifted from Sam to Ra'id. He pulled the trigger halfway, much as you would with an SLR camera to adjust and set the focus. The telemetry display readjusted…

* * * * *

"They are not for my benefit, but for my brother's. He is not responsible for anything I have done."

Sam was listening with a sense of satisfaction that he might be pulling this off. Then he heard two pops, not unlike firecrackers firing. Instinctively, he looked around for the source. When he turned to Ra'id, he glimpsed him sinking onto the table, still and silent.

* * * * *

"What the fuck was that?" hissed the sniper. "Target is down! Target is down!"

As he scanned the area. "Sir, *I* did not take the shot."

The image the people in the War Room were watching was a little nauseating. It went from left to right, up and down, focusing on the doors and windows of the hotel; and then up to the roof of the hotel and then to the right!

A silhouette appeared. The scope centered rapidly to show a thin man with dark slicked-back hair, holding a rifle aimed directly at the viewers, or rather the sniper. "Oh fuck...," exclaimed the sniper, just before the image jerked and flew in an erratic whirl until it stabilized, focusing on a pea pebble encrusted rooftop.

* * * * *

Sam, dumbfounded, could not quite make sense of what he was looking at. Ra'id was slumped over the table, blood oozing onto the glass tabletop, pooling from two wounds.

It was only then that instinct took over and he ducked, looking around to see if he could be the next target. Almost immediately, he realized that he was reacting stupidly. He was literally out in the open and if he had been the next target, he would have been killed by now. Hesitantly, he started to rise from his position and noticed Melinda running from the restaurant door toward him, seemingly in slow motion.

* * * * *

"What in hell's creation just happened?" yelled President Alexander as he rose from his chair to stand in front of the image on the display screen.

"Sir, I'm not sure!" said Broom. "I believe Al-Eissa was taken out by someone else. Our man as well."

Carl Broom tapped onto his microphone, frantically shouting, "Anyone! Status report!"

A voice, devoid of emotion, reported over the intercom, "Target *is* down. Buckner is secure and we have agents getting to our sharpshooter."

* * * * *

Melinda had reached Sam, gun in the extended arm position, panning the area in case of a further assault, expertly covering and coaxing Sam to the security of the hotel interior.

* * * * *

"Sir, we have Agent Milford and he is dead! We are extracting the body."

* * * * *

Carl Broom was doing what he did best: managing a crisis situation. Through the intercom connection with the team members in Sana'a, he quickly outlined the exit strategy. The goal: get the hell out of there leaving no evidence they had been there at all.

Ra'id's body would be left *as is* for local authorities to try to determine what had happened, or more likely, cover up.

While the team on the ground brought the van around to the service entrance of the hotel, to collect the body and the rest of the group, Broom was contacting the cargo hangar at the airport to get the plane ready to take off as soon as they arrived. The 5th Fleet Commander was advised that it was time to launch the fighter escorts from the base in Bahrain, in order to meet up with the plane carrying the team once it was over the international waters of the Mediterranean.

Chapter 55

An hour later at the island compound, Al-Kabir arrived and was putting the final touches to the demonstration he had planned for the Board members. Mohammed had been busy ensuring that everything was in order: from the coding in the laptop with the master instructions, to the state of the supercomputers which did the number-crunching, to the maser which converted them to the harmonic waves, to the connections to the satellite transmitters which would link up to the relay satellites some twenty-two thousand miles above them. Everything was running well and within operational parameters.

The Sheikh turned to Mohammed. "How soon after we complete the demonstration could you process another three samples?"

Mohammed was a little stunned by the request, but he thought for a moment and said, "Assuming the heat sinks around the maser cool down quickly enough, the computers should be able to calibrate the algorithms for the microwaves in about three hours for each sample. We should be ready early tomorrow morning."

"Very good! I've decided to accelerate our program. I want you to pull up samples US001, US023 and US87. They will be our next targets."

Concerned Ra'id was not there yet and that he might have to prepare the operation by himself, he sheepishly responded, "Yes sir. I will as soon as possible."

Chapter 56

The four-engine FedEx jet was at twenty-five thousand feet and climbing when it crossed the southern shores of Yemen over the Gulf of Aden and turned west toward the Red Sea. The crew had picked up an unexpected package. Orders had come from FedEx Head Office, which in turn, had come from the Secretary of States' office. They were to become the medical evacuation team for a group of American tourists, caught up in a peaceful protest in Sana'a, which had turned violent. During the mêlée, one of them had been gravely injured.

The pilot and copilot said nothing, doing what they could to expedite the boarding of the six muscular, well-armed *tourists*, the single female, someone called Sam. And, oh yes, a body bag.

An hour later, they were exiting the airspace over the Suez Canal and were soon joined by an F-117 Nighthawk Stealth fighter. The FedEx pilot and copilot, seated in the cockpit area, could not believe what they had been suddenly involved in. Needless to say, this would grant them bragging rights for years to come.

In the rear cargo area, the group was sitting silently, next to the body of their teammate. It was Sam who broke the silence. "Melinda, Ra'id said something about the second lab being on some island, Kamaran Island I believe, not far from Sana'a. I think he was also ready to tell me who was behind all of this. Then…"

Melinda's eyes opened wide. "OK, *that's* what we've been looking for! Did he mention anything else?"

Sam thought for a moment. "No, nothing more about the lab or weapon or the operation. He did try to explain *why* he had done it and mentioned his brother."

"Ok. It's a start. I'll be right back." She got up off the floor of the cargo area and manoeuvred around some of the bundles of boxes, tied down in nets to prevent them from flying in the event of turbulence.

Through her *com*, she contacted Broom and filled him in on the information Sam had given her and then returned to sit next to him.

Sam looked at her. "We had him! He was ready to cooperate. Who shot him? Who could have known he was coming to the hotel to meet me?"

Melinda put her hand on his. "We don't know."

The rest of the flight to Rome was completed in silence. On arrival at the FedEx's scheduled destination at their terminal in the Leonardo da Vinci Airport, the team and body were quickly transferred to the same Globemaster they had taken originally, when they had had such high hopes. Now, it would take a dispirited team home.

✳ ✳ ✳ ✳ ✳

Just as they approached the Atlantic Ocean over France, Sam noticed the level of water in the bottle he was holding began to tilt. The other agents woke from their snooze and the group leader stood to go to the cockpit. He returned and announced that the plane was being diverted to Tel Aviv and that instructions were forthcoming.

Part 5

Chapter 57

Broom was on the *com* with Melinda. "We found the lab. I'm sending high definition pictures we took with our satellites over the region. The communications officer on the plane should be getting them as we speak. The officer approached Melinda with a series of pictures he had printed on board.

"I have them, sir!"

She waved Sam and the team leader over to her. "I'm looking at them now."

Sam could only hear her side of the conversation. "Yes, I see it," pointing to the aerial photo of what looked like a series of buildings, lined up in military fashion. She recognized two of them as Quonset huts and all were within a compound area in the middle of the desert.

"Let me look for that one," she said, sifting through the pictures until she spotted the one Broom was referring to.

"Yes I see them," indicating the three satellite dishes within the walls of one of the structures. She listened for another five minutes.

"Thank you, sir. I'll relay your instructions to the team." And then, she disconnected.

"Sam, they found the island Al-Eissa spoke to you about. Kamaran Island is off the coast of Yemen, just as he said. It would seem he was being straight with you about that part. These pictures came from our eyes in the sky and as you saw, it has to be where the laboratory is."

"How can you be sure?" asked Sam, remembering Frankfurt.

"Well, you saw the picture of the satellite dishes. They aren't there for someone to be able to get HBO!" The other team members chuckled but quickly stopped with a single look from the team leader.

"These other pictures show heat signatures within the area. If you'll notice, there are a few small red spots around this building, more here, and about twenty spread around the perimeter and the two Quonset huts. They represent the people in the compound, probably guards."

"What's really interesting is the amount of heat being generated by the two huts!" This was evident by the deep red hues emanating from the buildings.

"Look at this one," she suggested, pointing to one of the rectangular structures.

"See how it is a very deep blue compared to a few of the other ones, which are a light blue, while the rest are simply dark gray. The one red hut is probably the power plant, pumping out the electricity required to run the mainframe computers and, the other more than likely, is the weapon. The computer room sits within the deep blue area because it requires a lot of cold air, while the living quarters are only cooled to comfort levels. There is no doubt that this must be the site. We haven't found any comparable heat signatures anywhere else on the island."

"Why there?" asked Sam.

"Can you think of a better place to hide this lab? And we may just have tracked down the money trail. It seems the main tenant on the island runs a tourist resort about five miles northeast of this compound. They also have a license to run a desalination operation we assume is in one of the two huts."

"Who are they?" Sam asked.

"We think it's a corporation called the Foundation for the Promotion of Islamic Culture. Intelligence is still tracking them down, however, Broom says they are huge, with influence throughout the region. Probably not all *social*.

The team leader interrupted, "So what is the plan?"

Melinda responded, "At the moment, Broom only said that we are to rendezvous at the military airport in Tel Aviv with Agent Cohen. The Israelis are taking over the assault. We'll be there as support."

Sam questioned her, "Why the Israelis?"

"That was one thing Broom was clear about. The US can't and won't be seen to *invade* an Islamic country, not after Iraq. And the Israelis have a beef they need to settle over their eight soldiers. It's understood by the Yemeni authorities, that this is a straight in-and-out operation, with no Yemeni casualties, especially now that Al-Eissa is dead. They have no knowledge of the purpose of the lab. As far as they are concerned, the people in the lab are foreign nationals developing chemical and biological weapons."

"So, now I suggest we get some sleep. Once we arrive in Tel Aviv, there won't be many *Z's* in it for us for a while."

Sam lay down on top of the sleeping bag he had been provided and turned on his left side to face Melinda who had taken the spot next to his. Leaning up onto his elbow, he spoke quietly, "Something is bothering me."

Melinda looked up at him."About what?"

"The dead soldier… I noticed the rifle he had when they brought the body down from that rooftop. It isn't like the ones carried by the others."

"You're wondering what his mission *really* was." Melinda responded.

"Yes. I don't want to be paranoid: was he along to protect me or…?"

"I'm not privy to any special order he may have been given, but I would guess that, considering the fact someone else was there to take out Al-Eissa, the weight of the evidence would suggest Broom anticipated the situation and tried to make sure you were protected."

"I would like to believe that, but I'm not naïve enough to think there couldn't be more at play." Sam lay back down on his side and, after a moment, closed his eyes. Melinda's remained open, staring at Sam for another minute. She was thinking he was a civilian, caught up in this business of hers, so dangerous and seemingly casual about taking lives. Yet, Sam had shown resilience and an inner strength that she was learning to appreciate. With a slight smile on her lips, she too closed her eyes and tried to sleep.

Chapter 58

"Gentlemen, welcome!"

A string of limos and SUVs lined the main lane at the center of the compound. The board members had all flown in to the Island airport, and then transferred to the compound in vehicles leased by the Sheikh from the mainland: there weren't enough vehicles on the island to accommodate the delegation.

Sheikh Al-Kabir was standing in front of the barrack which housed the lab itself. Before going in, he led the group on a tour of the facilities: the huts, the refrigerated computer room and then the satellite dish building, taking pride in the impression he was making.

He knew he needed to fully impress them; he had to be seen being able to get anything done. He had to be seen as a musical director, capable of orchestrating one of the most audacious political coups ever conceived. He was to create a new political entity, which would soon direct world politics, and all without firing a shot. There would be a few casualties, but unlike other wars of independence, these would be less random and each would serve a specific purpose.

The people who were going to die shortly were those who stood in the way of progress. They were the ones who bowed to foreign interests, keeping the Muslim world in a position of weakness, thinking they could influence the Western world by eking out a little more or a little less oil, in the hopes of affecting the decision-making factors around the world. These individuals had little understanding of power: the *real* power that came with the ability of annihilating one's enemies, rather than just costing them a few more dollars to run their automobiles. All the while, they filled their pockets with the wealth the black gold commanded on the world markets and thought they were actually running their countries.

Not that wealth was a bad thing. The Sheikh was one of the world's richest men, though he went to extreme lengths not to be on the Forbes list. He would show these corrupt human beings how to use wealth, not so much to make more, but to affect history in a meaningful way. The new Islamic Federation would be led by true believers, commanded by none other than himself! Some of his Muslim brothers had experimented with democracy. The majority though, craved for strong leaders who could, with guidance from Allah, rally them behind a single cause: the supremacy of Islam!

As the group found its way back to the laboratory, "...and though the process might seem simple, its implementation is extremely complex as you have seen. I will now show you the nerve center of the operation."

Entering the barrack behind the others, the Sheikh walked around to Mohammed. "May I present Doctor Mohammed Al-Kammin? He will be running the demonstration for you."

"Is Doctor Al-Eissa not here?"

Just then, the door opened and in walked Vincenzo. He simply nodded his head to the Sheikh, acknowledging the fact that the deed was done.

Looking back at the members, the Sheikh continued, "No, unfortunately the doctor in unavailable. His uncle is in hospital dying and he requested our permission to leave so that he could look after him and his funeral arrangements. He should be back tomorrow. However, Doctor Al-Kammin is fully capable of operating the system."

The Sheikh then gestured to the group to observe the interior of the laboratory. On the six lab counters behind them, they could see what looked like twelve old doorchime buttons, each connected to a wire leading to a distribution box next to the laptop Mohammed was busy working on.

237

Glancing up from the display screen, Mohammed spoke, "Sir, I am ready."

The Sheikh then turned to the group. "Gentlemen, if you please, walk over to the tables and you will find a few names you will recognize next to a button. Some of you have only one name you will recognize, while others will have two or three, depending on the transition strategy that has been put into place. The rest of the plan will be initiated within a day or two."

The board members walked from table to table, stopping when they identified their correct station.

Once everyone was in position, the Sheikh smiled, knowing that in a moment, the twelve would not only take an active part in the plan and, by doing so, also commit personally to him.

"Gentlemen, the moment of truth is now here. You will create your own fate with your actions, according to our plan. You will soon be called upon to lead your respected countries and this is only the first step, one of many. Much will be expected of you by your people... By our people!"

Looking back at Mohammed, "Doctor Al-Kammin will now *prime* the weapon and on cue, you will simply depress the button before you. The computer has been programed to take the first name from each of your lists, then the second and then the third, and send the codes to the weapon. It is that simple." All the board member smiled and nodded to each other, knowing they had the power over the lives of those who had kept them from attaining their goals.

Mohammed at the ready, the Sheikh simply stretched his left arm out to the side and flicked his hand once upward, signalling Mohammed to begin. From close by outside, came the whirring hum of the maser.

"What you are hearing, is Allah whispering." The Sheikh then brought his arm forward and pointed his index finger downward, instructing the group to press their buttons.

238

The whirring hum radically increased in volume and intensity, making one or two of the board members squint and cover their ears.

Having to raise his voice to be heard, the Sheikh continued, "Now hear the howl of Allah!"

The loud hum continued for fifteen minutes and then subsided slowly to silence. None of the board members had moved or said a word, until the Sheikh broke the quiet. "It is done. You have begun the great revolution and now, the hard work begins. When you return home tonight, be prepared to become the leaders of a new world."

Mohammed was busy watching the settings on the computer display.

The Sheikh looked at him briefly and then turned back to the group. "Now, I would guess you are wondering if you have actually done anything."

As if on cue, one of the participants' cell phone rang, surprising its owner. The Sheikh gestured to him to answer. No sooner had he done so, that another rang, then another, then all of them. They were getting confirmation of the deaths of their targets from their contacts back home.

The Sheikh had a huge smile of satisfaction on his face, prompting similar smiles and shouts of approval from everyone in the room: everyone but Mohammed. A fact which did not go unnoticed by the Sheikh.

Still smiling, the Sheikh continued, "Now, let us retire to another building to celebrate before your departure. Vincenzo will lead you to it and I will join you within a minute."

No sooner had everyone left than the Sheikh turned to Mohammed. "What is it?"

"Sir, I will have to confirm with direct observation, however, the settings on the diagnostic program which runs automatically after each use of the maser, indicate that

239

several of the heat sinks which cool the unit have overheated. I am hoping they have not been damaged."

The Sheikh did not show any sign of anger. "What would happen if that were the case?"

Mohammed did not hesitate. "If the damage is severe, the next time we use the weapon, it could cause an unrestrained spike in temperature in one part of the cooling component, possibly leading to what you could call a *blowout* at the site of the damage. Because the frequencies we are dealing with are quit close to the light spectrum, they are very powerful and, if uncontrolled by our computer program, they could destroy the maser and release all the energy. Everything within a mile would disappear!"

The Sheikh did not blink. "And our other three targets?"

"They will have to wait until I have confirmed the extent of the damage and repair it. Worse case scenario, I would say one day, maybe two. Hopefully, Ra'id and I can accelerate the repairs once he returns."

Now the Sheikh showed signs of frustration. "I would suggest you see if there is damage and advise me immediately. I assume Ra'id will be returning tomorrow or the following day. We cannot wait, so please begin without him." He turned and stomped out of the building, leaving Mohammed standing there, open-mouthed.

Chapter 59

President Alexander was already sitting on one of the sofas in the Oval Office when Carl Broom was shown in by Mildred. "Good morning Mr. President!"

Alexander pointed to the other sofa and Broom quickly sat. "Ok, what do we have?"

"Sir, we've identified the shooter." Handing the President a few photos, Broom continued. "His name is Vincenzo Provani: ex-Italian military, black-ops. Our contact at Interpol tells us he was trained in explosives, strategic operations. His claim to fame however, is that he was one of the best snipers they had."

The President's eyebrows rose. "I have a feeling that's not all."

"No sir, it isn't. He was dishonorably discharged when he took out a target *after* he had been ordered to stand down. As a result, it seems he became a *gun for hire* by anyone needing a job done, mostly in the Middle East. Then his tracks go cold. He hasn't surfaced until his picture was taken by our man in Sana'a."

"What about this foundation you mentioned in your report?"

"We're working on that." Broom continued. "On the surface, it seems to be *legit*, doing exactly what the name says: supporting Muslim groups and individuals everywhere. They are funded by almost every Muslim country in the world, and there seems to be a lot of cash flowing. So far, though, the only link between the Foundation and any of this, is the tourist resort it runs on Kamaran Island. We are operating on the presumption that its close proximity to the compound isn't just coincidence!"

"And the lab itself?"

"The Israelis have a team waiting for our people to show up. They should be landing as we speak, but it will take at least a day to prepare for the assault on the compound. One possible problem though: we are getting rumors that the Yemeni authorities are having second thoughts about letting the team in."

Broom's Blackberry vibrated. He quickly looked and saw it was a text message saying *Urgent!* "Sir, I need to take this." Alexander just gestured what Broom interpreted as permission to proceed.

Broom's eyes widened. "Sir, not good news. It seems the weapon is operational. Some eighteen government officials have just been killed and our satellite over the island has recorded a huge spike in the heat signature there."

"Good God!" gasped Alexander.

"The strange thing, sir, is that they are all in Middle Eastern countries and not just from one in particular." Looking down at his phone once more, he added, "Correction: now there are twenty-two deaths." He looked up at the President. "This is serious… Very serious. They have proven they can strike at multiple targets in a multitude of locations. I'd say they have also indicated there is some sort of purpose or cause here rather than random killings."

"Explain."

"Well, it looks like all of the victims are in Muslim or Arabic countries. I recognize a few of the names. They are relatively highly placed in their respective governments. It's as if there's a *coup d'état* taking place, in more than one country at the same time!"

Alexander paused. "Then it's started. What has me concerned is that we don't know if the coup is being coordinated by a loose conspiracy of rogue nationals in each of these countries and the weapon is under their control, or if it is the work of some individual group, perhaps this

242

foundation, wanting to take down those governments? And to what end? Either way, I'll be taking our defence status up a notch, from DEFCON 4 to 3, though I'm guessing that will be of little use against this weapon. And I think it's time to position the 5th and 6th Fleets in closer to allow us to move quickly if we need to."

The President walked over to the door to Mildred's office and looking in, gave her instructions to call in the Chief of Staff, the Secretary of State and the Vice President. Just as he was to close the door, he turned back to her. "And get the Speaker of the House as well: tell him to pack lightly."

Mildred was taken aback somewhat. "Sir, the wives?"

"No, I'm guessing that in this situation, they aren't at risk."

Returning to Broom, "Taking out that lab is your number one priority! No matter which of the two scenarios I mentioned is correct, we need to move up the destruction of that facility before it's too late. I just wish we could send in a bunch of cruise missiles and be done with it. Unfortunately, at the moment, world reaction would be too great. There might come a time when that will be our only choice."

He turned to walk to his desk. "Now, I need to deal with the fallout from the killings and the impact it's going to have, not only in the Middle East, but on the global level as well. Thank you, Carl."

Broom left and the President prepared to head to the bunkers below the White House. They were designed to take a direct nuclear hit and still protect the occupants, allowing the President to continue to run the government from there. The War Room was part of the facility and he assumed, or *hoped*, it would protect him and the others from this weapon.

Chapter 60

The plane had landed at the Sde-Dov Airport some fifteen minutes before and had quickly taxied to the hangar where the Israeli commando team was assembled. The air was somewhat cooler than that in Sana'a earlier that day. Even though it was nine in the evening, the temperature was still eighty degrees Fahrenheit!

As Sam and the others exited the plane using the tail ramp, he got a glimpse of his surroundings. Nothing very special, really, he thought. They were at the southern part of the airport complex, in the hangar zone. This approach strip was lined on the south side by two large, eighty-foot airplane hangars, and on the opposite side of the strip, by one which was at least one hundred twenty feet wide. Planes were parked on either side of the two hangars and from his vantage point, Sam could see more hangars to the rear. He estimated that the airport was smaller than the Ben Gurion Airport they had flown into the last time he was in Israel.

Looking westward beyond the end of the access strip leading to the main runway, he saw the Mediterranean and it took his breath away! The full moon hung in the sky, eclipsing the stars which seemed to have dropped onto the surface of the water and twinkled on the crest of each wave. The long luminous path back to the full moon's position was the picture he had in his mind of what he would see somewhere on a Pacific island, next to a sultry beauty lying close to him in a hammock, sipping on a Mai Tai; he hoped it would be Melinda.

She glanced at him, then to the sea and the moon. "Not good!"

He looked at her with an expression of surprise which quickly turned to one of understanding when he realized she wasn't commenting on his reverie, but on the combat situation they might face, if they had to attack while the moon was out.

As they walked toward the narrow opening of the hangar door, he could see the lights were blazing inside. He had to squint until his eyes adapted to their intensity. What he saw was amazing: There were no fewer than a hundred soldiers, some hooking up equipment, while others were peering at a dozen computer monitors, all set up on portable tables in the middle of the hangar. Around another table covered with what looked like maps, were a dozen or more soldiers dressed in SWAT uniforms, obviously part of the assault team. And in the middle of them was Agent Cohen. The activity was dizzying and Sam had to mentally adjust to the fact that this was a much larger operation than the last in Frankfurt. It was obvious that the Israelis did not underestimate the logistics and that they had pulled out all the stops.

Agent Cohen happened to glance up at the individuals moving toward him. When he recognized Melinda and Sam, a welcoming smile lit up his face as he moved around the table to greet them. Large hugs for Melinda: something not lost on Sam. There were also equally sincere hugs for him.

"How are you, my friends? As you can see, we have been at it for several hours now and our plan for the assault on the compound is almost ready. Come and see."

He walked them around the table and introduced them to several of the assault team. In spite of the fact that they were all much shorter than their German counterparts, Sam could see the cool intensity they all demonstrated. They were built much like Agent Cohen and Sam figured he would not want to be on the *wrong* side of these individuals!

245

Agent Cohen pointed to one of the maps on the table. "The assault team will comprise of twenty-five members, including you. We have been ordered to attack as soon as possible. I do not know if you have been informed: the killing has already begun!."

Sam and Melinda looked at each other and both turned to Agent Cohen, shaking their heads in the negative. "That's all right," said Agent Cohen. "We just learned about it as well. It would seem there are up to twenty or more individuals, all in Islamic countries, who were vaporized a few hours ago." Sam thought that that might not be the correct word to use, but so be it!

"We've advised our government and yours that we cannot lead an assault against the island until just before daybreak, in part because of the full moon and because the guards will be most vulnerable at that time."

Agent Cohen continued, "I would suggest you get some coffee and something to eat while we finalize preparations. We will bring you back in a few hours to brief you on the operation and the roles your will play." Coolly and without presumption he added, "Now, please allow us to complete our planning."

With that, the assault team was again hunched over the maps on the table, while others ran back and forth from the computers linked to the satellite system high above, bringing the team up-to-the-second reports on topographic information and body movement within the compound.

Sam and Melinda took Agent Cohen's suggestion and headed to the temporary canteen area for something to eat and drink. The setting was simple: a table with five trays of kosher sandwiches, each labeled. Sam went for the smoked salmon and cream cheese bagel and the roast beef with horseradish sauce, while Melinda chose one of the avocado and salad on tomato bread. Both opted for coffee, black, rather than tea, knowing it would be a long night.

246

As they sat at the small circular table, Sam marveled at the activity around them.

He then turned to Melinda. "You OK?"

"Yeah, this is a little more than the usual Homeland Security mission, but we do train for similar types of projects." She waited a moment. "I do have to admit that the possible outcomes of this one are rather unique! How are *you* doing?"

"Well, if my background were that of James Bond, I'd be in my element. This however... In any case, after Frankfurt, I would guess this team will take nothing for granted. I trust Agent Cohen, so my jitters are pretty well in check."

Sam started to move his hand over to hers catching himself in mid motion, realizing that this was not the time nor the place for a show of affection. Melinda caught the gesture from the corner of her eye and smiled.

Sam took a bite out of one of his sandwiches, and had a sip of coffee, then cleared his throat. "When you say you've trained for this, can you give me examples? And how did *you* get involved with this in the first place?"

Melinda was about to drink some of her coffee but put her cup back down on the table without having done so. "I'm not sure that I can actually go into the details of some of the operations I've trained for, though I can tell you why I got this assignment." She took a quick gulp of coffee and a mouthful of her sandwich and then gestured with her finger to *hang on* for a second.

Swallowing her food, she continued "I can tell you I didn't exactly volunteer for the assignment. In fact, I have a feeling it was a question of getting the short straw from the group in the division. I told you that I've taken some ribbing for being right, significantly more often than my male counterparts, both while I was in the Secret Service division and again when I moved up to Intelligence and Analysis."

247

Sam nodded his understanding and Melinda could tell by his eyes that he was genuinely interested in or impressed by her career path.

"Well, I think when the first soldier was killed, and because of the way we were told he died, my immediate supervisors didn't take it very seriously when approached by Israeli intelligence, other than the fact *they* thought it important enough to include us. I think my superiors thought it would be a wild goose chase and that the cause would be easily explained. I felt otherwise and because I happened to have an opening in my docket, they simply appointed me as the Department's liaison on this case! I really think some of the guys were hoping this wouldn't figure well on my resume and that they could distance themselves from the hunt."

Sam looked incredulous. "You're kidding aren't you? That would just boil my blood."

He smiled at her and said, "I have a sneaky feeling this is going to turn out completely differently for you."

Melinda smiled back and she was the one who reached over and gently patted his hand. "Thank you! I'm glad you feel that way; and I think you're right! All the more reason for me not to fail at this: not just for myself, but more importantly, for the lives of all the people who could be targeted. I'll admit this weapon really gives me the willies."

Before Sam could respond, one of the assault team members approached them. "Agent Gordon, we need your input from this point on in our planning."

"Yes, of course." Melinda rose and turned to Sam. "I'll fill you in as soon as I can!" Then she went over to join Agent Cohen and the group.

"Ah, Agent Gordon," Agent Cohen said with a smile. "The next phase of our planning needs coordination and approvals from your President." About twenty yards away, Sam sat on his own munching on his sandwich, with the look of pride in his eyes as he watched Melinda.

248

Chapter 61

"Yes, Mr. President, Agent Cohen has just sent you a detailed plan for the assault." Melinda was looking at the President on the video link which connected her directly to the War Room. "It's four o'clock in the morning our time, and the plan is to strike no later than seven this morning. Sorry for keeping you up so late sir!"

"Don't worry about that. It isn't the first time, nor will it be the last that we spend a night in this room. And, may I remind you that you've been up for a while as well."

Melinda smiled: "Ditto on the late night."

The President turned to the Chief of Staff who was reading intently on his iPad the list of the requested equipment he had just received from the Israelis. The admiral looked up at the President. "Not a problem sir. The carrier strike group from both the 5th and the 6th are in position to intervene if necessary and to support the assault. The requested equipment is pretty much standard and already on board. The choppers are fueled and waiting."

The President turned to the Secretary of State who was huddled with Vice-President Graft. "Gentlemen, anything new?"

It was the vice-president who spoke first. "Based on our *intel*, there's an awful lot of chatter coming from the countries where the killings took place."

He looked at the Secretary who added, "Sir, we have word that at least one country, Libya, has declared a state of emergency after a flurry of communiqués between those countries involved. They know something is up but aren't too sure *what* yet. The militaries of seven of them are already on the move and it would seem they are being deployed within the capitals at strategic sites. I would say they are trying to secure their positions. And I've already received four calls from ambassadors asking if we know anything about what is going on. I've told them that we are aware of the events which have taken place, that we are making queries and will be in touch shortly with any answer we may find."

The President nodded and then turned to the screen, but not before glancing at Carl Broom. Broom was on his BlackBerry, feverishly texting to his team back at Homeland Security. "Carl, anything else?"

"No, sir, not at the moment. We are a *go* back at the office."

"OK then," looking at Melinda and Agent Cohen next to her. "Let's get this operation moving."

Without a word and with a look of grim resolution, Agent Cohen turned to his men and made a whirling gesture with his finger in the air, to indicate they were leaving.

Melinda walked over to Sam. "Are you ready? It's time!" Sam smiled hesitantly, and picked up his packsack and followed the rest of the group out of the rear of the hangar.

There on the tarmac between the hangars was a monster of a helicopter, just now starting up its engines. Agent Cohen caught the look on Sam's face. "Magnificent isn't it! It's a Yas'ur or what Americans call a Sea Stallion."

The beast was two storeys high at the rotor level and at least thirty to forty feet long. Its six rotor blades had to measure about sixty feet in diameter and were by now turning just below the *whoop-whoop* noise level generally associated with helicopters blades, rotating faster and faster, "It carries four crew and up to thirty-eight troops: a total of some eight thousand pounds of personnel or cargo." Agent Cohen beamed. "It's our workhorse," and as he led Sam and the group to the open door on the side, he passed his hand over the Star of David painted on the fuselage.

In spite of the maintenance of the airstrips, dust and sand had been blown onto the tarmac, only now to be kicked up into the air once more by the rising helicopter. Regardless of its size, Sam felt a little confined inside, sitting on a small bench with half of the assault team, facing Melinda on the other side along with the rest of the group.

The flight would be relatively short, taking only about an hour and a half to get to the carrier strike group out in the Mediterranean, just off the entrance to the Suez Canal.

As they approached their destination, Melinda waved Sam over to her side and the portal window in the access door. Sam looked down onto the sea below.

Though it was just daybreak, he could nevertheless see the impressive sight of the carrier strike group consisting of six cruisers and destroyers, surrounding at a respectable distance, the darling of the group: the USS George H-W Bush, a Nimitz-class supercarrier.

Despite the dawn their running lights were still on and Sam noticed that the carrier tower was farther back on the ship than he had expected. He made himself a mental reminder to watch more recent movies or documentaries.

Melinda informed him that the *Bush* was just under eleven hundred feet long and about two hundred and fifty feet wide, with approximately one hundred and fourteen thousand tons of displacement. Sam looked at her. "Is all of that part of your training?"

"Not quite! Just part of the information I got during the briefing back at the hangar. We need to have a working knowledge of every piece of equipment we will have access to in this operation. You'd be surprised what could save your life when you least expect it. Now, I can finally fill you in on the assault plans. There isn't much of a chance you can drop out now." she said with a smile.

251

Chapter 62

Mohammed had awoken at about five-thirty in the morning, unable to fall back asleep. He had stayed up quite late the night before, mulling over his situation and what he was involved in.

He knew something must have happened to Ra'id. Mohammed had had no communication with him for two days, which was unusual for them. They had been in daily contact for at least three years, never *not* knowing what the other was up to or where he was. They were like brothers!

He had run through all the formation Ra'id had shared with him that day at the hospital with his uncle. Mohammed found it hard to believe that the Sheikh could be the man described by Umayr. Wadi Al-Kabir had shown himself to be such a generous and loving man. If Umayr was right, this was the man responsible for coordinating for the mugging and the death of Ra'id's parents, as well as for orchestrating the release of information he knew the Israelis would act upon, leading to the death of Samihah.

No wonder Ra'id was so furious! Not so much with his dying uncle, who, though he had informed the Sheikh about where Ra'id's parents and Samihah would be, never thought the information would be used in such a way. It was no small wonder that Umayr had stepped in as he had to look after Ra'id and Ali.

The Sheikh however, was a different thing all together. Ra'id had been betrayed by the Sheikh and by his own naiveté, and felt he had to redress both. Mohammed had agreed to help.

If Ra'id were still alive, he would most certainly avenge the three deaths by killing the Sheikh. As for himself,

Mohammed had decided he would find a way to destroy the maser and the computer program which controlled it. But how?

He had thought about blowing up the maser with dynamite. Where would he find some? Then there was the issue of the guards: all mercenaries were hired because of their ability to kill. How could he get to the maser with them patrolling the grounds 24/7? And then there was the issue of Vincenzo, who, since the departure of the board members and the Sheikh, had not left his side, other than for *potty breaks* and sleeping time. Vincenzo scared him!

Then it struck him. He had one way and one way only to destroy the maser: sabotage it to explode, as he had warned the Sheikh could happen if it overheated. That would mean that the whole compound would be destroyed, along with the maser, the antenna array, the guards, Vincenzo, and himself.

The realisation that US001 could only be the President of the United States, and that his death in this way, would most certainly lead to war, perhaps a world war, left him no other option.

So he had gotten up, showered and then gone for breakfast. A minute or two after he had entered the dining room and given his order to the cook, the door opened and Vincenzo walked in with a smile, looking just a little dishevelled. He had been awakened by one of the guards as soon as Mohammed had stepped out of his barrack.

"Good morning Mohammed. You are up soon this morning. Is everything ok?"

Though Mohammed felt hemmed in, he tried to keep his calm.

"Yes, thank you, Vincenzo. I was anxious to verify the condition of the maser and initiate the three programs the Sheikh has ordered. Each code has been entered and we should be able to proceed within an hour or so."

Vincenzo's smile widened, "That is wonderful news. A good breakfast will be a start to a good day!"

Chapter 63

The Yas'ur landed smoothly on the rear of the aircraft carrier. No sooner had the exit door opened and Agent Cohen exited, did the commander of the ship arrive, instinctively ducking below the rotor which was winding down to a stop.

Warmly shaking Cohen's hand, Captain Macdonald said, "Welcome to my ship. I understand that you and your team are not here and that we are not talking at the present. I would like to offer you some *non-existent* coffee and breakfast, if you like."

Agent Cohen stepped out of the way of the group, waving Sam and Melinda over to his side. The rest of the team seemed to ignore the four and simply walked directly toward the front of the flight deck, where five more helicopters waited.

"Thank you, sir. As you can see, we are merely in transit, although I would like to introduce you to Agent Gordon from Homeland Security and the direct liaison between us and the President, and this is Sam Buckner, a consultant attached to the operation, on loan from Canada." The captain shook both hands and then led them out from under the rotors which were now still.

While they walked toward the front of the ship, Sam looked around, taking in the sheer size of it. It was one thing to hear the dimensions and to see the ship from four thousand feet up. To actually be on the deck, seeing the tower rising high above and what seemed like city-block-size elevator platforms for the planes, Sam was again in awe.

He thought, "How long ago was it that I agreed to join the task force. First Germany, the White House, Yemen, and now this!"

255

As they were walking, the captain pointed to the five helicopters they were approaching. "You're going to love your ride! These are state-of-the-art flying machines. They are modified Sikorsky UH-60 Black Hawks."

Sam quickly looked at the captain with a deer-in-the-headlights look. He was about to speak, when the Captain interjected, "I know what you are thinking. The movie about the botched operation in Somalia."

Sam nodded in the affirmative.

"Don't worry. These aren't anywhere near as *rustic* as those helicopters were. These have a nickname: Airwolf! They are longer and sleeker, and run even more quietly than the Eurostealth." That didn't mean much to Sam, but Melinda eyes expressed understanding.

Sam could see that these were no ordinary helicopters. The first thing he noticed was the extended, elegant shape of the fuselage: totally different from the dinosaur that had shuttled them in to the carrier. The next thing he noticed, was that even in the early morning sun, the helicopters didn't reflect sunlight. Every part was painted a mat charcoal gray, and no matter how many angles they had, no light was reflected.

The rotor axles, both the main and the rear, were covered with a cowl and the exhaust vents from the engines were recessed, with just a small exhaust port being visible. And the rotor tips were angled downward in a forty-five degree pitch.

He had tuned out the chatter from the Captain and Agent Cohen and returned to reality when Melinda touched his left arm. "Are you OK?"

Sam looked at her. "Yes, yes I am. It's just a lot to take in. I'm used to the same small lab, day in day out, other than three hours a week in the lecture hall. This, this is amazing. I love it."

The rest of the team had already reached the helicopters and had efficiently loaded their equipment. This left Sam, Melinda and the last two team members to hop into the fifth helicopter. Agent Cohen was the last to board, but not before shaking the captain's hand and winking with a smile, thanking him for the *non-existent* support!

In sequence, each lifted from the flight deck and, rather than rising into the sky, they moved quickly ahead of the ship and dropped to about forty feet above the water level. The plan was to travel at low altitude to evade radar, and fly approximately ten miles to the east of the Suez Canal and the Red Sea, all the way to Kamaran Island. The flight would take about two hours at the speed the helicopters were traveling, and to Sam's relief, would not have to bank and adjust too often to the terrain.

Chapter 64

The President, the Vice President and the Speaker of the House, George Samson, were in an intense discussion at the far end of the War Room. Standing facing each other and speaking in a whisper, so as not to be overheard by the others in the room, they were reviewing the issues around the line of succession, assuming the President would, indeed, be killed. Though the military and the intelligence people were all busy going about their tasks to ensure the success of the current operation, no one needed to be told what that discussion was about!

Of the large monitors on the wall, one was displaying the relative positions of the 5th and 6th Carrier Fleet groups, the assault team's helicopters and the location of the compound on Kamaran Island, each linked to their code names by a pencil thin line, similar to tactical displays on flight combat games. The screen would refresh every two to three seconds and it was clear the assault team was moving quickly toward its target.

Next to it was another monitor showing roughly the same view; this from a satellite far above the target area, displaying an infrared version of the other, in real time. The heat signature of the two fleets was clear. That of the assault helicopters was barely visible, in spite of the fact that there were five of them in tight formation.

A third screen focused more tightly on the compound: other than a dozen or so human shapes moving in and around the area, most of the buildings were displayed in a cool blue, indicating a lack of activity.

"Sir," it was Admiral Constab, Commander of the 5th Fleet, brought in to coordinate the support operation for the mission. "They are about twenty minutes from the target."

The President nodded in the direction of the admiral to acknowledge the update and turned back to the two before him. "Ok then gentlemen, we are in agreement." Looking to the Vice President, "I'll leave it to you to inform the Secretary and the Chief of Staff so they will be in a position to do their jobs *if* the need arises."

With that, everyone in the room took their seats and prepared for the action to come. The President stifled a yawn, sipped his coffee and looked up at the monitors on the wall.

Chapter 65

Mohammed finished his breakfast in silence. As he rose, he looked up at Vincenzo sitting across from him. "I need to inspect the maser one last time before we fire it up." Vincenzo had a mouthful of croissant and simply nodded in agreement.

Exiting the barrack and going down the two steps to the ground, he checked to see if anyone was there. Seeing no one, he walked quickly to the Quonset hut which housed the maser. Reaching the entrance, he keyed in the access code, looked around once more and entered.

As he walked over to the maser assembly, he marveled at the simplicity of the process. He and Ra'id had conceived the invention after seeing a small boy playing space cowboys with friends, all firing *ray guns* that had red and yellow flashing lights inside a transparent plastic barrel, with a series of whirling disks on a shaft, producing crackling arcs making a *Crrrrrrr* sound every time they pulled the triggers.

Ra'id had stopped in his tracks and reached over to Mohammed, stopping him as well. "Did you see that?"

"Yes I did. Are you thinking what I'm thinking?"

"I think so. The electric discharge of those whirling disks is creating that snapping sound. We're talking about a particular frequency range. So, if we could produce multiple," Mohammed continued the thought, "simultaneous frequencies at the right sonic resonance," and Ra'id finished the sentence, "we could disrupt a group of the DNA sequence of a simple test organism, such as fruit flies."

And that was the launch of the concept to find a cure for AIDS; now look at what it had led to. Mohammed shook his head in disbelief and approached the equipment.

There, in front of him, was a series of horizontal cylinders, grouped in clusters of five around a central shaft, much like the bullet cylinders of an old six-shooter. There were a total of ten clusters, circling like spokes on a bicycle wheel and connected by a series of cables leading to much larger, vertical cylinders in the center of the building.

The horizontal cylinders housed the servos which in turn spun a series of a hundred adjustable disks in each cylinder, something like the disks in the boys' *ray guns*. Each disk could have its diameters and the speed of the spin adjusted by the master computer program, in order to produce a small arc, creating a specific frequency or electric signature. Put them all together in harmonic layers, like onionskins, and the frequencies produced could be unlimited.

The large central cylinder was built in two-halves. Fundamentally, it acted much like the old radio vacuum tubes, but was so much more sophisticated: Ra'id had once compared the difference to that of an amoeba to a human.

The electric signatures produced by the whirling disks would be delivered to an amplifier above the maser; this then, was connected to a lithium nitride plate at the top of the container filled with methanol, which would act as the medium for the transfer of energy to the bottom lithium nitride plate. The discharge between these two incredibly efficient ion conductors produced the harmonic waves which were tuned to the specific DNA code.

Mohammed moved between two of the cylinder clusters to the maser casing. Instinctively, he again looked around to see if anyone was there. He was alone. He then turned, pulling out a small wrench from the inner pocket of his jacket. He reached to one of the bolts helping to secure the two halves of the casing. He loosened one, then two more

261

next to it. Then, he put the wrench back into his pocket and slowly backed away, hesitantly looking at his executioner and the end of a brilliant concept.

Exiting the Quonset hut, he was met by Vincenzo. "And I hope everything is OK?"

Mohammed looked at him directly and without smiling or giving a hint of the double meaning, "Yes it is. Everything will work as planned."

He turned away from Vincenzo and headed toward the laboratory, not walking like a man facing his death but walking purposely like a man facing his destiny. A destiny he now realized had been set into motion the day he had met Ra'id.

What a shame, he thought to himself. So much potential for good, now a tool for pure evil. At least, my death will be a deed for good.

Chapter 66

Melinda looked up toward the helicopter's engine and hearing only a barely audible swoosh, leaned toward Sam. "We're in stealth mode!"

Sam had also noticed that the sound from the engine had dropped dramatically as had the sound of the rotors. They could actually hear themselves think.

Agent Cohen rose and faced the group of four in his team. "Let me summarize the plan: We are coming in from the northwest and will be flying at three-zero feet over the mangrove forest the island is famous for. Just behind the compound is a low ridge which will give us the cover we will need to surprise the mercenaries guarding the area. The other four *helos* have their designated landing areas, as do we. They will take out the guards and secure their quadrant of the compound."

"*Our* task will be to land as close as possible to the building housing the computers. The temperature in that one is too low to accommodate workers, so we believe the scientists will be in barracks close to this one and that is the one we will look for. We will split up into two teams: Agent Gordon, Doctor Buckner and, pointing to a member of the assault team, Four, will take the barracks to the west. I will take the barracks to the east, assisted by Number Five."

He checked his watch. "ETA in ten minutes." Turning to Sam, "Doctor, I wish we could provide you with a weapon. Your role will be to tell us what we have, once we have secured the laboratory. Until then, I would suggest you stay well behind out of harm's way. Your Kevlar suit should keep you safe in case we miss one of the *bogies*."

For the first time, Agent Cohen laughed loudly. "I am only kidding you. Don't worry, you are in good hands."

Still laughing to himself, he returned to his seat and looked out down to the mangroves they were now over, already teaming with wildlife, waking to the early morning sun. Agent Cohen would have preferred a night operation, but a daytime operation was something he was used to: the better to see the enemy!

*****

Mohammed was sitting on the tall stool in front of the master computer on the counter. It was time to start warming up the maser and make sure that the supercomputers were ready to feed it the sequence of codes and instructions. He needed to make sure the servos were all working properly and that each disk could adjust correctly and produce the *spark* which would be its contribution to the harmonic wave.

As always, Vincenzo was looking over his shoulder. That, in itself, didn't really bother Mohammed because he could tune him out. What bothered him was the thought of the pistol he kept hidden in a holster under his sports coat. Mohammed had no illusion that Vincenzo had used it before and that he wouldn't hesitate to use it again!

Mohammed moved his mouse to bring up the program needed to warm up the maser. A low humming sound, emanating from the servo clusters, soon came from the direction of the Quonset hut. It would take about ten minutes to get up to speed.

Mohammed was concentrating intently on the screen when he felt Vincenzo's hand on his shoulder, making him jump and turn to look back. "What is the matter?"

Vincenzo didn't answer, just bringing his finger to his lips, *shushing* Mohammed to remain quiet, and looking up and around at some invisible fly.

Almost immediately, Vincenzo reached for his two-way radio and coolly spat out instructions in Italian, "Heads up! We have company." Turning to Mohammed. "How much time before you can send the codes?"

Mohammed looked quickly at the screen of the computer. "About eight minutes!"

Vincenzo returned the radio to his mouth and again in Italian, "Look sharp! We need at least ten minutes. I don't care what it takes, give me ten minutes! It's time to earn your salaries!"

*****

Admiral Constab spoke up, "Mr. President, there's a spike in the temperature within the Quonset hut! It looks like they are firing up."

Every eye turned from the tactical display of the assault team approaching the compound, to the screen revealing the infrared layout. Where there had been a cool blue outline, there now was a light yellow hue becoming brighter and brighter.

The admiral continued, "Sir, I believe we need to move onto option two now."

The President looked at each person around the table. "How long do you think it will take the assault team to take control of the weapon?"

The admiral responded, "We are advised by the assault team leader that, based on the information regarding the number and the position of the guards, he believes it would take no more than ten minutes to assume control."

Again the President looked around. "Can anyone guess how long before that weapon fires?"

This time, no one voiced an opinion and the President, with as much frustration on his face as in his voice. "That's what I thought! This is *not* the position we were supposed to be in! Too much is at stake here."

265

Turning to the Chief of Staff, "General, I'm raising our security level to DEFCON 2! I was hoping not to have to use our fallback option. You need to tell our people in the 6th Fleet to prepare to launch the cruise missiles. How long before they reach the target, once launched?"

The admiral responded calmly, "We estimate the flights to take about eight minutes, sir."

Carl Broom quickly asked, "Sir, what about our people?"

"I know, Carl! We need to give them a chance to capture the equipment, intact if possible. If it becomes evident that they can't do it in time, we'll have to abort the operation and launch the missiles. If we can't have it, no one else can."

The President looked around the table. "I gather your silence means you would agree." Seeing no dissent, he ordered the admiral to advise the team of his decision and to be prepared to abort at a moment's notice.

*****

Viewed from the perspective of the mercenaries, the scene must have been horrifying. The five *stealthified* helicopters, which had been in very tight formation coming in on the ridge behind the compound, had at the last second, just as they breached the crest, fanned out somewhat like the five fingers of an outstretched hand, and headed to very specific, predetermined landing locations.

The mercenaries could barely hear the attack helicopters. However, the flashes of fire that suddenly erupted from below and to the sides of the helicopters, were unmistakable: a flurry of rockets was launched from all but the aircraft Agent Cohen, Melinda and Sam were in.

Thirty seconds before the start of the assault, the pilots had turned on their tactical displays, all linked to the

266

same satellites feeding the displays the President was watching. Even before they could have a line of sight on the targets, the pilots already had a bearing on the infrared images of the guards ahead. Each missile had a specific target to strike and would seek out its prey. The plan was to eliminate as many of the guards as possible within the first few seconds of the assault, leaving what they believed to be the area where the laboratory was, intact.

The mercenaries had been caught totally by surprise. The ten on the *graveyard shift* did what they could, shooting wildly at the black airships streaking in. The brief moments between the initial spark of the missile launches, to the time the guards met their Maker, did not give them much opportunity to think about what was happening.

It did, however, give the guards in the inner compound time to pour out from their barracks and spread out toward the sounds of the helicopters as they made their landings.

Once on the ground, the pilots kept the rotors turning, churning up the dust, making the choppers and the assault teams difficult to see, all the while coordinating their teams' movements in the direction of the oncoming red dots which were the enemy.

*****

Back in the War Room, the tactical display monitor had shifted to a live feed from the camera on the lead *helo*. They had seen two of the helicopters move ahead on either side and to the front, with rockets blazing toward their targets. Though they couldn't see the two at the rear, they could witness their rockets finding their targets.

All five of the choppers landed, one in each corner of the compound, with the lead helicopter taking the center ground. By then, the camera could only record the dust flying, so the President ordered the monitors to display the infrared view.

They could observe the glowing bodies of the assault team moving quickly and with purpose, from building to building, behind which or within which the guards had taken positions. Most of the mercenaries were visible, since the roofs of all but the newly renovated structures had long ago fallen within themselves.

It became evident, looking at the bodies in motion toward the center of the compound, and those of the immobile images of the dead mercenaries, that the team was making quick work of the guards.

Chapter 67

Things were happening very quickly for Sam. One minute they were flying over the ridge that had protected their approach, the next, all hell had broken loose around them! Looking out of the windows of the helicopter, he had witnessed the missiles launching and the blinding flashes of the explosions as their helicopter descended into the middle of the compound.

No sooner were they on the ground than the doors opened and Agent Cohen, followed by the team mate he had called Number Five, jumped out and headed off to the west side of the compound.

Melinda quickly headed out, stopping briefly to get her bearings in the dust-filled air, then waved to Sam and Number Four, pointing to the east side.

Before Sam could jump out, Melinda stopped him with her right hand while covering her mini cheek microphone with her left. "I know what Agent Cohen said about your role here. *I* think it would be a good idea if you had some type of protection."

With that, she reached under the back of her Kevlar jacket, and took a Glock 17 out from her belt. She pulled the slide back, loading the first bullet into the chamber. "Do you know how to use this?"

Sam took the gun, looked at it for a moment and released the safety. "I've handled a few of these before. But that's another story."

With a wink, he got out of the helicopter.

In a crouching position, they ran to the side of the closest barrack which looked as though it had been restored. Moving with their backs to the wall of the barrack, their guns at the ready, they advanced quickly to the door. Number Four reached into one of his pockets and pulled out what seemed to be a small gray cube of putty with a little electronic device connected to it. Ignoring the key pad next to the door, he attached the cube to the door handle and then moved over a few steps, again positioning himself in a crouch.

Melinda quickly gestured to Sam that they should do the same. A moment later, a whoop sound was heard and the lock assembly disappeared, sending the door swinging inward on its hinges.

A cold blast of air rushed out of the dark room and Sam knew they had just found the air-conditioned computer mainframe. Both Melinda and Number Four quickly covered for each other to look inside and realizing no one was waiting for them, they indicated it was time to move on to the next building.

Sam peeked in and noticed the level of activity in the computer mainframe, thinking this couldn't be good.

"Number Four!" It was the helicopter pilot.

"A bogey just came out of the shadows... Not one of ours... Coming up on your one-eighty!"

As soon as the warning came over the *coms*, all three of their heads swivelled to look back. It was Sam who was the closest and the first to see the barrel of a gun sneak out from the corner of the building.

A tingling of fear shot up his spine and he couldn't help but hold his breath. His mind went to Melinda next to him and instinctively, his right arm rose, his gun pointed in the direction of the danger and just as the mercenary appeared, Sam pulled the trigger twice. The enemy soldier dropped like a sac of rags, catching Sam by surprise. It had happened so suddenly!

It was also the first time he had killed another person.

Finally, he exhaled and slowly lowered his gun.

"Good God, this is real!" Sam thought to himself.

He felt Melinda's hand on his shoulder, reassuring him he had done the right thing. It was only then that he realized that his life as a sheltered academician would never be the same. He quickly shrugged aside his thoughts, and followed the other two to the next building.

They followed the same procedure as before and again, there was no one in the barrack. This one, however, seemed to be living quarters.

It was then that Sam heard the whine coming from somewhere toward the rear of the compound. Tapping on Melinda's back to get her attention. "Do you hear that?"

"Sounds like a generator or something similar," she responded.

"No, it's something else. I noticed the mainframe computer was really active and that thought the noise was normal. But now that I hear that other sound. I think it's the weapon has been initiated. If I'm right, we have very little time before it's fired."

*****

Vincenzo had been pacing the floor, looking his watch and listening to the chatter on the communication device which connected him with the mercenaries protecting the compound. It was becoming evident to him, both by the level of the sounds of war around him and the fact that fewer and fewer of his men were responding to his questions, that the noose was tightening.

"How much time before we can launch the codes?"

Mohammed looked at the display on the computer monitor. "It will take three minutes before the charge is at maximum."

"Then, all we have to do is press the button?"

Mohammed felt a chill run down his spine. "Yes, and the weapon will fire. Nothing will be able to stop it."

271

He instantly knew he had made a mistake by giving him that much information, even though he realized that it wouldn't make much difference for himself or anyone else in the area.

*****

"Sir, the temperature is rising dramatically again!"

"Thank you Admiral. I think I can see that for myself."

The President paused. "Sorry Admiral. I hope you can forgive a moment of anxiety!"

"No problem sir! But, I think we are at the threshold of decision. Not knowing how long we have, I recommend the cruise missiles be deployed."

"You're correct of course. Damn! I wish we could have we could have salvaged the weapon."

Looking briefly at each person around the table, Alexander turned to the admiral. "All right, do it!"

*****

Agent Cohen stopped dead in his tracks and cupped his earpiece. "Seriously! We are so close!"

Listening a little longer to the voice at the other end, he responded, "Yes sir, understood."

As he swore to himself inwardly, ever the consummate soldier, he implemented the optional plan. "Team leader here. Abort the operation. I repeat, abort the operation and return to the helicopters. We have *incoming* in ten."

"Copy 7"

"Copy 20"

"Copy 12," and so on. Each of the assault teams responded and began to move back to their rendezvous points with the helicopters: all but Number Four.

Before he could acknowledge the command, Melinda had *signed*, with a slicing motion across her throat, not to respond. They were approaching the last renovated building in their quadrant. She felt this would be the one they were ultimately looking for. "How much time do we need to check this one out and get back to our ride out?"

Number Four whispered, "Four minutes at most."

Melinda looked back at Sam, eyebrows raised and head cocked sideways, asking, "Do we?"

Sam understood the risks and quickly weighed the odds. "Let's go for it!"

Melinda turned to Number Four. "Let them know we will catch up to them."

As they approached the door to the barrack, Number Four relayed her instructions. Instantly Agent Cohen barked back that his orders were not requests! Melinda simply turned off her *com*, followed by Sam. Though Number Four did not, he did continue on to the door.

*****

The President didn't have to ask for an explanation of what he was watching on the infrared display. "Who's not following orders?"

It was Broom who answered, "That's Dr. Buckner, Agent Gordon and one of the assault team." Looking at the President, "Shall I order her back to the *helo*?"

The President paused for just a moment. "No, let them finish what they started. There's too much at stake here. And besides, we can destroy the cruise missiles before they strike, can't we?"

273

Looking at the nods of agreement around the table, the President sank back into his chair and stared at the monitor and the red forms moving within the compound.

*****

Following the same procedure they had taken with the other buildings, the three reached the last barrack, as the helicopters lifting off. The explosive charge was placed on the handle and they all assumed a protective, crouching position. As soon as the door fly open, Number Four quickly moved in front of the opening, with Melinda taking the backup position to his side.

*****

Vincenzo was standing over Mohammed's shoulder, looking at the display on the computer monitor: 80% charged, 85% charged.

The explosion and the door flying open totally startled Mohammed. He instinctively jumped from the stool and hid next to the counter.

Vincenzo's reaction was different As if on cue, he reached for the gun in his holster, raised it toward the door that was opening and fired.

It took but a fraction of a second, and Number Four fell backward, dead before he even hit the ground!

Sam watched in shock as he saw the soldier take the bullet in the forehead and fly back, off the stoop and onto his back on the dirt road.

Melinda's training took hold and from her position, low and to side of the opening, she opened fired, launching a barrage of bullets in all directions in the room. She quickly rushed inside and ducked behind the first counter, about three yards from the one on which the computer sat.

She looked back and seeing Sam peeking in, she put her hand up in a *wait* motion, reached around the counter with her gun and fired the rest of the bullets in the magazine in the direction she felt the killer was. She immediately put another clip into the magazine, and fired three more bullets, then waved Sam over to her side.

He bolted into the room and slammed up against the counter beside her, not quite knowing what he was supposed to do after that.

Vincenzo had ducked behind the counter he was next to, pointing and directing Mohammed to stay low, move to the rear of the room, and hide. He, in turn, covered Mohammed's retreat with a burst of gunfire.

Melinda half whispered and signed what she was planning: she was going to approach from behind the counters and along the wall leading closer to the target. She put her hand on Sam's shoulder, in part to calm him, in part to indicate he should stay put. Then she left him and moved around the counter.

Sam felt he needed to do something, so he glanced around his side and shot two rounds in the direction of Vincenzo. The feint seemed to work. Sam saw a man rise and point a gun in his direction, obviously waiting for the next volley.

It was then that Melinda decided to move. She sprang like a cheetah and dove over the counter behind which Vincenzo was rising, hoping to knock him down. She barely missed the computer and was almost onto her target, when Vincenzo, startled by the move, tried to reverse his aim at the person flying toward him. Though he didn't succeed in getting a fix on Melinda, he simply followed through with his motion and caught her on the side of the head with the muzzle of his gun.

275

It caught Melinda by surprise and after the *crack* she felt to the side of her head, everything went black. Her body slid over the edge of the counter and onto the floor.

Sam looked around the corner of the counter just in time to see Melinda being struck and her body dropping to the floor with a thud.

Rage filled him instantly!

He saw *the man* slowly turn toward Melinda and realized he was going to kill her where she lay.

Sam simply lost it at that point! Any and all feelings of self-preservation disappeared. He rose from his position behind the counter and sprinted head-on into *the man* pointing his gun down at Melinda.

The hundreds of hours of running along the lakeside and working out at the gym paid off. In a moment he had reached his target and hit him soundly with a full tackle at rib level.

The hit to his right side, just below the arm he had levelled at Melinda, caught Vincenzo by surprise. The impact was strong enough that it broke two of his ribs and caused his arm to fly away from Melinda, flinging the gun out of his hand to somewhere at the rear of the room.

Both men went crashing to the floor in the aisle between the counters. Sam had a glimmer of elation that he had pulled it off. He hadn't accounted for Vincenzo's military training.

As the two rolled and punched each other wildly, Sam realized that, in spite of the injuries he had inflicted on his adversary, this tall, lanky man, was no pushover. He, himself, had no hand-to-hand combat training, but it was obvious that the other did.

His only hope was to use his weight advantage and try to keep his opponent on the ground, in a position for him to try to deliver the knockout punch. Within ten seconds, Sam found himself on his back with the vampire-like man above him. From the corner of his eye, he saw *the man* reach back to his right boot, and pull out a knife.

The fear returned and Sam knew this could be it for him. The adrenaline in him surged and he was able to grab the arm clutching the knife with both hands and hold it away. He noticed a slight grimace on *the man's* face and knew his tackle had indeed hurt him. Sam used his left hand for a quick jab to the man's ribs and instantly felt the arm holding the knife weaken.

Before he could capitalize on the moment, *the man* quickly flicked the knife from his right hand over and into his left. With a vicious look on his face, he pointed the blade toward Sam's exposed right flank. Sam closed his eyes, waiting for the *coup de grâce* that would end his life.

Not quite comprehending what was happening, Sam heard three gunshots and felt *the man* fall on top of him, a sickening gurgling sound coming from his chest. Sam pushed him off of him and looked around. There, still lying on the ground and with quite the gash on her temple, was Melinda, gun in hand and arm extended in his direction. Lying next to him was Vincenzo, deathly still.

Sam got up quickly and went to Melinda, who was having problems steadying herself, trying to cope with the mother of all headaches. Helping her up into a sitting position on the floor, he cradled her in his arms.

The moment was interrupted by a rustling sound somewhere behind the counter they were leaning up against. Sam thought, he's not dead and he's coming for us.

He grabbed Melinda's gun and reached around the corner, fully expecting to see *the man* getting up to finish them off. No, he was still lying there. However, from the corner of his eye, he saw another shape peer over the last counter at the rear. The gun was immediately raised to point at the new apparition.

"Whoa, please! Don't shoot!" It was Mohammed, with his hands up over his head. "Is it over?"

"Who are you?" barked Sam. Before he got an answer, the stranger's eyes moved to the opening in the door and froze, raising his hands up even higher.

Sam quickly jerked back to face the newcomers, leaning on the counter and holding the gun with both hands, ready to shoot. He recognized the two entering the room with their assault rifles sweeping back and forth, scanning for any danger: Number Five and Agent Cohen.

Both had rushed to the barrack after sending the other four helicopters away, leaving one behind.

They found Number Four on his back, obviously dead from the gunshot wound to the head. Looking inside the room, they had seen Sam's reaction to the person at the rear of the room, but determined he wasn't an immediate threat. The body on the floor assured them he wasn't a problem either.

Agent Cohen yelled to Sam, "Dr. Buckner, anyone else in the building?"

"No, just Melinda and some guy at the rear as far as I can tell. She's hurt!"

Speaking to Mohammed, Agent Cohen took charge. "You! Clasp your hands behind the back of your head, turn around and walk backward to me."

He and Number Five both charged into the barrack: Agent Cohen to apprehend Mohammed, while Number Five to administer medical attention to the gash on Melinda's temple.

Both Sam and Number Five then lifted Melinda and helped her out of the building. Agent Cohen had Mohammed secured, wrists tied behind his back. Only when they were all outside did Cohen demand to know who Mohammed was and what he was doing there.

" I am Dr. Al-Eissa's associate. I can answer any questions you may have once we have left the area. I've sabotaged the weapon and it could explode any moment."

The look on his face showed he wasn't bluffing.

Agent Cohen let out a Jewish curse that needed no translation. Looking at his watch, "Either way, we are out of here. The Cruise missiles are six minutes away. And you're saying we may have less time?"

Mohammed nodded in the affirmative.

Agent Cohen tapped on his *com*. "Get the helicopter up to lift-off speed now. We're coming."

Just then, they heard the weapon's whine increase to a loud wail. Agent Cohen looked up into Sam's eyes with a questioning look. He then turned his head to look into the barrack, only to see the shape of a man leaning on the counter over the computer. *The man* wasn't dead after all and had managed to initiate the weapon.

Agent Cohen did not hesitate: one shot to the man's temple assured him he would never play dead again.

Waving the others to head to the helicopter, Agent Cohen then bent over Number Four and grabbed him by the right arm, lifting him onto his shoulder in one smooth motion and, as if he was carrying nothing, started to run to catch up to the others.

Just then, Sam stopped and looked at Number Five. "Can you get her back on your own?"

"Yes," was the response.

"Where are you going?" Melinda yelled back to Sam, who was already halfway back to the barrack.

"The computer." was all he said.

He ran into the room, jumped over *the man's*, half thinking he would reach up and grab Sam's leg to stop him. He reached for the laptop and, not waiting to disconnect it from the power source, he turned and fled from the building, running for all his worth toward the helicopter which was already half levitating to leave.

The door was open and Sam simply lunged head first into the helicopter, twisting in mid-air and landing on his back, sliding between the legs of his fellow passengers.

The helicopter was forty feet up when Sam finally relaxed his grip on the laptop he was holding tightly to his chest.

*****

"Sir, the heat signature is off the chart!"

President Alexander jumped out of his chair. "Are we too late?"

Not waiting for an answer, he turned to the admiral. "How far out are the missiles?"

The admiral checked the computer monitor before him, with the tactical information showing the statistics in numerical format rather than the image. "The first is four minutes away and the next three will arrive at ten-second intervals."

"Anyone, best guess as to whether or not that weapon is firing or if we still have enough time?"

Again the admiral responded, "We can't really say sir! Not having any idea of how much energy it needs to actually fire, we can't estimate the time it takes for it to get to firing capacity."

His face the color of ash, the President sat back downand just stared at the wall monitors. He wiped a bit of perspiration from his upper lip, saying nothing.

It was Secretary Broom who was sweating the most and squirming in his chair. He had taken his jacket off a while back, and, in spite of the air conditioning in the room, his white shirt was drenched. He tried to get up out of his chair, but was unable to do so. He let out a groan from deep down in his gut and grabbed his head with both hands.

Everyone around the table stopped to look, quickly realizing that Broom had been targeted and that even here, deep under the White House, he had been reached by this incredible weapon. Every civilian in the room seemed to have the same reaction of horror at what they were witnessing. They pushed away from the table, still sitting in their chairs, trying to get some distance from Broom in an instinctual move of self-preservation.

The military people had all witnessed death and their reactions were more of resignation, knowing they could do nothing to help Broom or to save themselves if they were being targeted. In spite of the coolness they exhibited, the President could see in their eyes that they were in both, denial and shock.

All of them in the room were used to having or taking control. Now all they experienced was complete vulnerability.

Meanwhile, Broom's face was contorted in abject agony. By then he was already dead and did not feel the sizzling of each of the molecules in his body.

It was the President who spoke first, in a tone denoting both fear and anger. "What has just happened."

Looking around, "I thought we were protected here. So can someone tell me how this is at all possible?"

Admiral Constab's advisor leaned forward to whisper something into his left ear.

The admiral listened and then turned to the President. "Sir, if you would allow, I think there's something you need to hear. He has a background in Physics and might have something to contribute."

Alexander looked at him. "Go on."

The lieutenant that spoke up, "Sir, I should have thought of it before. May I present a theory. I'll keep it simple and brief. Much as a radio station can transmit an electromagnetic signal, which then is intercepted or cut by an antenna, an electric current is created which mirrors the signal exactly. The radio tuner then isolates the signal and the amplifier gives it the energy to move the magnets in the speakers, reproducing the original signal or sound."

The President interrupted him. "Ok, so much for the high school science lesson. What are you saying young man?"

"Well Sir, the signal from the weapon would seem to be emitted from a satellite, which means it is *just* an electromagnetic wave."

The President was getting frustrated. "So, you haven't said how that or those signals got down here and found Broom!"

"Sorry sir. It's the wiring here. Though the bunker was designed to survive a nuclear bomb and the EMP it would create, the wiring is hardened *not* to melt, and therefore, can continue to carry the signal or current. All of the cables and wires here, linking us with the rest of the world, are carrying all the signals, including the one from the weapon. *That* signal was tuned to Secretary Broom's DNA, which became the tuner for the signal or current. With nowhere else for the it to go, it degraded or transformed into heat. That's what killed him."

President Alexander leaned back and pondered for a moment. "So what you are suggesting is that we need to cut all the power and communication devices in the bunker and no one else can be affected?"

"Yes sir, that's it, theoretically speaking."

The Vice-President broke in. "Mr. President, we have to assume you could be the next target. We can't give them the symbolic victory of killing the President of the United States. If it means shutting down the power for a few minutes, or at least until the missiles strike, we need to do so."

Nods of agreement were expressed around the table.

Looking at his watch. "We have two minutes to the first strike. Is that right?"

The admiral nodded.

Alexander took out his handkerchief and wiped the perspiration on his brow. "OK, let's do it!"

Admiral Constab looked up at the President. "Sir, what about the team?"

Alexander took a moment to respond. "Let's hope they are as good as advertised."

He then turned to the shadow behind the smoked glass panel and made a thumbs-down motion with his hand, indicating it was time to pull the plug.

Ten seconds later, the main breakers to the power panels were pulled and all went dark, with only the battery operated emergency exit lights kicked in, leaving the room and its occupants in an eerie reddish glow.

*****

"You idiot! I can't believe you went back for that." Melinda was livid, but the pain she felt in her head forced her to tone down the volume of her comments to almost a whisper.

Sam smiled in a boyish way and winked. "This is what we came here for, isn't it?"

And looking toward Mohammed, "plus, he is a bonus!"

His smile quickly disappeared when he looked next to him and saw Number Four's body. Looking at Agent Cohen, "I'm truly sorry for what happened to him. He was a brave man."

Agent Cohen simply responded with, "You need not dwell on his fate. He, as all of the team, knew what could happen. That's what we do. The difficult part will be informing his family. It is the worst part of my duties."

The helicopter was about one mile away when the weapon reached the critical temperature and blew up.

What looked like a miniature nuclear bomb rose above the compound. Had they been able to look back, they would have seen the shock waves emanating from the center, much like the waves in a pond when a stone is dropped into it. In this case, the water waves were replaced by waves of dust!

It took but a few seconds before the sound blast reached the *helo*, tossing it violently forward, up and down.

The explosion created an EMP which caused most of the electronics in the helicopter to spark and sizzle. The pilot simply turned to the group. "Hang on, we're going down..."

Chapter 67

(Four days later)

Sam exited the elevator on the third floor, walking with a bit of a limp and carrying a bouquet of twelve red roses. Looking both ways, he noticed the nurse's desk to the right. The nurse behind the counter watched him as he hobbled over. "Sir, are you OK?"

"Yes, I am. I should have used my cane, but both my ego and the flowers made it a non-starter." Leaning on the counter, "I'm looking for Assistant Secretary Gordon's room."

The nurse looked at the room roster sheet. "Yes sir, she's in room 3-0-2."

Sam thanked her and walked slowly down the hallway, trying not to limp too much. Reaching the door, he knocked gently and pried it open, peeking in to see if she was awake.

Melinda was lying with her eyes closed, well aware of her surroundings.

When she heard the knock and saw the door open slowly, she turned her head in its direction and seeing Sam, flashed a large beaming smile. "Hey there. Come on in."

Even with a bandage wrapped from the top of her head down to her eyebrows, Sam couldn't help think how amazing she looked. "Hey, how are you feeling?"

Just then he had a flashback and was in the helicopter when it was hit by the EMP and went down. The pilot had done a great job trying to keep it level. They hit the ground fairly hard, their only saving grace being the fact that they struck a sand dune and not a rocky outcrop.

No one was killed, though every one except Agent Cohen sustained minor injuries: Sam wrenched his right knee and bruised his left shoulder when he flew up from the floor on which he was still lying and literally hit the ceiling.

Melinda, already injured, was strapped into her seat with her back facing the front of the helicopter. The crash caused her to suffer a whiplash and her head hit the wall separating the passenger area and the cockpit, compounding the gash on her left temple while causing a mild concussion.

The pilot broke his right arm, while Number Five and Mohammed suffered heavy bruising to the chest, where the seat belt crossed their ribs.

The helicopter had come to rest on its side and when the dust finally started to clear, Agent Cohen and Number Five climbed out by way of the side hatch and began to pull the others out, starting with Melinda.

Once everyone was out and away from the wreck, they could all detect the smoke billowing up from the island a little over a mile away. No more than fifteen seconds later, a massive explosion in the compound was seen from their vantage point, followed by three more.

Agent Cohen had spoken up, "Has to be the cruise missiles. We were lucky."

Turning in the other direction, they all could see the running lights of four helicopters moving in their direction. The rest of the team had returned to find their comrades.

Melinda snapped him out of his moment of reverie. "As well as can be expected, I guess. Where's your sling?"

"At the hotel, along with the cane," he smiled sheepishly. Remembering the roses, he leaned over to kiss her gently on the lips. "That was for you. And this is for Assistant Secretary Gordon," handing her the roses.

Melinda laughed. "Thank you. They are beautiful." She put the roses aside on the night table. "I still can't believe how this has all happened. I can't help think about how horrible it must have been for Secretary Broom. I liked him, even though he was rather *stiff*, if you know what I mean. He was a straight shooter."

Sam shook his head. "I only wish we could have stopped it from happening."

Melinda reached up to him and put a finger on his lips, as though trying to take away his guilt. She added, "We both tried, without avail."

They both fell silent for a moment.

Melinda broke in and tried to change the subject. "My new boss came to congratulate the team and my role in the mission, and to inform me of the President's decision that I be promoted to the position of assistant secretary. He was been told how close he came to being the next victim. From inside accounts, it seems the President was *really* shaken by what happened down there."

"No kidding," said Sam. "Based on the DNA code number Mohammed had programed into the weapon, the next targe could only have been the President!"

"Glad you brought up Mohammed."

Melinda interrupted Sam, "Did you hear? He's missing."

"What do you mean *missing*?"

"After we returned to Tel Aviv, as you know, the Yemeni government pulled strings and pressured the US to hand him over to them, as a Yemeni citizen, stating they would see to his punishment. The President agreed, only because we had the computer with the master logarithm, thanks to you."

Sam smiled and nodded.

"Well, it seems once he was on Yemeni soil and incarcerated, someone worked their magic and the following morning, he was gone."

Sam shook his head in disbelief, looked around and finding a chair, pulled it up closer to the bedside. "So what does that mean? Do we have to worry about another weapon somewhere?"

"No, we don't believe so. We have the core program and the two labs we knew about have been destroyed. We doubt whoever put this together would have built two backup weapons: too much money would be involved. As well, Dr. Al-Eissa is dead and we are on the threshold of finding the money trail. It would seem it ends at the doorstep of the foundation that ran that tourist resort, not far from the compound. The new secretary is heading up the task force to confirm this and take them down. Which brings me to my first task as Assistant Secretary: when I leave the hospital and resume my responsibilities, I'm charged to find Mohammed and bring him in."

Sam looked at her with a puzzled expression. "I thought you said he wasn't dangerous?"

"Yes and no. First, he was involved in a lot of murders for which he needs to account. And he knows too much to be allowed to roam free. The President wants him in our custody until we know *all* he does. And speaking of the President, after witnessing what the weapon could do and actually seeing how Broom died, I'm told he was traumatized. It seems he has decided that the weapon can never be built, not by the US, not by anyone. The laptop has been sent somewhere where it will never see the light of day! Something like the *blackhole* of a warehouse in the Indiana Jones movie."

Just then, the telephone next to her bed chimed. Melinda reached over and picked it up. "Yes, this is Melinda."

It was Agent Cohen calling to check in on her condition and to extend an invitation. "…and our three governments would like to acknowledge your contributions in the success of our mission. You and Dr. Buckner are invited, as guests of the grateful people of Israel, to receive the recognition of our country, that of the United States, and of course for Dr. Buckner, that of Canada." Melinda covered the receiver with her hand and mouthed that it was Agent Cohen and that they were going back to Tel Aviv.

"Now, because of the nature of the mission, remember that this ceremony will not be made known and can never be mentioned."

"Yes, I understand," replied Melinda. "I'll inform Sam and we will wait for the details of the meeting. I think I can speak for the two of us," winking at Sam, "when I say that we are truly honored by this gesture."

Sam held his hand out, indicating he also wanted to speak to Agent Cohen. Melinda handed him the phone.

"Hi, this is Sam," he said. "Listen, I need to thank you for everything you did for me and Melinda. We owe you our lives and I for one, will never forget it."

He nodded to the invisible man at the end of the line. "You are welcome. It *was* quite the experience."

He paused for a moment. "And one last thing, something has been on my mind for a while now. I don't remember anyone, at any time, having said what your first name is. We've always called you *Agent Cohen.*"

Smiling into the receiver. "I'd like to think we were on a first-name basis by now. What is your first name anyway?"

Agent Cohen chuckled a little. "My name is Shmu'el, Shmu'el Cohen. You can call me Samual or, Sam!"

He let out a hearty laugh and said, "Good-bye my friend," and hung up.

It took Sam a second or two to have the irony of the situation sink in. Looking at Melinda, "Did you know?"

Melinda smiled. "Yes, I did. But you never asked and I didn't think it was that important."

The two had a good laugh, after which they went silent for a moment.

It was Melinda who spoke first, "So, what do you have planned for the near and distant future?"

Sam looked at her and gave her a hesitant smile. "Well, funny you would mention that! I spoke with Jalal yesterday and it seems our project has come up with some solid evidence that would support my theory. So, I'm looking at publishing our findings and then, I see a book in my future!"

Melinda chuckled. "Well, I am acquainted with a future famous author, am I!"

"Maybe not as famous as controversial."

Melinda looked at him quizzically. "And what does that mean?"

Smiling devilishly, "You'll just have to wait until the book is out. As a teaser, let's just say that it might upset some of the more religious types!"

"Well then, I expect a signed first-edition copy from the author!"

Sam nodded and then the reality set in. "So I have the feeling we won't be seeing much of each other for a little while?"

Melinda gazed up at Sam with a gentle look in her eyes. "Well, my new job will keep me pretty busy. I'm not at work quite yet! I've been given a couple of weeks of paid holidays to recuperate! And I doubt we will be going to Israel until I'm officially back to work." With a flutter of her eyes, "So, where would you want to go?"

A week later, the two were lying on their lounge chairs looking at a spectacular sunset. The view of the Pacific Ocean from the small deck which surrounded their lagoon-over-water bungalow at the Te Tiare Beach Resort in Huahine, French Polynesia, was just what the doctor had ordered. The peace and quiet there was the extreme opposite of the turmoil they had experienced the last month or so.

The stitches from Melinda's injury had been removed just prior to leaving and were barely visible beneath her hair. Sam was no longer limping, and any and all stiffness was gone.

They were sipping on a tropical drink, which had just been delivered by canoe to their bungalow. Sam's drink happened to have an umbrella.

He looked at it with disgust. "This doesn't suit a guy who has just saved the world!"

Melinda chuckled as he took it and threw it into the gentle waves lapping at the pillars supporting the thatched-roof hut.

As they sat there, with the sun just disappearing beneath the waves on the horizon, he leaned in close to her to kiss her gently. He then put his hand on hers, resting them on her armrest while they watched the night fall upon them.

For some time, neither of them spoke.

Sam squeezed her hand and rolled his head toward her, moving his eyes a few times in the direction of the room, he said, "Well, shall we?"

Chapter 68

At the same moment, on the other side of the world, the sun was doing the exact opposite.

Sheikh Wadi Al-Kabir was sitting at the desk in his Capri mansion office. He looked somewhat disheveled and dark circles framed his bloodshot eyes. He had not had much sleep since the time of the assault on the compound.

He knew of its demise and the death of Vincenzo, and that saddened him. Not because he felt a personal loss. It was more because he had relied on Vincenzo to cook and look after the mansion, besides some of the *special* jobs he would do, without question. In fact, the Sheikh had eaten little since satisfying himself with the leftover bread and cheese in the pantry.

"Yes, I know the position I put you in when I asked you to orchestrate Mohammed's escape." He was speaking to the board member from Yemen.

"You did well... Where is he now?"

The Yemeni official said with trepidation, "We do not know. In spite of the fact he has a week's head start, we don't believe he has left the country."

"Keep looking! Spare no expense and keep me informed. We need to know what he might have said or who he could have implicated."

He hung up and started dialing the manager at the Swiss bank he did business with, in order to begin the process of moving his cash assets from around the world to where he thought was the safest and most discreet location.

He felt the stress of the situation and quickly wiped a few beads of sweat off his brow and upper lip. By the time he realized something was wrong, his jaw had already clamped shut and his eyes were bulging out of their sockets.

*****

Parked in reverse outside the retractable gate and protected from view by the tall stone walls on either side of the laneway, a black-paneled van sat idling, with a strange sound emanating from the rear.

Looking inside the cab through the side-view mirror, one could see the sombre face of a young man, looking back as though he was able to see through the gate and into the house.

Mohammed had indeed left Yemen and had followed Ra'id's instructions to a tee. When the two had spoken in private while at the hospital before his uncle died, Ra'id had described everything which had been revealed regarding the Board and the Sheikh. He had admitted to the rage he felt about having been manipulated as he had been: from the death of his beloved parents, to that of the love of his life, Samihah. He loathed his uncle's role in the whole plan, though he realized that he too had been used. The Sheikh, however, was the devil incarnate.

Ra'id had decided to get his revenge by using the very weapon he had been duped into creating. He knew the Sheikh and all the board members would be at the demonstration and that it would be a success, prompting the Sheikh to have a celebratory meal afterward: plenty of opportunity to collect DNA. He would then program fourteen codes: one for each of the board members, one for Vincenzo, and above all, one for the Sheikh.

When he decided to meet with Sam, Ra'id had asked Mohammed to look under his pillow where he would find an envelope: in it would be a set of instructions and some money he had retrieved from his uncle's home the night of the *reveal*. At the hospital, Ra'id had asked Mohammed to complete his personal jihad, should *something* happen to him.

After the luncheon the board members had shared, he collected the forks and had processed the codes required to target each of them. As a precaution, he had e-mailed them to the personal e-mail address he and Ra'id had used when they wanted to communicate with each other without any concern of being intercepted.

However, when Mohammed realized he might not be able to get away from the compound and had decided to destroy the weapon, the exercise was rendered moot and he resigned himself to his fate. Then came the assault and his escape from death. He saw the light at the end of the tunnel and swore to himself that he would not stop until Ra'id's murderers were all dead. He might not have the weapon at the compound available to him. He *did* have the van however.

After their jaunt into Israel, Ra'id and Mohammed had driven it back to Naples and had parked it in Vincenzo's *cousin's* wrecking yard. A healthy payment to Hanz had ensured the vehicle would not be tampered with.

Now here he was, looking back at the mansion through the side-view mirror. He looked at his watch. It had been five minutes since he had flipped the switch on. That was sufficient, he thought. He leaned over to the switch on the dashboard and turned it off. Reaching over to the passenger seat, he picked up a clipboard. The sheet on it had thirteen names. He crossed out the first at the top and put a checkmark beside the name of the person he was to visit next.

Later, the black van moved slowly onto the winding lane. It stopped at the end and when the coast was clear, it turned east toward the cliff-hugging road back down to Capri Town.

What's next for Sam and Melinda?

If you have enjoyed "The Osiris String", you can look forward to my next novel.

Sam and Melinda are back! But this time, it's Sam who is looking over his shoulder. The book he wrote and published, based on the research he was doing in "The Osiris String", becomes a best seller and the focus of a fast-growing movement.

But not everyone is applauding. The conclusions Sam has reached have angered the religious right in the US.

One paramilitary group, deeply entrenched in conservative ideology, has sworn to eliminate Sam in a effort to curtail the trend he has started and which threatens everything they believe in.

Look for "The Divine Formula"!

Here is a sneak preview of the sequel in the Sam

Buckner Adventures: **The Divine Formula.**

Prologue

Mohammed Al-Kammin had been on the run for four months.

He was also on the hunt: looking for the men whose names were on his list. He had already *visited* two of his former investors, including Sheikh Wadi Al-Kabir, the mastermind behind what would become life-shattering events, and leading to the death of the people Mohammed cherished the most.

Having twice taken care of business, he now had to deal with the remaining eleven members of the board of directors of the Foundation for the Promotion of Islamic Culture: They needed to pay for their sins.

Mohammed was, or had been, Ra'id Al-Eissa's partner in developing an invention that promised to cure HIV. Ra'id conceived of a way to excite, with harmonic microwaves, the HIV genetic code to the point of combustion, without affecting the infected host cell. It wasn't a far stretch of the imagination for the Sheikh to see the potential of the invention. He used his tremendous resources to manipulate Ra'id's life in order to persuade him to convert his invention into a weapon able to kill anyone, anywhere, in order to control world politics through intimidation and assassinations and clear the way for him to establish an Islamic federation.

Two laboratories had been set up, the primary one in Frankfurt, Germany, and a backup lab on the small island of Kamaran in Yemen. However, both had been destroyed during raids by German and Israeli Special Ops teams, led by Homeland Security.

Before Ra'id was killed, under orders from the Sheikh, he had learned of the latter's betrayal and involvement in the deaths of his parents and that of his beloved Samihah. As a result, he had asked Mohammed to take up a *jihad* to punish those responsible, a request which Mohammed had accepted without hesitation.

Going *underground* for almost three months before surfacing and taking out the second person on his list, Mohammed was now on his way to Saudi Arabia to find the third.

Still driving what looked like an old, beaten-up Mercedes van, he maintained the pretence of being a used-furniture vendor.

The vehicle was nothing like it seemed to be. Both sides had large motifs of old furniture painted on them, with the company's name, "Mustafa's Pre-Owned Furniture", written in Arabic in the lower-right corner of the signs.

When he and Ra'id had originally used the vehicle to avenge Samihah's death at the hands of an elite Israeli commando team, the van also had the name posted in Hebrew, considering they were *visiting* their targets in Israel.

A few scratches and dents on the bumpers and sides completed the look of a well-travelled vehicle. The four rear tires, two on either side, seemed to show the stress of the vehicle's age. In fact, the tires were rated for the additional strain of a series of lithium-ion batteries hidden within the frame of the vehicle, adding nearly twelve hundred kilograms to its weight.

The interior of the rear cab was just large enough to accommodate a variety of old pieces. Two antique tube-type radios, an Art Deco Grunow World Cruiser Tombstone radio and a larger floor model antique Philco AM radio were secured by bungee cords to the front wall. There was a single bed with box spring and mattress lying flat on the floor to one side, with an assortment of boxes piled on top. A Louis XV armoire stood against the right side wall, next to a Crystal Ice

298

Box from Freemont, Nebraska. There was barely room for anyone to move within.

These items too, were not what they seemed to be. Hidden under and within the old furniture were the components of the portable version of what was the deadliest weapon ever created: not as deadly as a nuclear bomb or the Ebola virus, but more like a *designer* weapon, able to target anyone, just for being who they were, using their DNA.

The drive to their destination felt that much longer without music because the truck's radio functioned as the control unit for the equipment in the rear. Cleverly camouflaged within the pieces of furniture were the different parts of the weapon. The two radios had working dials and control knobs, but, hidden inside and crammed tightly within the speaker cavities were the oscillators and capacitors for the maser. In a false back at the rear of the armoire were concealed the components for the computer which coordinated the process. The coil assembly in the box spring below the mattress was actually the antenna array. The maser which created the microwaves was itself in parts, hidden inside the walls of the metal icebox. As for the boxes piled on the mattress, they were filled with dishes and pots and pans to add a final touch of realism.

When in close proximity to the target and with the switch flipped on, a pulse of incredibly complex harmonic microwaves would be emitted and would simultaneously excite every cell in the victim, literally frying him, or her, within a matter of thirty-odd seconds.

The target he had just killed had recently been appointed chairman of the Supreme Council of the Armed Forces of Egypt, after the upheaval that had been

299

caused by his predecessor's demise: all part of the Sheikh's master plan.

Colonel General Mahmoud Hassim was one of the thirteen members of the board of directors of the Foundation for the Promotion of Islam and had been groomed by the Sheikh for almost seven years. He was to assume the new position and prepare the *coup d'état* which would let the council reclaim the power it had been forced to relinquish by the president.

Mohammed smiled to himself, thinking *that* would never happen now.